BOUNCE
THE WIRE!

BOUNCE
THE WIRE!

PAUL ANDREWS

authorHOUSE®

AuthorHouse™ UK Ltd.
1663 Liberty Drive
Bloomington, IN 47403   USA
www.authorhouse.co.uk
Phone: 0800.197.4150

Published by AuthorHouse 08/09/2013

ISBN: 978-1-4918-7535-3 (sc)
ISBN: 978-1-4918-7536-0 (e)

CHAPTER ONE

It was never quite like this at the Felix Centre, the British Army's Bomb Disposal school, thought Tommy, as he edged further forward to scrape more of the loosely packed sand and earth away, hoping, maybe perversely, to expose a small corner of what he believed to be yet another pressure plate device, this would be the fifth time this week. Finger tip searching they called it at the school, it sounded dead easy sat in the air conditioned classrooms listening to one of the Instructors, a guy Tommy knew well, explaining the types of device currently being used and more importantly how to deal with them, safely and quickly. The days of being able to take a few hours to deal with a suspected device were a luxury of another place and time, here any time spent not moving was a time of concern and no little danger. Even on the exercise areas being assessed as being suitable to carry out high threat Bomb Disposal operations, this finger tip searching hadn't posed too many difficulties, true enough the only penalty back then was being called a clown by the directing staff and the possibility of not being deemed suitable for Ops, now the penalty was rather different and probably final.

"What have you found Boss?" Marty asked passing him a bottle of water, "another plate", he told his number two, a position of real responsibility, the number two role, carried out by junior non commissioned Officers, called for tact, diplomacy, common sense and a fair amount of military combined with technical ability, particularly here in the dust, dirt and chaos that is Southern Afghanistan, sometimes having to deal with out of date equipment that showed a remarkable ability to break down at the most inopportune moments, impatient operators and even more impatient commanders who demanded to know when the operator would be finished, as well as worrying about being shot at by people who didn't even know them. All this whilst keeping an eye on the boss, dreading, but being ready for the unexplained and unexpected explosive sound of something going wrong in the danger area, which would see the number two rushing headlong into an area they knew hid at least one improvised explosive device, or to use the ever loved military system of acronyms, IED and who knows what else, the only concern being to save and remove the boss from the danger area by any means possible. It was often said that a good number two was worth his weight in gold, or in this case her weight. The bond that developed between an operator and a number two allowed for a sense of intimacy and trust that Tommy sometimes wished he had had in his now failed marriage. Marty busied herself preparing the equipment that would be needed on the next manual approach, whilst Tommy went away to brief the commander as to what was going on.

Here comes the ATO now said Captain Elliot as Tommy hurried over to where the Commander was holding an impromptu orders group, "what have you got for us then ATO" asked the captain. As Tommy or ATO as was referred to in this company related what had been found, he found himself wondering how he had gotten himself into this position. Leaving school with only few desultory O' levels to his name and little idea what he wanted to do, he had stumbled from one factory job to another till aged twenty he had wandered into the Army, Royal Navy and Air Force careers offices all pretty much co located just off the Dock Road in Liverpool and in one foul swoop expressed an interest in all three. It was the Army that answered first, and so it became that Tommy Byrne became Private Byrne, quickly nicknamed Scouse by the ever imaginative instructors, enlisted into the Royal Logistic Corps, he wasn't even sure what Ammunition Technicians actually did in the RLC but he had been sold on tales of Brave Bomb Disposal types fearlessly cutting the red wire with only a few seconds left on the clock. Now of course some years later and a number of sometimes intense operational tours including Northern Ireland, Iraq and Afghanistan under his belt he knew exactly what an ATO really did, it was often not very pretty, very often hazardous and seldom involved cutting wires red, blue or any other colour by hand.

"So let's get this straight" said Captain Elliot as Tommy finished talking, "some local villager stops this patrol and tells us that he saw some strangers acting suspiciously right on the route we were supposed to travel, acting on this info the search team found a patch of ground that appeared to be disturbed and now on further investigation you tell me that you have found, and are about to render safe another pressure plate device. Why did he tell us? What's in it for him? I now have the best part of twenty guys' stationary in an area I would choose not to be, we have been here for maybe, what twenty five minutes and we will be here for another twenty at least." "That's about the size of it" said Tommy, "I deal with the bomb you look after me and my team". "Bleeding Rupert's" he muttered walking away, using the soldiers jargon for all

Officers, under his breath and wandered off to do just what he was here to do.

Marty had everything laid out for him as he jogged back to suit up, although to be honest he only wore the bare minimum protection, heat, speed and the need to be able to move into cover quickly played a large part in deciding what level of protection would be worn, not that he couldn't operate in the full suit but nowadays nobody did, not out here. He would not be the first operator to receive incoming sniper fire on a manual approach to a suspect device. Ready to go he issued last minute instructions to his escort, gulped down a bottle of water and set off taking care to not snag his firing lines as he did so.

Tommy was woken by the shrill sound of the duty phone ringing, stumbling from bed still only half awake he answered, "Scouse, it's me Steve" Steve Thompson was the Senior Ammunition Technician in Country and as such the link between the operators, regardless of rank and senior commanders at headquarters. The familiarity between operators was sometimes difficult to grasp, particularly with the infantry units they served, where observance of rank structures was never relaxed and first name terms were only rarely used and almost never between Officers and enlisted men. To be fair the Ammunition trade observed these tried and trusted rules but bent them sometimes to suit their own particular traits. I have some bad news, Chris Evans was killed yesterday evening, as the words sunk in, Tommy remembered speaking with Capt Chris Evans, only last week when he had dropped off some recovered firing systems he had been tasked to. Chris Evans a quietly spoken man maybe twenty seven years old or so, and now dead! "How, where, what happened?" the questions came at once, "We are still not sure" came Steve's measured reply, Tommy knew that Steve would have been out most of the night trying to make sense of what had happened, if for no other reason to ensure it didn't happen again. "He was tasked to a suspected Command Wire device along Route Violet; it would seem he had identified and was dealing with the firing pack when he was caught up in an explosion, there was no evidence of anything else in the area, he had carried out all the normal search drills before approaching the pack, it would appear the pack was booby trapped, but we don't yet know how". "How are the team?", asked Tommy, "Not doing too well" replied Steve, "you know Chris, he was a good boss to have around and his team have taken it pretty badly, his number two was first on scene after the explosion and tried to patch him up as best he could but from what I have seen he had no chance. I have stood them down from any operations till further notice, and have asked Brigade to task a reserve operator to take over the position. That will take some time, can I ask you and your team to take up any tasks that crop up in the meantime". Tommy knew that although asked as a question, it was never really anything other than a command, "yeah sure Steve no worries", he answered, "who else knows about Chris?". The jungle drums would soon be beating the news and Tommy wanted to make sure that his team found out from him and not over breakfast in the mess hall.

Wednesday morning found the team in the main military stronghold of Lashkar Gah readying equipment for another mission supporting a patrol who would be out of the base for a few days, flying out originally to a pre cleared landing zone then going off into the hills and valleys around the areas, showing a presence, carrying out a number of search operations winning hearts and minds if at all possible, but mainly trying to stay out of serious trouble. The patrol commander had requested EOD support for the task and given the high possibility of the searches uncovering either bomb making equipments or actual devices then EOD Command had approved and tasked call sign Lima 21, Staff Sergeant Tommy Byrne's team accordingly. To be honest Tommy and the team didn't mind going out with the patrol, it got them away from the routine of the base, and anything out of the ordinary made the time go that much quicker, six month tours very often seemed to last, at least in the mind, a whole lot longer than six months. Another factor was the sooner the team got out on patrol again, the sooner they would stop being constantly reminded that one of "our own" had recently been killed. One of the advantages of being a very small and some may say elite trade which perversely was also one of its problems, was that pretty soon everyone knew everyone else. The pre mission briefs revealed nothing untoward, the Intelligence guys proved themselves to be as accurate as ever by predicting the patrol could expect IEDs and possible small arms fire from small gangs of insurgents possibly supported by out of country assets. A threat briefing something akin to saying "expect excitable children around Christmas time"!

On the move out to the landing zone, Tommy gazed out of the tailgate of the chopper as they swept over the open plains below, occasionally sighting nomadic herdsmen as they moved their meagre flocks from one grazing area to another, the landscape seemingly endless, beautiful yet dangerous. The threat from Surface to air Missiles although small was real and pilots often took evasive actions mainly to avoid setting patterns, but also in an attempt to unsettle the stomachs of the non fare paying passengers in the back, the load master safely strapped in and in essence in charge of these passengers, gave a countdown of five minutes to the patrol commander as they approached the drop off. The team busied themselves retrieving equipments', bags and anything else they had stashed aboard, aware that the chopper would not return to deliver items left behind once it had flown off.

Safely on the ground, a quick communications check, shake down and head count saw the Patrol set off, initially at a brisk pace, conscious of the fact that a helicopter touching down is not a quiet affair and having touched down they tend to either drop off or pick up troops. It would not take long for any locals in the area to identify that a patrol were on the ground and to put in place a less than welcoming committee. Tommy and his small team were positioned somewhere near the middle of the patrol, he had his head on its customary swivel looking everywhere and nowhere at the same time, looking for something out of the ordinary, though to be honest he had lost any idea of what was normal these days.

He was troubled by a number of things that seemed to be happening just recently, and he wasn't the only one, aside from Captain Chris Evans, a number of other IEDD operators had been finding that the enemy had started to get an idea of just what actions a Bomb Disposal technician would be carrying out to any given device, and as such had a number of successes, a month ago one of Tommy's mates had been slightly injured when a countdown timer had functioned inside a device during a render safe procedure. Full forensic exploitation had yet to be carried out on the remains of the bomb, but Tommy and other operators in the area had no doubt that something had been rigged so as to target one of them, by someone who knew precisely what they would be doing. Tommy as well as every other soldier on the ground knew that it was commonly expected that whenever a patrol went out, they assumed they were being watched. Watchers, or to use the military parlance, dickers, very often youngsters, would be paid to watch a patrol, find out where they went, what they did, where they stopped etc, anything to determine a pattern which could be used by insurgents to launch an attack. One of the drawbacks of having locally employed civilians working inside the camps that you could never be certain that the dickers would be outside the wire. However for someone to know what and when Tommy or any one of his mates would be doing, necessitated more than just casual observance, and that what was worrying Tommy as he kept up his swivel headed patrolling.

The first scheduled stop was in a town called Barghana North of Lashkar Gah, the patrol had been tasked with a search operation of a suspected insurgent logistics base, the team were not expecting any unpleasant surprises but these days it never paid to be too complacent and as such Tommy was to go in with the main search element. Security was to be provided by a joint Afghan Army and British Military mentoring team already in the area, backed up by the rest of the patrol not directly involved in the search. The supposed logistics base was in a secluded compound at the North end of the town, records showed that a family had lived there for some time but recent reports indicated that on a number of occasions outsiders had been observed arriving and departing the mud walled compound at odd hours, it was not known what was the purpose of these visits but the suspicion was that the unknown visitors were holding a series of planning and resource meetings to coordinate future attacks against the Afghan security Forces and the Military in the immediate areas. Tommy and the patrol knew that valuable information could be learnt from searches of this nature, it was a real opportunity to gaze in to the insurgents crystal ball and get an idea of what type of attacks and devices could be expected in the near future, this ability to be forewarned allowed the would be targets to be forearmed and better prepared. No one believed that the emplacement of insurgent bombs and the attacks could ever be fully prevented. But even if one attack was stopped then that had to be regarded as a success. The main search team lined up outside the target and after a confirmatory check that the way in was not booby trapped gained entry through both front and rear doors simultaneously thus preventing any "squirters" it had been known in the past for someone inside to "squirt" through a window or a back door as the search team gained entry thus making a quick getaway. Of course the security element outside would be aware of that possibility and would be on hand to cut off any would be escapee. The house was empty but showed signs of recent occupation, bedding on the cots and signs of recent cooking fires all pointed towards someone having lived and eaten there only recently. Tommy never got used to the conditions in which some the villages were forced to live, he often wondered if he had been born into this way of life would he now be planning ways of attacking the soldiers that had invaded his land. The first room revealed little in the way of useful intelligence with the exception of being able to gather DNA samples from the bedding and some cooking utensils, which would later be uploaded onto the database and may go some way to identifying who had been here or prove a link between whoever had slept in this bed to an incident elsewhere. The second room was more promising; with a box containing two cell phones and a handful of computer discs, along with an assorted collection of documents and what appeared to be receipts. Tommy's knowledge of the local language was limited at best but the interpreter the patrol had brought along with them insisted that was just what they were. A shout from the back of the house roused Tommy from his perusal of the contents of the box, "ATO over here" Tommy moved through the house to find one of the patrol looking into a manmade hole in the ground, the hole had been covered by a wooden panel and roughly camouflaged with matting. Tommy took his torch and peered down into the ground, despite first appearances the hole was actually quite large and was easily big enough to allow a reasonably sized man to climb down there. From his vantage point Tommy could make out three Afghan cooking pots with their lids off and the insides filled with a light brown granular substance, these sort of cooking pots had been used many times to hold an amount of high explosive which could then be triggered by any number of means to cause a large number of fatalities to any exposed personnel in the immediate area. Tommy shone his light deeper into the hole and saw what appeared to be a number of battery packs and other components, all of which he would be expected to make safe before being moved, after why else was he here? After a check of the floor space immediately below the opening Tommy gently lowered himself in the hole, taking care not to move anything he did a quick tally of what he could see inside, he had clipped a small voice recorder to his jacket which not only saved time but allowed Tommy to move and log things at the same time. Aside from the cooking pots and what he assumed to be firing packs, Tommy saw an array of switches, batteries and what appeared to be military training pamphlets'. Once settled and happy that he had sufficient and safe space in which to work he called Marty down to join him and settled into a tried and trusted routine of recording, photography, inspection and once he was satisfied that items were safe to be moved, placed into forensic bags and lifted out of the hide. The explosives would be subject to a controlled demolition nearby everything else would be removed for further exploitation and a full detailed technical assessment back at base. As this process was going on, the remainder of the compound was being subjected to a full search, utilising search teams, ground penetrating radar specialists and specially trained dogs.

The hide was almost complete, Tommy and Marty between them had recovered significant amount of bomb making equipment and paraphernalia, the only things left were the cooking pots, these as far as Tommy was concerned posed little in the way of danger. The teams had recently taken possession of new and lightweight X ray machines, bomb technicians had used radiography for many years but the equipment was heavy and not always suitable for the rough handling it was subjected to on patrols. As Marty prepared the equipment Tommy went up top to warn the Patrol Commander what was about to happen and that he needed the area around the hole cleared of non essential personnel to prevent any chance of his guys being hit by stray Gamma or beta rays or whatever the technical term was. That done he checked that everything was in order, rather than move the as yet uncleared pots he had planned to move the x ray machine to each in turn, and then once he was happy that they were safe to move he would move them all in one go. There was no reason to expect anything untoward inside the pots this was more of a routine exercise to confirm their safety and to provide a permanent record of the contents. Marty positioned the machine next to the first pot and taken care not to trip on the cabling that snaked out from the generator that would fire the x-rays climbed out of the hole, after a quick look around to ensure that there was no one in the danger area Marty pressed the fire button. The machine emitted a series of clicks as it fired the pre set number of pulses, almost immediately the earth around Tommy seemed to open up and he was hit by an enormous noise and rushing of hot burning air he found himself being thrown violently backwards his last sight was of Marty flying towards the opposite side of the hole seemingly in slow motion, the noise lasted an eternity he could feel his hands and face burning, he landed heavily and struggled to make sense of what had just happened, he could make out a shape, barely recognisable as Marty nearby, she lay on her front, Tommy still unable to properly focus, could make out something was wrong but his brain wouldn't let him make sense of what he was seeing, slowly as if time had stopped, he realised that one of her legs was bent at a seemingly impossible angle and part of an arm had been torn of in the blast. Soldiers rushed in shouting and yelling but Tommy, his ears still ringing from the noise, couldn't make out what they were saying, two ran to Marty's side and began to pull medical packs from their webbing another was at Tommy's side asking him what had happened. As Tommy was half carried half dragged out of the immediate area by the patrol he could see the team medic working frantically over Marty's prostate body, he struggled to get up but was unable to move and he slumped down unable to register what had just happened. "Chopper in bound" came a shout from somewhere; a helicopter had been called to evacuate the team. Tommy stared towards where the medics were still desperately working on Marty yelling at her to breathe pummelling her chest while another was attempting to stem the blood flowing from her torn and broken body.

CHAPTER TWO

ommy woke in a bed to see a nurse standing over him, "Hello Tommy, do you know where you are?" she said, Tommy looked around him but all he could see was screens around the bed, "Bastion?" he ventured, Camp Bastion was where a majority of British casualties were brought to immediately after sustaining their injuries, it was possibly one of the best equipped hospitals for its size anywhere in the world, the staff had performed miracle after miracle keeping people alive whose injuries would have certainly meant death had they been injured and treated anywhere else. "Yes" she replied, "let me get the Doctor for you"," Wait" Tommy said as she turned to walk away, "My number two, Marty how is she?" The nurse glanced around, "Let me fetch the Doctor" she said. Tommy's heart sank, had he killed her somehow, he remembered her badly injured body being worked on by the medics, she must have died of her injuries, injuries he was somehow responsible for. The nurse returned and with her, presumably the doctor she had gone to fetch, "Hi Staff" he introduced himself as Doctor Miller, and proceeded to ask Tommy how he felt, "like shit Doc" said Tommy, "what has happened to Marty, what happened to me?" He continued. The Doctor looked back at him and answered in a matter of fact tone, "LCpl Allen has been stabilised here and once we are happy she is strong enough to travel will be heading back to the UK on a casualty transfer flight, she is in a bad way, she has some damage to her internal organs and we have kept her in a self induced coma to aid her recovery process, she will live but she was been badly damaged in the explosion, the medics on the scene did a fantastic job to keep her alive, she is a lucky girl". Tommy surprised at the Doctors candour was devastated by the news that Marty was in such a bad way, "you on the other hand were remarkably fortunate" went on the Doctor, "you have some burns to your face and arms, which may require some form of surgery, you suffered concussion and a nasty gash to your head, some minor cuts and bruises elsewhere, but otherwise you got away relatively undamaged. You will possibly suffer some form of hearing loss as a result of the blast, but we won't know till we can carry out some proper testing once the immediate effects have gone. We should be able to release you pretty soon, you will be transferred back to the UK to recover both physically and mentally, and that will be arranged through your unit and in consultation with ourselves here at Bastion, no need for you to do anything but get better. Your Commanding Officer and a Warrant Officer Thompson have been in touch and when you are fit enough would like to come to talk with you."

Tommy lay back his head throbbing not just with the after effects of the blast but more so with the news that Marty's life had been irreparably changed and he was to blame, but for the life of him he did not know how he could have been so stupid as to not assess the cooking pots as anything other than containers for the explosives they contained. How could he face her again, would she ever forgive him, he had never felt so alone and so helplessly useless. He began to go through the events in the hide one more time trying somewhere to see the clues that would point towards the cooking pots as being what they truly were. He remembered sorting through switches, batteries, even a handful of detonators but nothing steered him towards the pots, he had purposely left them till the end believing that a quick x-ray to confirm the filling and the image to be kept and included in the post action report, before he could take them outside and dispose of them safely.

Steve's head popped through the screen, "hey Tommy you doing alright" he asked with real concern in his voice, Tommy simply looked at his friend and shrugged and answered "no not really, what the fuck happened out there?" I was hoping you could tell me replied Steve. Tommy went through the task as best as he could, Steve kept silent throughout simply nodding at times and at others looking slightly quizzical, once Tommy finished, Steve shook his head, "and there was nothing that pointed towards some type of anti handling switch anywhere" he asked, "no", repeated Tommy "and besides we never moved them, everything we moved we had a good look at first, both of us. The pots were left to last simply because to move them would have meant working across the other bits and pieces first and I didn't want to run the risk of something being dislodged whilst we shifted the bloody things. There were no intact devices, not even partially constructed devices; it was just a storage room for whoever built this thing, at least that's what I thought," concluded Tommy sadly. "We have sent in a post blast team" Steve said "and given what has been going on recently I tasked Brian to head it up." The post blast teams were a forensic exploitation team, usually headed up by an experienced Bomb Disposal operator, supported by military police, infantry tacticians and intelligence analysts. The teams were meant to be deployed following any kind of explosive device either functioning or being found and rendered safe, however given the current tempo of operations they were now only tasked to significant events, one where loss of life had occurred or where an unusual device or new enemy tactic had been used. Brian Owens, a very experienced operator had been a chef in his hometown of Glasgow before he joined the army; he and Tommy had served together had played football together and on a few occasions gotten drunk together. Tommy knew he was the best man for the job, Brian would get to the bottom of what had happened and if blame were to be apportioned would not shrink pointing the finger should that be necessary. "He should be back later today", went on Steve "once we know the score we will keep you in the loop, as it stands right now Tommy, no one is blaming anyone, we just don't know what happened, I cannot see anything in your report that points to anything other than a find, we have had no intelligence saying we should be aware of rigged cooking pots. We have no previous attacks that would fall into those criteria, we simply don't know what happened, but we will", promised Steve. "Our main concern right now is to get young Marty back home, the Boss has spoken with the Regiment and the families Officer has been round the to the house, She is strong and has not given up fighting just yet, and nor should you" added Steve sensing the deep despair lurking just below Tommy's outward facing facade. Steve then dropped some "gifts from the lads" he had brought with him on to Tommy's bed, and said he would be back soon. Tommy tried to clear his head by leafing through the lads' magazine that had been left, this after throwing away the gift wrapped ear defenders, the sheets of toilet tissue, the get well "you skiving bastard" card and thoughtfully, a gift token (out of date) for Costa coffee, the closest one being in Dover! That someone had jokingly placed in between the pages, the army sense of humour was so far removed from that of the civilian world, that what would seem heartless and possibly cruel to some outside of the military was a thing of necessity in the world of bombs bullets and bandages!

Doctors and nurses came and went, the screens were removed sometime later that day, pills were taken, notes recorded and Tommy barely took notice of any of it so far immersed in his private world of self recrimination and blame was he. At one point he again asked how Marty was doing but the reply was the same as previously. He ran through the task again and again in his head looking for the one thing he had missed. The next day began just as the one before had ended, with the duty doctor doing his rounds looking at Tommy's head wound, asking the nurse to have his burn bandages changed and Tommy wishing he could turn back time, how often had that same wish be prayed for in these wards he wondered. Steve and Brian came in at around ten thirty, they immediately and ominously to Tommy's thinking, placed the screens back around the bed and pulled up chairs as close as possible. "How are you doing mate", Brian asked in his distinctive Glaswegian tone, "yeah yeah" replied Tommy, "what have you found?" "You were targeted" Brian replied grimly. What? exploded Tommy, "we found one of the pots pretty much intact" continued Brian, "the second one had functioned probably due to its proximity to the one you were x-raying, but the third was only slightly damaged, obviously given what you had told Steve you were doing when the device functioned and the fact that this pot had been thrown about by the blast, we were not about to move it or consider taking x rays, we put it to the sword", the sword was an explosive entry tool used to open up hard cased containers, fire extinguishers, beer barrels and in this case cooking pots. "After we had her open we were able to take a look inside, and we found amongst a power source and initiator, a homemade electronic switching system which, when we were able to test it, turned out to be an x ray sensitive switch, rigged to function on receipt of a single x ray pulse. Pretty crude in its design and no secondary arming system inside but there you have it, someone has built a device designed to function when it is x rayed. Now the question is who else apart from ourselves uses radiography in the field? Who was the intended target? And how did they know we would be doing that in that compound?"

The enormity of what he had learnt dawned on Tommy as Steve and Brian left promising to return soon, who would have that level of insight and knowledge of render safe procedures. British laws allowed for a large degree of anonymity for sensitive operations including Bomb Disposal techniques. Tommy had attended court more than once to offer expert witness testimony where details or precise procedures where never discussed in an open forum and even the reports that every operator reluctantly completed after every task never revealed exactly what actions had been carried out, instead a series of codes were used, each code referring to a specific action which were changed every few years. The thought that one of their own would give up that type of information was simply impossible to believe and Tommy immediately dismissed it, but who and how were questions that shocked him to the core. He knew that the Commanding Officer would have sent out a flash signal to every operator both here in theatre and to the Regimental Headquarters in the UK warning that procedures had been possibly compromised and to exercise extreme caution, the danger that operators would be tempted to disregard standard and proven actions in order to be unpredictable, was that those standard procedures had kept people alive for many years and to go against them may be counterproductive and actually produce the very effects that whoever was responsible for the breach really wanted, that of the death and maiming of Bomb Disposal operators. The news that he had been deliberately targeted and not unsafe ought to have eased Tommy's conscience, but he still found himself wondering could, should he have done things differently. He knew he would probably always have those doubts and that Marty most likely would too. The doctor came in shortly after and expressed pleasure in Tommy's progress, the stitches would need another week or so but the burns to his face and arms were mending well, when asked about Marty, the news was slightly better in that she had rallied slightly and was now out of immediate danger, she was being kept in a medical coma to allow her body recovery time and would be flown out to the Military Hospital in Birmingham in a day or so.

The next day saw a surprise visitor in the shape of lieutenant Colonel Doyle, the senior ATO in theatre and Tommy's Commanding Officer; accompanied by a smiling Steve Thompson, "hello Staff" he said as he approached the bed, "how are you coping?" "Not bad sir" Tommy answered "be glad to get out of here to be honest" he added, and it was true, Tommy had never been one for reporting sick and spending days in bed. "Well I think we will leave that decision to the doctor" said his CO, "but I do have some news that may cheer you up" he said pulling an official looking letter from a folder he was carrying. "The promotions board sat yesterday and I am very pleased to announce that you have been selected for promotion to Warrant Officer Class Two, and on a personal note, not before time" said the CO, "well done mate" Steve piped up, Tommy was stunned, in all that had been going on he had totally forgot that the board was due to sit, he had been qualified for promotion for some time and now that he had been selected, it opened up a whole new career path for him. "Thanks Sir" he managed to answer before Steve pushed a hip flask into his hands, purely medicinal he said, good for shock he added with a smile. Save some for me chipped in the CO tacitly giving him the go ahead to have a drink which probably broke at least three standing orders in theatre. Once they had toasted the good news, the CO pulled up a chair and told Tommy that he was to be flown home for convalescence and any further treatment before he could expect to be back carrying out operational duties. Despite Tommy's protests that he was fine and would be happier to get back to his team, what was left of it, he thought grimly to himself! Both Steve and the Boss were adamant that he was to fly home, take some well deserved time off, get well and see what happens then.

The flight back to Brize Norton was uneventful, given his status as a casualty Tommy was excused he usual Royal Air Force administrative run around that they seemed to relish in, instead he was escorted to a private waiting area accompanied by a travelling nurse who would be responsible for the well being of all the walking wounded, Tommy was surprised at how many casualties there actually were, apart from a number of friends, who had been, in some cases very badly injured, and on too many occasions killed whilst carrying out Bomb Disposal duties, he had never seen much evidence of wounded service men and women returning to UK, of course there was a big groundswell of support for those who had paid the ultimate sacrifice with ordinary people stopping in the streets and paying their respects as a military cortege, the vehicles and closed caskets strewn with flowers, passed by, the media never seemed to pay much attention to those who returned from overseas as multiple amputees, broken minded or suffering with hideous burns to most of their bodies. Tommy assumed that whilst it was right and proper to have people remember those who had given their lives for their Country, it was harder for the public, or possibly the Government to stomach seeing young men and women return condemned to spending the rest of their lives physically or emotionally crippled. The cavernous body of the Hercules aircraft was partitioned with a large screen, with soldiers returning home on leave or after completion of their tour at the front of the aircraft and those with medical needs towards the rear. The plane resembled a small hospital with beds, resuscitating machines, surgical lights and a whole team of doctors and medical staff who continued their life saving support through even the most turbulent flights, Tommy had never given much thought to what made someone a hero, but to his mind he was seeing it now.

A Duty driver from Regimental Headquarters in Oxford was waiting in the casualty processing centre, a new and very busy addition to Brize Norton's arrival hall, Tommy was processed swiftly and allowed to leave the centre on the understanding that he reported to Selly Oak hospital in Birmingham for assessment the following day. Tommy's first action after having got into the car was to phone his Mum back home in Liverpool and promise to come up and see them as soon as he was able to, he had called her from the hospital in Bastion simply to prevent her hearing the news that "Our Tommy" had been hurt from someone else, she was understandably worried but Tommy reassured her that he was ok, he knew of course that once he returned home he would be unable to even boil the kettle himself without his Mum, Sister or any number of concerned Aunties fussing over him. The journey from Brize to the small nondescript camp that housed the Headquarters of all British Bomb Disposal operations took less than forty minutes and Tommy soon found himself standing outside the Adjutants office waiting to go in and talk with the Regimental CO, Lieutenant Colonel Wilson was a no nonsense type of Officer who appreciated straight talk and returned it in similar fashion, this to the discomfort of some but to the guys on the ground it was a breath of fresh air. His first action was to get his Adjutant to bring a chair across and to order a tray of coffee, sit down Staff he ordered, "How are you feeling?" "Pretty tired" answered Tommy truthfully "and looking forward to getting out this uniform and into a pair of jeans and a sweatshirt to be honest, Other than that not bad" he continued, "heads a bit sore and these burns dressings are getting on my nerves, but give me a few days and I will be ready for work again", he added hopefully. "Well first things first said the Colonel, let's see what the hospital say tomorrow, and then you have a month's leave to take before you go anywhere, on top of that you need to complete a posting preference now that you have come off the board, which by the way I am delighted for, very well done" "thank you sir" said Tommy automatically, thinking a month with his Mum and he would be willing to be posted anywhere, not that he didn't love her but she had a tendency to "mother" which, whilst ok initially soon got to be a bit much. "I was thinking about postings" continued Tommy "and quite fancy staying within the Regiment and taking over as Troop Warrant Officer somewhere?" Before leaving Afghanistan, Steve had tipped Tommy the wink that the Troop Warrant Officer position at Nottingham Troop had recently become vacant and as it stood had not been filled. The colonel smiled at that and then asked Tommy just what the feeling was on the ground over in Afghanistan, he, of course had reams of official reports and documents from all levels of analysts and experts but he wanted to know how his men were feeling, what did they need?" "hmm" started Tommy, "well to be honest sir, the news that we are being deliberately targeted is a bit worrying, we always know we are at risk, of course we are, but this is different. When Chris, sorry, Captain Evans was killed the feelings were the usual, sadness and wondering "what went wrong", but now it seems as if he was set up, and then we have

Marty and myself getting caught out by a rigged cooking pot, again on purpose, it is all getting a bit skittish over there. Other than that the lads are doing a great job, kits working pretty well and we are gearing up for spring offensive, it looked as if we were getting on top of things for a while, just hope this new threat doesn't set us back again. Do we have any idea where the leak is coming from" he asked the Colonel. "No we don't, not yet anyway, but we will do, I have asked the Intel guys to start looking and the Military Police will be coming over tomorrow at my request and I shall be putting them in the frame, but as yet, we have nothing, this may of course just be a coincidence and not be anything more sinister than good fortune on their part". "I hope so" said Tommy in reply. "What time are you at the hospital tomorrow?" Asked the CO by way of changing the subject, "eleven thirty" said Tommy, "well I intend to pay a visit to LCpl Allen tomorrow, I shall get my driver to collect you from the mess at nine thirty, get some rest Staff and we will see what the experts say tomorrow, in the meantime I shall give manning and records a call and explain that we have spoken about your posting preferences and I see no problems with you taking over as Troop WO at Nottingham and would be delighted to have you continue within the Regiment in that role." "Thank you Sir" Tommy saluted and left the office, before heading across to the mess he called in at the SAT's office, the SAT was the Regimental equivalent to Steve Thompson in theatre. Tommy wanted to know what else had been going on whilst he was away, and as such the SAT was the guy in the know.

The next day Tommy was dressed and ready to go, he had spent a fitful night, images of Marty and booby trapped cooking pots filled his dreams, he had spent most of his waking hours wondering whether or not he would get the opportunity to see her at the hospital, he also wondered whether she would actually want to see him today or any other day for that matter. The doctors examined Tommy and remarked he had indeed been very lucky to have not suffered more serious damage in the explosion, his stitches could come out in a weeks' time and he would be assessed by a burns unit at the same time to gauge the long term effects of the damage to his face and arms. He seemed to have developed some minor loss of hearing but other than that was given a clean bill of health. He was asked whether or not he had been advised that the Psychiatric department could offer some help should he feel the need, he immediately denied he had any need of a shrink and that any appointment that was made for him to see one would be a complete waste of time. Once he had a fresh prescription of pain killers he headed off to the critical injuries wing, where he had arranged to meet the CO and his driver, as he passed the nurses' station on the way to the waiting room, he took a gamble and popped his head around the door and asked the most kindly looking one there, how Marty Allen was doing. The nurse looked up and asked what Tommy's relationship to Marty was? He figured that honesty was the best policy and explained he was the operator who had also been injured in the explosion, and that he had just been released from medical care and was hoping to hear some more good news? The nurse opened a cabinet and pulled out a folder, "she will be ok," she said looking at Tommy with a warm smile, "she has been seen by the surgeons and will need to have further surgery, she will not be running any marathons for a little while, but she should be able to live an almost normal life once she fully recovers, it may take a little while but she should get there with the proper care and treatment. She will be able to receive non close family visitors in a few days; maybe you could ask her yourself then how she is doing?" "I am not sure she will want to see me" said Tommy hesitantly, unsure why he found himself opening up to this particular nurse, must be those new painkillers messing with his head he figured. "Give me your number" said the nurse "and I shall see what she says". Tommy rattled off his mobile number thinking as far as pick up lines go, it was as good as he had heard, still he thought he always did have a soft spot for tall nurses despite the wedding band she was wearing! And if she was simply using his number to tell him that Marty never wanted to set eyes on him again, at least he would know for sure.

During the drive back to Oxford the Colonel informed Tommy that he spoken with the desk Officer at manning and records and all things being equal the process of letting everyone who needs to know that newly promoted Warrant Officer Class Two Tommy Byrne was to be the Nottingham Troop's new Warrant Officer would begin very soon. Once Tommy was back in his room at the mess he busied himself getting everything in order to go on leave, he didn't have that much to pack, years of military life had left Tommy able to pack swiftly and travel light, he left his mobile number with the Operations Room clerks and walked to the nearby train station, his car was in a secure car parking compound in Liverpool, left there before he set off for Afghanistan a few short months ago. He found the train journey more stressful than usual, the noise and confusion of a busy train station seemed to set his nerves on edge, and he reckoned that living in a small enclosed environment for so long must have left its mark. As the train pulled into Lime Street station in Liverpool, Tommy steeled himself for the homecoming that he just knew his family would have prepared, a house full of Aunts and Uncles all saying how proud they were and what a great job he had done, and didn't he look well, washed down with a bargain store buffet that his Mum swore by and most other people simply swore at!. He grimaced at the thought but then he remembered coming home from previous tours when he had been married, to a cold and less than welcoming house, and an even less welcoming wife, he knew which scenario he preferred.

CHAPTER THREE

ommy's phone rang a few days later; he didn't recognise the number but saw that it was prefixed with a Birmingham dialling code. "Hi is that Tommy Byrne?" asked a voice, "yes who is this" he answered, "Hello my name is Mandy, I am a nurse at Selly Oak, you asked me about Marty Allen the other day" the voice on the other end continued, "well I have spoken with Marty and she would love to see you if you can make it, she didn't know you were back in the UK, she is still very ill but making progress" continued Mandy, "she is still not really up to visitors, however given who you are and how very proud we all are of you guys, the doctor has said you can come in and see her, it will most likely help her as well". That's fantastic said Tommy, when would be the best time to visit her, well normal visiting hours are between one and two in the afternoon and between six and eight in the evening, however I have spoken with the ward sister and she has agreed to you coming down outside of those hours if you would rather avoid the crowds. Thank you for calling me said Tommy; tell Marty I shall be there tomorrow afternoon. Tommy spent the rest of the day worrying how Marty would react to seeing him again and to some degree how he would feel seeing her so badly hurt. He left Liverpool around mid morning aiming to miss the worst of the M6 motorway madness and with sufficient time to find his way to the hospital, park the car, buy something to take in with him and allow some time to drop by the out patients ward and see if they could kill two birds with one stone and remove his stitches a few days earlier than planned. He arrived at the nurses' station just after one forty five; Mandy was once again on duty and gave Tommy a smile as he introduced himself at the door. She offered to take him to the ward let him have a quick chat with the ward sister then he was free to spend an hour, but no more with Marty. Tommy suddenly felt more nervous than he could ever remember feeling, and when he considered how many times he had donned the bomb suit and made that long lonely walk to investigate a suspect device he found that both surprising and a little scary. Mandy, maybe sensing his unease, gave his arm a reassuring squeeze as they turned right out of the office and headed towards the ward. The sister in charge greeted Tommy and quickly filled him in on Marty's condition and what treatment she had been given so far, she also told Tommy that Marty had not surprisingly suffered some despondency and shown levels of depression since being brought out of her coma and learning the full extent of her injuries.

Tommy left the sister and walked across to the small room that Marty had been placed in, the door was open and he could see a small figure propped up on the bed her left arm a swathe of bandages and dressings her leg clamped by some medieval looking contraption and an array of machines and drips, as he approached he felt suddenly very afraid and almost turned on his heels and walked out of the hospital, he knew that if he did that he could never return and would never forgive himself. Marty spared him that decision however by, at that very moment of doubt and insecurity looking up and seeing him; he gave a grin and forced his legs to walk towards her. "Hey Marty" he said, "Do you think I pressed the button too hard Boss" she asked him her voice breaking with the effort it took to attempt a joke at even this most difficult time. "Marty I am so sorry", Tommy's voice cracked, "stop it" she interrupted him forcefully, "the Colonel has told me a little of what happened, you were not to blame, Tommy, none of us were". Tommy again marvelled at the strength of the girl, he had known from the first time she worked for him that she was a good number two, that she had something about her, never shirked from hard work, always willing to improve things whether that was equipment issues, her skills or even her ability to let Tommy think he was in charge, which was a skill every number two learnt from a very early stage in their careers. The hour passed quickly and Tommy was surprised to see Mandy standing at the door saying that Marty needed to rest and that he could come again another time. Tommy and Marty said their farewells, Tommy promising to return as soon as he could, Marty making him promise to stop feeling bad about what had happened in the hole, a promise both of them knew he would not keep. In return he told her to keep her chin up and to just concentrate on getting better saying that he would be in need of a good number two at Nottingham once he got there.

Tommy drove back to Liverpool and going over in his head what Marty had told him, she would need another round of surgery on her arm and would eventually be fitted for a prosthetic limb, the damage to her liver and spleen would need watching and she would never be as active as she used to be, however the colonel and the Welfare Officer had visited and assured her she should not be worried about her future in the army, the current operational theatres had resulted in a large number of men and women who had suffered injuries and there was a push to have these employed in administrative positions and teaching roles within the military where their experiences could be used. The money and time spent on training someone like Marty was quite considerable and to simply throw that away because they had been injured in the line of duty was both morally and financially wrong, providing that the soldier could carry out whatever duties had been assigned to them in this new position, then Tommy could see no reason to not keep them on. Tommy knew personally one operator who had lost most of an arm some years ago to a terrorist device, and was still on active duty, was still a very good operator, a fantastic instructor and a good man to boot, despite a poor taste in football teams, Tommy thought to himself.

Tommy survived a few more days in Liverpool and decided he had to get away and broke the news to his Mum that he was going off to the Brecon Beacons to do some walking and spend a few days camping, the change of scenery would do him good he figured and too many bowls of his mums home cooked Scouse, a Liverpool delicacy, was starting to leave its effects on him, so a spot of hill walking would keep him in the shape he had become accustomed to. Before he left he again phoned the hospital to see how Marty was doing and to leave a message telling her he would visit next weekend. Tommy drove down to the small town of Hay on Wye and having settled himself in a small campsite, set off on foot to wander round the hills and valleys of this quiet and peaceful rural piece of the Welsh borders. As he sat atop of Hay Bluff sipping a mug of hot coffee, he began thinking of how he had been set up, he was not sufficiently egotistical to think he had been personally targeted, he just happened to be the operator at that particular compound. He would not let himself believe that anyone of his fellow operators would have gone rogue, but someone had been telling someone how he and his mates dealt with various devices, and that was hard to accept. The selection process for being admitted to the world of Bomb Disposal included amongst dexterity, problem solving and fitness assessments, psychometric testing presumably aimed at weeding at those people who were not suitable for such high intensity operations, and hopefully to identify those who would pose a threat to themselves or others. However someone who had knowledge of the current render safe procedures had gone across to the enemy, or maybe, the thought suddenly occurred to Tommy, had always been part of the opposition. He thought back to the tasks he had done in his career, how many times had someone been watching what he was doing, making notes, Tommy concluded it would be almost impossible for someone to identify every action simply by watching from afar, no this had to be someone who had access to reports, code lists and knew of specific procedures relating to specific tasks. He tried to imagine what his mates would be thinking as they went out on missions knowing that someone had been deliberately setting them up, he knew that teams would still deploy, what other choice did they have?, but he also knew that they would be looking at ways to mix it up a little, to be unpredictable, if that meant that forensic evidence was lost, or the use of more powerful explosive tools were used, then so be it. Tommy finished his coffee and set off back towards the campsite, he loved the feeling of being alone in the outdoors, the sound of the country soothing and reassuring, despite being born a city boy he found himself more and more longing for the tranquillity of the outdoors.

Tommy woke early the next morning and after a quick shave and a cup of tea drove himself into town, planning to treat himself to a proper farmhouse breakfast. After ordering his fry up, he then turned his mobile phone on to check for any messages, almost immediately it rang, the caller ID showed up as Ops room. "Hello Tommy Byrne here", he answered, "Staff Byrne its Corporal Cooper from the Ops room, I have a message for you from the SAT, he has been trying to get hold of you since yesterday afternoon". "I have been out walking", Tommy said by way of reply, "what's going on?" "He needs you to call him as soon as you can", continued the caller. "Ok" said Tommy, "do you know what he wants"? Tommy was reluctant to call without knowing at least something about what was required of him. "No, sorry, Staff, I don't but it is probably to do with the explosion in Helmand yesterday afternoon". "What explosion, where, when" said Tommy as his breakfast arrived. Hang on Staff, the SAT has just walked in said Corporal Cooper, let me put him on. Tommy heard the controller explain to the SAT who was on the line, and then the familiar Welsh accent of Andy Jenkins sounded in Tommy's ears. "Hi Tommy, where are you?" "Hay on Wye" answered Tommy, "what's going on", "Tommy it's not good news, we have been hit again" said Andy, "yesterday morning a routine patrol was ambushed with a roadside IED and in the follow up, Echo 22, was taken out by a device that had been left behind", Echo 22, thought Tommy, Sergeant Frank Carter's team, he knew that Andy would have not wanted to name names over an insecure phone line, Tommy didn't really know Frank all that well, a newly arrived operator who had only recently passed the high threat course "he had carried out all the usual actions" continued the SAT grimly "but somehow the terrorists knew precisely what he would be doing and where. This is looking very similar to the device that killed Chris Evans recently. Can you get back to Oxford Tommy? The CO wants to talk with you"

Breakfast forgotten, Tommy left a five pound note on the table and walked out, how could this have happened again he wondered, and what did the CO want with him in such a hurry. One thing that Tommy had learnt in his years in uniform was that only rarely did good things come from Commanding Officers wanting to talk with Staff Sergeants in a hurry. The drive back to Oxford was slow and tedious, the welsh borders may be beautiful, but getting anywhere from there was a long slow process and it would seem that every time he managed to get onto a decent stretch of road, either a caravan or tractor would suddenly appear on the horizon to slow him down again. Pulling off the A34 towards the base Tommy felt a sense of unease, a sensation he had not experienced before. He pushed it to one side, telling himself he had gone through a fair bit these past few weeks, and he just needed to sort himself out. Before going across to the main headquarters building, he stopped by the mess to freshen up and put on a clean shirt.

His first port of call after entering the secure corridors that was home to the upper echelons of UK Bomb Disposal operations, was to the SAT's office, Andy greeted him and led him to the operations centre where all ongoing incidents were monitored and details of yesterday's attacks were being collated by analysts looking for the smallest clue that would tell them where the leak was coming from. The emerging facts were sketchy; it would seem that Frank had been on an operation nearby when the first roadside IED had functioned, the first responders reported that they were suspicious of a patch of ground that looked as if it had recently been disturbed. Frank had been tasked by brigade arriving with a military escort a short time after the initial call had gone out. In the meantime a wire had been discovered by medics treating the wounded, the wire ran from the edge of the road towards the high ground to the West. The high ground would have been an ideal vantage point for any insurgents lying in wait to initiate the device, the rolling hills allowed for plenty of opportunity to escape undetected and far enough from the effects of the blast to not be casualties of their own device as well offering an excellent field of view into the killing area.

Following the golden rule, Frank had not simply followed the wire, he had traced the wire with a small remote controlled robot to a point where the wire had been buried presumably to avoid detection by surveillance drones, at this juncture Frank had explosively cut the wire, after a period of time, Frank had walked into the area where the wire had been cut, and it would seem that a few minutes after he got there a large explosion in the area of where he had been standing occurred and he was killed instantly, his number two and escort had both stated that Frank had simply been confirming the cut and was standing still looking up to the high ground when he was killed. The post blast team had found little in the way of device evidence, the initial blast was fired from the high ground as suspected, and a standard car battery had been recovered from there after being spotted by a helicopter pilot flying the casualties out. However nothing had been found which would tell how Frank was caught out. "I have asked Steve to head up this investigation and to review all the attacks to date where Operators have been targeted" continued Andy, referring of course to his counterpart in theatre. "Now let's get you in front of the CO" said Andy with a knowing look in Tommy's direction.

CHAPTER FOUR

"**S**taff, Mr Jenkins come in", said the CO using the correct term of address all Officers are required to give to a Warrant Officer Class One in the Ammunition Technical trade of the Royal Logistic Corps. "How are you doing Staff, feeling any stronger for your leave?", he asked with some concern "You will have heard about Sergeant Carter", the CO continued, "Yes, and much fitter now thank you sir" replied Tommy sadly, although not well known to Tommy the loss of any young man was a thing to be mourned particularly when the young man in question was one of our own he thought. "We have had some interesting developments over the past couple of days, the death of Sergeant Carter only makes it more imperative we find out just what is going on over there", the CO began. "You obviously remember only too well the hide in Barghana", he went to say, "However you may not know that some of the evidence recovered has proven to be of interest to our friends in MI5. Now what I am about to say has to stay within these four walls", the CO stressed," it would seem that you bagged a number of receipts before you x rayed the pots", Tommy remembered only too well what had happened in the hide, but kept quiet as the CO continued, "It would appear that one of the receipts was from easy build components, a well known and internationally recognised electronic component supplier, the receipt was recovered from a forensic bag you had labelled as contents of rubbish bin, it had unfortunately been torn into a number of pieces before being thrown away", "you did well to find it and bag it Tommy", said Andy clearly impressed by Tommy's diligence and proficiency, "yes indeed, but a serial number was able to be recovered from the fragments" said the CO clearly annoyed by his SAT's interruption. "And that number has been traced it refers to one of a number of items that were ordered from an address in Leicester". Tommy wondered where this conversation was going, if this was now a police or security forces operation then why was the CO telling him all this, the reason soon became apparent as the colonel went on to say, "The powers that be have decided, and I believe it to be the correct course of action, to stage a covert intelligence gathering operation to try to find out exactly what is going on. The address is registered to a Mr Said Malik, Mr Malik is not known to the police, but it would seem that the house is also home to a number of his close family, cousins, uncles to name a few. A number of registered occupants have been flagged up, by Leicestershire police as having sympathetic tendencies to Al Qaeda and two of Mr Malik's cousins as being members of a particularly radical mosque in the city. The police and security services have had the house and the occupants under surveillance now for the past 24 hours; they want to conduct a search of the property when the opportunity next presents itself, they have the necessary permissions and experts on hand to gain entry, what they do not have", the colonel concluded with a long look at Tommy, "is, to use their words, a Bomb Disposal expert with current and in depth knowledge of operations in Afghanistan."

"Why me", said Tommy after taking a moment to digest all of what he had just been told, "I assume as I am here you are referring to me" he asked, "a number of reasons Staff, you have just returned from theatre, albeit a little earlier than planned, you are ideally placed to know just what type of devices and circuitry Is being used out there. You have carried out covert work before with various agencies so would have no trouble fitting in with the team already on the ground, and I figured you may have some personal interest in this particular job, I know you are still officially on sick leave and I cannot nor will I order you to take part in this, if you decide you don't want to, or feel you are not ready for it, then I will look elsewhere. Your decision will in no way reflect badly on you, it will not, and I promise you this, it will not be recorded in your records, the only people who are in this loop right now are us three, and the Operations Officer, if you do volunteer, then we will have to widen that net a little, but only a little", he promised, "as far as anyone else is concerned you are still on your post tour leave, which we will let you take once this is over" he added with a smile.

Tommy looked at Andy, who simply gave him a wink in return, what the hell he thought, he was getting bored at home anyway and if this gave him an opportunity to help put away those who were supplying the terrorist networks in Afghanistan then even better, besides which he had enjoyed his work with the police surveillance teams before, he remembered being involved in a long covert operation aimed at capturing an animal rights extremist a few years earlier, the job resulted in Tommy having to defuse a number of, to be fair he maintained, fairly simple incendiary devices, by hand, and the man responsible for them being placed in a number of high street department stores being sentenced to a very hefty prison sentence. Chasing electronic suppliers in

Leicester would be easy in comparison he thought, he would unfortunately later have course to review that sentiment, he was however in no position to know that just then. "Count me in" he told the colonel, "good man" said Andy and the CO nodded in silent agreement, "good" he said, "The Ops Officer has all the details you will be needing just now, the first thing is to get you across to Leicestershire Police Headquarters, where you can meet with the MLO, the Military Liaison Officer, from there you will be put to work, the Ops room will give you a secure duty phone which you can use to contact the SAT here, you can keep him in the picture of your day to day activities and will be your point of contact back to Regiment, he will of course keep me fully updated". With that the CO wished him luck and asked them to send in the adjutant on their way out.

On the way to the Ops room, Andy and Tommy discussed what equipment he should take with him, the task was being sold as an advisory position, but both men knew that the line between advising and actually having to do something was often easily crossed. The Ops Officer had clearly been warned by the adjutant of their pending arrival as he was waiting for them with a folder already open on his desk, the folder was worryingly slim in Tommy's opinion, containing just a couple of typewritten sheets of A4 paper and a couple of photographs, still he guessed it was still early days. The MLO was to be found at Leicestershire Police Headquarters in Enderby; Tommy was to report to him for a full briefing, the Regiment would phone in advance of Tommy's arrival to ensure that he was expected. The file contained little way in the way of useful intelligence, photocopies of the torn receipt, names of the occupants of the house under observation and an official request from the police for military support throughout the operation, codenamed Operation Vanguard. Tommy told the Ops Officer he intended to grab some equipment and pack a bag, before driving the short journey to Enderby, aiming to be there within a couple of hours, Tommy checked his watch amazed to find it was almost four thirty in the afternoon, was it really only a few hours ago he was waking up in tent on the Welsh border he asked himself.

The MLO was a big bear of a man with huge hands, who introduced himself as Terry, Terry was clearly a man who knew how things operated as the first thing on the agenda was to stop in at the station cafeteria and order two all day breakfasts and two mugs of tea. Tommy and Terry made small talk swapping tales of suspect devices in Afghanistan for tales of pub fights in Loughborough; it almost seemed to Tommy he had had the safer job given some of the tales Terry was telling. Once they had finished eating they made their way to the briefing room, there Tommy was brought up to speed on events thus far. It seemed that the surveillance team had secured an observation post in the upstairs room of a ladies hairdresser situated almost directly opposite the house. The house was currently occupied and no one had entered or left for two hours now, which was not unusual. Tommy's role in Op Vanguard was to be on standby for when the entry team were in a position to gain access to the property, once inside he was to position himself with the team leader and offer technical advice on whatever was found. The men who had featured on the anti terrorist watch list, were not thought to be overtly dangerous, the acts that had gotten them noticed were limited to passing out leaflets calling for all British Muslims to rise against the UK government, and pamphlet's raging against US and UK military involvement in the Middle East. The two who attended the radical mosque were regarded as being more extreme in their views but had not to date been charged with any offences. Terry went on to say that one of Mr Malik's cousins, a Salim Barzam, was a second year electronics engineering student at the nearby university, and that police would be speaking with his tutors in the morning. Tommy asked about the receipts that had brought them to the house in the first place, explaining that he was in fact the guy that had found them in the bin, Terry explained that forensic tests were still being carried out by in theatre assets, Tommy knew all about what forensic testing could be done, and how long it sometimes took, but it appears that some bright spark back at Brigade had picked up on the relevance of the torn receipt, and after identifying its point of origin had notified the MOD in London who had in turn turned it over to the security forces. Easy build had been very forthcoming and although unable to identify who had placed the order it was able to at least say where the order had been dispatched to, "what we don't know" said Terry "is how the torn receipt ended up in the waste paper bin in the compound you were searching". Tommy asked the, to him obvious question, why didn't the police simply round them all up and question them? "We run the danger of spooking whoever did order the items if we do that" said Terry patiently, "We cannot simply go in and arrest everyone in the house" he added; "we have no proof that anyone there even ordered the stuff leave alone sent anything to Afghanistan, no, what we need is to link the receipt with someone at the address, ideally find proof of handling and posting if we can" Tommy looked through the files that Terry had given him, it seemed weird looking at a photocopy of a piece of paper he had last held shortly before his world and certainly Marty's life had been forever changed. The scrap of paper had been torn into a number of pieces and not all had been found, but what was shown was part of a package number, M084A, Terry explained that easy build had confirmed that was the company's packing details for a component named LM555, the LM555 was widely regarded as a highly stable device for generating accurate time delays, Tommy knew that triple five timers were used for many things and was a favourite of terrorist groups all over the world, favoured for its cost, its ease of use, its accuracy and the simplicity in which they could be bought.

Once the briefing was over, Terry took Tommy along to where the operation was being run from, there he met the Officer in overall charge of the operation, who said he would take him along to meet the rest of the guys shortly, they were being housed in an low cost motel close by the address so they could react quickly, a room had been put aside for Tommy and all costs would of course be met by the police, Terry laughingly warned him that any "extras" however would come out Tommy's pocket. Tommy explained that his car was currently in the police visitors section and asked if it could be secured within the main police station car park for the duration of the operation, which was agreed and the necessary car pass arranged, once Tommy had moved his car and retrieved his bags he was then driven to the motel to meet the team.

The team led by a sergeant Al Rayne were relaxing in the lounge when they arrived, introductions were made and they went over the planned entry procedures they had been working on, the house had two main access points, the rear door being regarded as the best option as it reduced the risk from casual observers, it would not be the first time that a well meaning passerby had disturbed and compromised a planned covert raid, once inside the premises, to which they had obtained detailed floor plans albeit a few years old, Tommy and the team lead were to be situated in the hallway able to respond immediately to any request from either floor. The rest of the team had been detailed areas of responsibility and were well practised in leaving thoroughly searched premises leaving no clue as to them ever having been there. It was debatable, it was explained to Tommy how robustly evidence recovered in this manner actually stood up in court, but anything recovered from these operations was never used as the only evidence produced and was very often the precursor for a properly executed Warrant authorising an overt police search team to fully search a house lifting everything from floorboards to false ceilings, none of which could be carried out in a covert manner.

The initial plan was to simply have the surveillance team to continue to watch the house and whenever someone left to have a mobile unit keep them under observation, once the house was empty and all occupants were under control then Al would be informed and the decision to enter would be left to him. If this became impossible to manage, then a contingency plan of a "staged" gas leak, requiring all the occupants of the street to be evacuated would be instigated. This was far from perfect but it was sometimes the only way to ensure that properties were vacated with sufficient time to allow Al and his team to conduct their clandestine business.

Briefing over, and with Al's phone number safely punched in to his mobile, Tommy took himself off to his room, and after unpacking, phoned the hospital to check on Marty, satisfied that she was still on the mend, and having left a message for her that he would be busy for a few days but would visit as soon as he was able to, he showered and changed before heading downstairs to have dinner. One of the advantages of working alongside specialist police teams was that they seemed to have a diet that centred around curry houses, and Leicester offered a wide range of such, and of course being locals the Officers found themselves being waited on with great diligence and attention by restaurateurs keen to attract such clientele. Tommy soon found himself very much at ease in their company, unsurprisingly, a couple had been in the army before swapping the green for the blue, the sense of humour and nonstop Mickey taking between all the guys on the team reminded Tommy of long evenings in the mess. The Officers were very keen to hear at firsthand about life in Afghanistan, and expressed admiration for the work everyone in uniform was doing over there. They explained that in Leicester, in common with many multi cultural cities around the UK, there was, amongst the younger generation in particular, an almost mythical respect for the brave freedom fighters waging a Jihad in support of religion. This support a direct result of a very clever propaganda campaign that was being waged over the internet, and was able to pour hundreds of heroic stories relating how these warriors against all odds were driving the infidels from their lands. These stories were then beamed into the bedrooms and study room of Britain every night feeding and corrupting these young impressionable minds. Tommy thought to himself that he hadn't seem much in the way of bravery when these freedom fighters drove a battered pickup truck laden with explosives into a busy market square timed to detonate when hundreds of civilians were busy buying whatever their hard earned wages could afford in order to feed their families. What he had seen, and still saw in the dark small hours of the night, were the shattered bodies of people cut down in their prime, the blood stains splattered across walls and pavements, he had heard the tormented screams of children blinded and afraid or the quiet moans of agony uttered by women with their legs and arms torn off and he had felt the naked fear and terror in the air, these images and sounds he was certain never got past the cutting room floor. Tommy had never had much time for politics, he had gone into Iraq without really knowing why, he had never believed that it was simply to prevent Saddam unleashing his fantasy weapons of mass destruction, he was there to do a job, and it was a job he was good at. What he did have time for though, was the sometimes old fashioned concept of courage and honesty. If these people wanted to fight him or the British Army, or any other Army for that matter, then come out and do it, not to hide behind closed doors and target innocent civilians. Tommy like a lot of his colleagues had developed a strong hatred for suicide bombers who in a misguided sense of religious zeal or worse, sent themselves into underground stations or department stores and cafes in order to inflict as much damage as they could on the people who were unlucky enough to be there at that particular time.

The next day Tommy woke and decided that in the absence of anything useful or fun to do, he would once again re start his fitness regime, after a couple of miles throwing himself around the woodland nearby and as many push ups and sit ups as he could manage, not as many as he used to be able to do, but not too shabby all things considered he conceded, he staggered back to his room showered and headed down to the breakfast bar where a couple of the team were quietly drinking coffee and reading the newspapers, the news headlines were the usual strikes and strife and hidden away on the third page was a short piece explaining how another Bomb Disposal exert had been killed on active duty, the reporter went on to say that Sergeant Frank Carter had been killed whilst dealing with a terrorist device when the bomb he was working on detonated prematurely. Al came in and announced that there had been no change in the situation at the premises' and suggested that he took Tommy along to the observation post in the hairdressers so he could familiarise himself with the layout of the house and surrounding area, the old army adage of time spent on reconnaissance is seldom time wasted, seemed to hold true in the police force also. Al parked his car a short walk away from observation post and after confirming with the control room via a concealed radio that he was now out of his car and was on foot heading towards the observation post, codenamed "ranch" they set off, Tommy who had been fitted with his own covert ear piece so he could at least listen to any transmissions, heard Al and the guys in the "ranch" agree that as they approached the rear door, a countdown would be given by Al so as to ensure that the door would be opened without Tommy and Al having to stand around possibly drawing attention to themselves. "That's me, one hundred meters" Tommy heard Al say quietly into his microphone clipped to his inner collar, "fifty, thirty, ten, five" and as they approached the door it swung open allowing them both inside and was immediately and softly closed behind them.

The post had been established following well rehearsed patterns two men on duty at all times, armed with high performance cameras, radios, log books and the usual concealment paraphernalia that would prevent anyone happening to look up at the hairdressers top floor window being able to see that there were two men up there pointing assorted cameras at the house opposite. On the wall were recently taken photographs of all the current occupants of the house, their names, and other useful information including any known aliases were printed below. Tommy read the names, aside from Said Malik and his cousin Salim, there were, Hussain Chowdhry, Imran Mazar and Rahim Mazar. The house itself was in line with all the others along the road, a detached four bedroom residence built around 1970, the front garden was paved to allow for off road parking and the rear was enclosed by a wooden fence and entered by a single gate, which opened inwards Tommy was informed. Al went on to say that "no alarm box had been seen outside the property and nothing had been seen as any of the occupants had entered, to indicate that they were punching a code into an alarm panel", these panels were usually placed within easy reach of the front door and was often visible to anyone who wanted to take note of such acts. "No dogs to be concerned about, either at the target or in the houses both side and the path leading to the back door was paved and not gravelled" which Tommy knew, made for a quieter approach.

"Stand by" said one of the two operators at the window, "we have the front door opening, I have Zulu 1 and Zulu 2 leaving the house, that's Zulu 1 into Charlie 1" his every word was being broadcast on a secure network and Tommy knew that at that very moment surveillance operators' both on foot and in vehicles were listening in, ready to move from a static watching role to a more complex mobile one. The code names Zulu 1 and 2 referred to two of the named occupants, namely Salim and Imran, Charlie 1 was the vehicle that had been parked in the driveway, "Zulu 1 and 2 mobile in Charlie 1 Northbound towards Granby Street" "That leaves three in the house, come on you buggers, go somewhere, anywhere will do, just get out of the house for a few hours" said Al with some feeling. However no one in the house seemed to hear Al's heartfelt plea and the front door remained resolutely shut. Charlie 1 onto Granby towards East gates Tommy heard over his earpiece, the transmissions now being sent from operators who would be following the suspect vehicle and others who were being prepositioned along possible routes by Officers manning the control room to pick up the tail as the car came into their area of operations. Tommy knew that a surveillance operation often involved dozens of Officers and vehicles; he had been on one task where at least six unmarked police cars, and one mobile control unit had followed a suspected terrorist for over forty miles undetected on a busy motorway by means of continually swapping positions leapfrogging the car in front and rejoining the motorway ahead of the suspect car. He was not envious of the controlling Officer's task; it was no easy thing to manage all the moving parts and to ensure that the suspects were both unaware of being followed and that they remained under police control. Tommy heard the various call signs report that vehicle and both occupants were moving North and eventually pulled up outside a small lock up, one of a block of twenty single storey storage units that could be rented by the month, just off the Blackbird Road, Zulu 1 and 2 were then observed going into the unit after first unlocking what looked like brand new and heavy duty padlock. Surveillance operators would remain on scene and retain control of suspects and the vehicle until such time as they were safely housed, even then they would be kept under observation. Al and Tommy made their way back to the motel, where Al briefed the team, and between them came up with a rough and ready plan to conduct a covert search of the lock up if permission could be obtained.

The rest of the day passed quietly, Salim and Imran, had after spending just under an hour in the lock up travelled back to the City, Salim had been dropped off at the university and was kept under close observation, returning home a few hours later, in the meantime Imran had gone into town and had been seen buying a pack of replacement headlight bulbs from Halfords. Al had driven back to the headquarters to seek permission to conduct a reconnaissance mission on the lock up that night, an operative had been tasked with getting as much information from the owners as possible regarding rental agreements, duration of contract, methods of payment and most importantly from a search perspective, details of internal layout, alarms and potential obstacles. A second operator had conducted a walk by the lock up and had been able to identify the make and type of padlock that had been fitted, that information had allowed the police specialist entry team to purchase an identical one and then spend a few hours practising defeating the lock and more importantly being able to lock it again after the task had been completed. The idea being that, there should be no evidence of anyone ever having been inside the lock up when any of the suspects returned there.

Al returned to the motel a few hours later having gotten the necessary legalities sorted out and the team busied themselves preparing for the nights task. Tommy was to again be on standby, this time in a car positioned nearby, and prepared to be taken on to target should the need arise. The team were to gain entry, record everything that was inside the storage unit, photograph all items of interest and if possible gather forensic evidence from keypads, telephone handsets or any other common touch items, then once complete, leave it appearing undisturbed. A number of contingency plans were discussed relating to an array of "what ifs" what if they couldn't gain access? What if they were compromised by a duty watch keeper? Even down to, "what if they find a bloody great big bomb?" this from one of the former soldiers on the team, to be answered immediately by a colleague saying that with the size of his arse he could simply sit on it and we would all be saved! Al settled the team down and after confirming with the ranch that all suspects were secured, they went out to prepare the vehicles and to set off unseen and unheard into the night.

Tommy checked his watch, fifteen minutes past midnight, he was sat in a parked car some five minutes away from the lock up, he had heard the team communicating with the guys on the ground who had staked out the area around the storage unit before the team arrived confirming that it was all quiet and also ideally placed to give an advance warning of people approaching the area. After being given the all clear the entry team made up of three people had made their way to the lock up, carefully avoiding the muddy puddles that the recent rainfall had left behind, a wet footprint left in a sealed unit would be just one way of alerting the suspects that someone had been inside whilst they had been safely tucked up for the night. The padlock had proven to a little difficult but the hours spent rehearsing had obviously paid off as before too long all three were inside the lock up and were conducting their initial assessment. Tommy heard the entry team leader inform control that they were inside and about to begin operations. The only sounds now were the radio checks every thirty minutes instigated by the control room, and one warning from an operator that a lone male had been spotted walking towards the lock ups, it turned out he was simply looking for a quiet spot to spend a penny, that done he turned around and made his way home blissfully unaware that his nocturnal naughtiness was being watched by at least two undercover Officers. After an hour the radio in Tommy's ear chirped into action and he heard his call sign being requested, a sealed package had been found inside a tool cabinet, the Officers couldn't open it without risk of compromise and wanted to know whether Tommy had bought his x ray equipment with him and if so could it be used to identify the contents. One item of equipment that Tommy and Andy had agreed on taking before he left the Regiment was the newly issued lightweight radiography kit, this was packed in the backpack at his feet and once prepared could produce an image within sixty seconds of the package being x rayed. This allowed for the contents to be identified or at least be identified as not containing a bomb, without any fear of compromising the search teams' presence. The only downside was the risk of exposure to the x rays themselves which posed a risk to personnel in the immediate area, the risk was small but none the less a risk anyway, normally Tommy would have simply asked that all non essential personnel move away from the area however in the cramped confines of the lock up this was not feasible. This was one of the "what ifs "that had been discussed and it had been agreed that as Tommy approached the lock up, two of the team would exit as he entered leaving the minimal people at risk, Tommy would then try to shield them machine as much as possible with whatever he could find within the unit, the main threat coming from the end of the machine that the x-rays were actually emitted from. Before Tommy could be escorted to the target, the other operators on duty had to once again pre position themselves to ensure that the area was and remained clear during the insertion and extraction phases of the manoeuvre. This done and the team warned of the pending arrival of Tommy they set off, the trick was, it had been drummed into Tommy to act as if you belonged there, nothing stands out more than someone who is obviously loitering around or wandering about aimlessly. Again the countdown sequence was used and within a few minutes Tommy found himself inside the lock up having seamlessly swapped positions with the two coming out. The team leader had been stood by the door as Tommy arrived and had immediately put a hand on Tommy's shoulder and guided him onto a mat that the team had placed in front of the door.

Adjusting his eyes to the gloom he could make out a number of tool lockers and storage cupboards along the wall, a low level workbench with assorted tools on it and what appeared to be a tailors mannequin stood against the rear wall, he could imagine the shock that would have produced when seen for the first time by the entry team. The leader a taciturn man who had introduced himself as Bob led Tommy to one of the storage cupboards and showed him the package in question, it was the size of small sports bag and had been wrapped in a plastic bag, the type of bag commonly used for garden waste and the like. The bag had then been sealed with tape, clearly whoever had done this did not want the contents either being seen or possibly being ruined in the cold damp air of the lock up. Tommy looked around and decided he would move the package to a position near the rear wall, this would allow for most of the dangerous emissions to be aimed outside, before he did that, he asked Bob if he was happy for this to happen, conscious that this was his area of expertise and he was the lead on this operation. Bob asked for a few minutes before the package was moved to take a few more photographs and record precisely where the bag was on the shelf, so as to allow him to accurately replace it once Tommy was finished. Whilst Bob did that, Tommy set about preparing his equipment, he had checked the battery levels and the condition of the generator before leaving the motel; however he once more went through the pre x ray check list. Satisfied everything was in order, Tommy moved across to the storage locker and after putting on a pair of surgical gloves he lifted the package, surprised at its weight or rather lack of it, he moved across to his work area and placed the package onto the drop sheet he had earlier placed on the ground. Before beginning the process that would produce the image, he had Bob move to the furthest point away from the generator as was possible given the space they had to work in, and made ready to fire. His mind suddenly returned to the time when he was last about to produce an x ray, and he froze just before he pressed the button, he shook his head to clear it telling himself angrily to get a grip, shocked at how his heart rate had just gone through the roof, the logical part of Tommy knew this was a completely different type of task, no terrorists or anyone else for that matter aside from the police knew he was in this lock up, no one knew he would be here x raying this package, there was no threat, yet Tommy found he was holding his breath and had tensed his whole body as the machine fired the first pulse. The machine went through its cycle and within a minute an image appeared on the small screen Tommy had placed by his side, the image could be manipulated to enhance its definition and clarity, colours could be altered and this latest model had a gizmo that allowed the user to take accurate measurements of individual items inside the package. Tommy took another couple of shots tweaking the number of pulses each time, there was no exact science involved in the number of pulses one had to fire through an item, but over time operators got to be very good at gauging the required number based on target size, weight and density. Satisfied he had captured every part of the package, Tommy returned it to Bob, who would be responsible for its replacement. He then turned his attention to the images he had saved, one thing stood out immediately, the package was not a bomb, nor did it contain any of the components you would expect to find within an IED, however Tommy could not hand on heart tell Bob what was actually inside the package, it appeared to be clothing, he could make out a metallic shapes that looked like zippers and others that just had to be buttons, he assessed the bag to contain at least trousers and maybe shirts possible two of each, Clothing would also explain the lack of weight he had noted on first moving the package.

The next morning the team gathered at a local police station to conduct an after action review, a few things had not gone as well as the team had hoped and it was an opportunity to improve the plan should they have a need to go back into the lock up at some point in the future. Bob then briefed everyone involved just what they had found on target, it was, at first glance not very exciting, but as Al reminded them all, it was sometimes the innocuous things that sometimes revealed the most light. The lock up had contained amongst other things a new workbench on which had been placed a soldering station with a fume extractor, assorted hand tools including wire strippers, snips, circuit board cutters and a helping hands set, which was in essence a weighted contraption that sported two small crocodile clips and a magnifying glass used for close up soldering work where you needed more than your allotted two hands to hold a soldering iron, the solder and the two items you were attempting to join together. In a box below the workbench were a number of batteries and battery connectors, various electrical toggle switches, assorted cabling and electrical tape, some of these were still in their sealed packs. One of the storage lockers had held three sets of disposable coverall, dust masks, and a box of surgical type gloves, another item that had attracted some interest was a bright yellow box that resembled a cool box but which had been adorned with a red cross and the words Human Organs for Transplant, thankfully the box had been empty. Tommy then revealed what he thought was in the sealed package, he showed the team the images he had taken and was able to point out the zippers and buttons to back up his assessment that the bag contained shirts and trousers, he was not able to tell from the image the colours and sizes inside but was pretty certain that there were two of each item. The team spent some time what these items meant and whether there was any merit in returning to the lock up another time, Tommy explained that apart from the perfectly legal home maintenance uses of the coveralls gloves and masks they were very often worn by terrorists during the process of manufacturing homemade explosives and constructing explosive devices. The presence of the workbench and tools although not alarming was of interest, the mannequin could be there for a number of reasons, as for the wrapped clothing and organ transplant box; no one had any sensible suggestions. Al concluded the discussion by saying that there was nothing in the lock up that could be used to Warrant detaining or even questioning any of the individuals being watched, It was decided that one way or another the house would be searched within 24 hours and based on what was found a decision to return to the lock up or arrest any or all of the men would then be made.

Tommy and Al were at the back of the observation post overlooking the house on Elmhurst Road, when three white vans with flashing orange lights and Gas Emergency Unit stencilled neatly along their flanks, pulled up at various points along the road supported by two police cars. As they stopped up to a dozen men piled out and as some began to erect barriers blocking off the approaches others proceeded to start going from house to house. As the gas board officials, who in reality were all serving Officers with a neighbouring police force, working under a mutual assistance scheme, with uniformed local police in attendance began to explain to the home owners what was going on a slow stream of people began to leave their homes and make their way to a nearby community shelter that had been turned into a temporary evacuation post, and was being manned by volunteers from a local charity. Al and Tommy watched their target house with interest, the surveillance team had watched as Zulu 3, Said Malik, had driven off earlier that morning and he was now under control at his place of work, the gas official had just knocked at the door and was explaining to Salim that there was a reported gas leak and everyone currently in Elmhurst Road was required to vacate their homes whilst a full and detailed search and repair task could be carried out. Every moment of this exchange was being recorded on video cameras currently being aimed at the front door by the concealed watchers. As Salim re-entered the property, the police Officer who had been at the door turned and mopped his brow with a white handkerchief, Al immediately got onto the radio and informed the entry team who were stationed less than a mile away that, Zulu 1 had been told of the "emergency" and was about to leave the house, the police Officer who had given the" all clear" sign continued along the road and positioned himself at one of the barriers that had effectively cordoned off the road. Tommy watched as Salim, Hussain and the two Mazar brothers walked out of the house each carrying a small backpack and made their way to the community shelter. "Zulus 1,2,4 and 5 now heading towards shelter, target is clear" reported one of the watchers, Tommy and Al made their way downstairs and dressed in official looking gas board uniforms made their way onto the road, at the same time a forth white van turned into the road and a further six officials jumped out.

Tommy was stood in the small hallway of the house he could hear the teams talking quietly as they systematically went though room by room, Al had gone upstairs to supervise the search of one of the bedrooms, the home looked ordinary enough, pictures of family members adorned the walls and a panoramic view of the Al-Haram Mosque during the Hajj dominated the wall above the fireplace. He saw Matt one of the searchers beckon him into the kitchen, he made his way carefully in to the small room and was immediately surprised at seeing four almost new refrigerators lined up along one wall they were all plugged in and running but as Matt opened each one in turn, Tommy saw they were all empty. Tommy knew; that one of the major concerns with the manufacture of some homemade explosives was the need to keep the mixture at a steady and low temperature. This could be achieved by ice cubes at some stages of the process and by keeping the finished product cool once the explosive had been produced. Four fridges was an awful lot of cooling space Tommy thought to himself. Sat on top of one of the fridges were two new coffee grinders neither of which showed any signs of ever having been used to grind coffee. The remaining cupboards were opened and apart from the usual crockery one would expect to find were eight new mixing bowls, thermometers and glass beakers all still in their original packaging. Tommy was watching Matt's team photograph all these items when he was aware of Al standing beside him, "you should see this Tommy "he said softly and led the way upstairs.

Al led Tommy to a small bedroom in which a box lay open on the floor, Tommy could see maps and photographs inside, but as he drew closer the reality of what he was looking at made him stop dead and he could feel the icy fingers of fear suddenly clutch his body, he knew then why Al felt he should take a look. The photographs, approximately fifty in total, were all neatly labelled showed Bomb disposal teams conducting their business; Tommy recognised most of the operators and number twos'. All of the pictures showed team members preparing or using equipment, or of operators being dressed in the bomb suit, a couple showed what looked like explosive devices being rendered safe by operators. The pictures were all taken on the mainland of the United Kingdom, Tommy knew that by the type of bomb van being used and the green and brown khaki uniforms being worn but also by the lack of body armour that would be worn in Iraq, Afghanistan or Northern Ireland. As Tommy leafed through the pictures he stopped at one that showed a young and very much alive Sergeant Frank Carter working on what appeared to be a Command wire device. Tommy could see a number of other uniformed personnel in the background and realised what he was looking at and where the photos had been taken.

The maps the usual Ordnance Survey sort that could be bought at most camping stores showed 1:50000 views of the West Midlands, Warwickshire and North Yorkshire. Also in the box were receipts for the lock up off the Blackbird Rd which showed that the lock up had been rented for three months, paid for in advance with cash in the name of Mahood Atcha, and another from a medical suppliers in Birmingham which specialised in medical uniforms and equipment again to be delivered to a Mr Atcha. Tommy returned the photographs to Al and returned to his station in the hallway trying to make sense of what he had just seen, one thing was certain; this was now much bigger than simply identifying who had ordered electrical components for which a receipt had been found in a mud walled compound in Southern Afghanistan. Al's team continued with their tasks copying hard drives and computer discs for interrogation by IT experts back at the station, going through drawers and cupboards, taking latent forensic evidence from various surfaces and objects for later analysis and possibly cross matching with DNA recovered from other scenes, and at all times leaving everything exactly as it had been found when they arrived, the photographs, receipts and maps were all scanned into the portable scanner brought along for that very purpose. Al got onto the radio and informed control that they were preparing to vacate the target and to get assurances that all suspects were still under control, he also requested the" gas leak" take another couple of hours to be repaired. Assurances received and approval for the emergency work to be continued granted, Tommy found himself walking back towards the van and then being driven to the main headquarters at Enderby, where a full debriefing had been hastily arranged. Sat in the back of the crowded van, Tommy had a quick chat with Al before telephoning Andy. Putting aside any small talk Tommy simply told Andy that they had a problem which could not be discussed over the phone but that he and Terry, the MLO, would travel to Oxford immediately after the debriefing and that they would need to talk with him the Ops Officer and the Colonel.

CHAPTER FIVE

Tommy introduced Terry to Colonel Wilson who in turn introduced the Ops Officer, Russ Harris, and his SAT, Andy, the five of them were seated in a secure briefing room on the top floor of the Regimental Headquarters, Tommy began by informing them what had been found in both the lock up and the house on Elmhurst Rd, and the conclusions he had drawn from these findings. He had given the same findings to the Police at the debriefing session after they had returned to Enderby. Once he had finished he sat back and waited for the response he knew would be forthcoming. "You are quite certain these pictures were taken on a validation exercise?" The Colonel asked. "They must have" answered Tommy; "where else would we have that many onlookers on a task?" Andy explained to Terry, that every British bomb disposal operator was required to undergo a validation assessment every few months, so as to ensure they were still in date and operating at the desired performance levels demanded of them. The operators were set a number of realistic training scenarios based on the current threats from around the world and to increase the realism Police and Fire Brigades from around the

Country as well as local Military Units were invited to attend and to supply witnesses, casualties, Incident Commanders and advisors. "What happens if they fail?" asked Terry, "in that case" Andy replied, "they are taken off the duty rota until such time as they prove themselves sufficiently proficient", "this after receiving an intensive programme of remedial training" added Russ. "The pictures show a number of simulated devices went on Andy, and the vehicles being deployed are normally used for operations on the Mainland, that coupled with the numbers of Police and other personnel in the background, I believe supports Tommy's assessment" "Do we know when and where the photos were taken" asked the Colonel, "and more importantly" said Terry, "who took them". Andy looked at Tommy who answered "probably somewhere near Ripon, these exercises move around the Country every so often, these seem to have been taken in winter, and the scenery suggests a couple of disused farmhouses on the North Yorkshire moors we used last time we were there. The date stamps on the pictures, although not conclusive evidence coincides with the dates of the exercise". The colonel nodded in agreement "They could have been taken by any number of people, Police Fire or even Military personnel, we even invite local landowners on occasions when we feel the need to promote a hearts and minds approach. The exercise controllers report should have the contact details of those attending the exercises; we need that sort of thing to comply with Health and Safety Regulations but also to ensure the caterers' provide enough food for the week" added the Ops Officer. "The thing is, we now have photos of operators performing, in some instances, very sensitive operations circulating around God know where and being seen by God knows who. We already have pretty damning evidence that my guys are being targeted based on what they will be doing to any given device", pointed out the Colonel forcefully, "Staff Byrne here is bloody lucky to be alive as a result of this targeting, these photos, whoever took them, seems to show us how some of that information may have gotten to the terrorists responsible for the emplacement of these devices" Colonel Wilson went on to say. "We also seem to have forgotten what else was found on target" said Andy with a rueful smile, "the presence of cooling systems, mixing apparatus, tools, protective masks and gloves all point towards someone at the premises' either having an extreme fondness for cooking or someone developing an interest in making homemade explosives, and possibly the means to initiate them, do we know what was found on the computer drives" he went on to ask Terry. "No, not yet" he replied, "I have asked the data boys to hasten their investigation and to get back to us as soon as they find something. In the meantime the five suspects have been assessed as being potentially dangerous and will be arrested should they demonstrate any signs of mounting any type of offensive action, they will continue to be subject to the surveillance operation being carried out under Op Vanguard, but armed Officers will be added to the team, and will respond should they be needed. The commissioner is very anxious to not have a major incident in his manor, but he accepts the views from his tactical advisors that we need to be able to spring the trap when we have sufficient evidence to arrest everyone concerned with this operation, if indeed it is an operation" he added. "It may well be worth asking the search teams to be on the lookout for any of the suspects looking to buy the chemicals required to make homemade explosives" suggested Russ, "Staff here will give you a complete listing of the more commonly used ones". "Obviously if this moves from being a watching brief to one where suspected explosives are being manufactured Staff, I will want you to let me know as soon as possible" added the Colonel, "I do not intend to remove you from this operation, but we will need more assets in place should this situation develop". "Very good Sir", replied Tommy dutifully. "Now" said the Colonel, "how do we find out who took these damn photographs and how did they come to be found in a house in Leicester". "Old fashioned Police work" Terry answered "and some luck" he added as an afterthought. The meeting finished with Tommy and Terry promising to call as soon as they had anything to report, and the Colonel asking Russ to set up a secure call to his counterpart in Afghanistan, as soon as possible.

On the drive back, Terry asked the question everyone seemed to want to ask, that of why did they do what they did, how can he walk up to a bomb and not be terrified every time, Tommy answered simply by shrugging his shoulders and by telling the tale of how he somehow fell almost by accident into the job, and he found he had some sort of knack for doing it well enough. He had no illusions of his courage or believed the hype that they were somehow superhuman, yes it was difficult at times and of course there were dangers involved, but no more hazardous than a lot of other professions for which he had utmost respect, fire fighters, police office to name two. The training was thorough and aimed at weeding out those not up to the mark, however he thought to himself, he sometimes had the impression that the current demand for operators meant that that some decisions were based on political necessity as opposed to operator ability. As for being superhuman he remembered some of the incredibly courageous acts he had witnessed being carried out by young soldiers and the work carried out by the nurses and doctors on the casualty flight home to Brize and in the hospitals all over the country and said he knew who he regarded as the real heroes.

Thinking of hospitals reminded Tommy that he had promised Marty he would see her again soon, he decided to take a chance and although not on the route back to Leicester, asked Terry if he could detour via the hospital, Terry replied that it would add another fifty miles to the journey, but if Tommy bought dinner tonight he was sure it could be arranged. With that Tommy phoned the ward to make sure it would be ok to visit at such short notice, and was pleased to hear the distinctive sound of Mandy's Birmingham accent as the call was answered, he was then doubly pleased to hear that of course she remembered him and that although irregular, was sure that Marty would be very pleased to see him again. Terry then called Al to explain where they were and give an estimated time of return, in turn he was told that Salim had returned to the lock up earlier that morning and dropped off a parcel that had been delivered to the target from a delivery company, he had then returned to the university and was currently still there, he then said that the IT reports should be with them inside a few hours, but other than that it was all quiet. Mandy had gone off duty by the time Tommy walked the now familiar route to the ward, and announced his arrival at the office, she had however warned the oncoming staff of his visit, Tommy was warned that there were other patients on the ward and the he should keep the noise down and would only be allowed thirty minutes as the doctor was due to do his rounds.

Mandy had clearly told Marty that she was to expect a visitor as she was propped up on the bed expectantly looking towards the door as Tommy walked in, he was amazed at how brighter she seemed, her hair had been tidied and the metal contraption around her leg had been removed, her arm was still heavily wrapped and it gave Marty a clumsy lop sided appearance. She motioned him to pull up a chair and asked him how he was doing, and what's this hush hush job he was on was. Tommy gave a loose explanation of what he was doing with the police omitting any reference to Afghanistan and the photos, she seemed satisfied with that and made Tommy promise to take care, even if it was just poking around empty houses. The thirty minutes passed quickly, Marty was to be moved very soon to an ordinary ward, and she was due to start a course of physiotherapy in a few days, Tommy expressed his concern for the unlucky therapist, for which he received a poorly aimed cushion that Marty threw at him, "you're supposed to be sick" he accused her laughing at her attempts to retrieve the cushion for a second attempt, "and you're supposed to bring me chocolates, grapes and copies of gossip magazines" she said, giving up on the cushion and settling back on the bed, "not bloody flowers", "you hate grapes" he complained, "that's not the point I am sick and I am female which makes me right", she said grinning at Tommy. Tommy knew when to admit defeat and promised to send every copy of "She" magazine he could find before his next visit. On his way out, he popped into the nurses' station and after thanking them for allowing the visit and for taking good care of Marty; he informed them Marty had asked him, to ask them, could she please be placed on the list of patients who were to receive regular visits from the hospital chaplain. Tommy walked away smiling, he remembered full well Marty telling him of how she had been forced to attend a strict religious school and had hated every minute of it. That would teach her to throw cushions; still he would probably be in need of the bomb suit next time he came to visit, he thought to himself.

CHAPTER SIX

Russ had ordered two of his clerks to go through the after action report from the last winter validation exercise held in North Yorkshire, and to identify every visitor who had attended over the course of the week. That would mean phoning at least nine different police forces and twice as many fire service headquarters, he told the two clerks that this was now top priority and to inform him should anyone not be fully cooperative. He would take care of the military visitors, thinking rightly that the response would be much more forthcoming if the request came from a Captain than if it originated from a Lance Corporal regardless of who had authorised the search. In the meantime the photographs had been scanned and were being pored over by photographic analysts who were told find out everything you can about what is going on in the shots, type of equipments being used, type of task, anything at all that you think may be of interest. He had not told any of his newly recruited staff; why they were doing what they were, but he did stress that it was of the upmost importance and may help to save lives both here and overseas. Before Terry had left, Russ had told him that once he had all the names, he would forward them onto him, and between the two services, they would attempt to identify who had been behind the lens. In the meantime Mahood Atcha was now subjected to a rigorous police investigation, Officers had gone to the rental company who managed the lock up and were trying to piece together a description of the man who had taken out the contract. Databases were being trawled in police stations across the county in the hope that someone, somewhere would eventually find out who Mr Atcha was, his links to the suspects in Elmhurst Rd and more importantly where he was now. The work promised to be long and pain staking and would require as Terry intimated old fashioned police work.

That diligence led to police discovering twelve men with that name in the Leicester area, each one was then individually investigated by a team of Officers, using electoral rolls, criminal record databases, anti terrorist watch lists and all other means at their disposal. The list was then whittled down to three likely suspects, one, a Doctor who worked at the local hospital, another, a man who was currently claiming unemployment benefits and finally a student at Leicester University. The Doctor was immediately ruled out after it was revealed that he had been suffering from a serious illness for some time and had not been able to leave his home for the past six months. When asked, colleagues had told police that Dr Atcha was a dedicated physician and had, before his illness regularly declared his abhorrence at the levels of violence and extremism that was carried out by some in the name of religion. Police Officers then visited the claims department of the unemployment offices and found that Mahood Atcha had been receiving benefits for three months, he lived with this parents in nearby Pickford Close, he had previously worked in a local pizza parlour before it closed down, he appeared to be a regular young man, not overly bright but always on time and well turned out. Police asked if the office CCTV cameras would have any images of Mr Atcha taken when he had last signed on," I am sorry" said the receptionist who had been dealing with the Officers, "but all recordings are routinely wiped after seven days" he is due to register at the claims office tomorrow morning though, we will have him on film then, if you want to come back". The admittance Officer at the university was able to tell Officers that one Mahood Atcha was recorded as being a former chemistry student, he had graduated last year, the records showed his last known address as 24 Pankhurst Rd in Loughborough and a passport style photograph taken shortly before his graduation showed a thin serious looking man with swept back hair and round rimmed glasses. Staff remembered him as being a studious man with few friends; he had been a member of the university Islamic studies group and often worked on their behalf distributing leaflets, and helping out at rallies.

Whilst Police were attempting to identify Mahood Atcha, Russ's team had been hard at work on compiling a list of visitors who had attended the exercise. They had been helped greatly by the fact that the photographs had clearly been taken over several days, so anyone who had been there for only one day was regarded as a less likely suspect. The list contained approximately sixty names including military, police and catering staff, all of whom had been at the exercise for at least two days. As Russ was preparing to phone Terry with the now finished list, his pager bleeped into life, an internal number was showing on the message screen, Russ called the number to hear the voice of one of the photographic analysts telling him he that they had possibly identified the photographer. Russ said he would be there immediately, as he approached the reproductive unit where the photography and mapping specialists worked he felt a sense of excitement and in some measure dread, he had tried to imagine the reaction if it turned out that it was one of his own guys who had been responsible for taking and distributing these pictures, he had attempted to convince himself that it was impossible, but was it? The analyst was waiting for him at the door, and immediately showed him to a desk on which a number of photographs had been enlarged and where possible enhanced. The analyst passed Russ a magnifying glass and pointed him towards one picture in particular. The image showed a bomb disposal operator working inside a suspect car, the operator had his back to the camera, Russ could see one of the teams remotely controlled robots parked to one side of the vehicle, the rear doors had been opened and the operator was doing something in the back of the vehicle, "what am I looking at?" He asked the analyst, "look at the front driver's side window", he was told, he did so, and there reflected in the window was an image, faint and not very distinctive admittedly, but still an image of someone taking a photograph. "Who is he" he asked "we don't know" answered the analyst, "but he is military, you can see the uniform", "Can we get this "blown up"" the Ops Officer asked, "make it any clearer possibly?" "We can try" came the reply, "very good well do that as soon as you can please, can I take this with me" he said pointing toward s the picture, "I will need to brief the CO". Clutching the picture in one hand Russ headed off to find his Commanding Officer, on the way he poked his head into Andy's office, "Mr Jenkins could you come with me please" he asked, and without waiting for a reply set off towards the Colonels office.

"Who is he Mr Jenkins, is he one of ours?" Asked the CO, "I doubt it Sir, for one thing our guys were either being assessed, assessing or being used as admin staff, we had five of the assessing panel down there throughout the exercise, but you know yourself, assessing a task is no easy matter and none of them would have been taking happy snaps mid way through a task. I was there for the duration as was the Officer Commanding of the North Yorkshire squadron who had staged the event. We were either hosting visitors or going around the exercise area getting a feel for every tasking, the admin guys, well they are pretty much full on for the whole time, building devices, preparing the tasks, delivering supplies etc, All those guys would have been busy, no this is someone who had the time to be able watch an incident and not look too suspicious taking photographs, which only leaves one option." "Military Support element", said Russ "looks like Sir" Andy replied. "This does not leave these offices gentlemen" said the CO looking at both Andy and Russ, "we will need to let Staff Byrne in on this Sir", Russ suggested. The CO came to a decision quickly, "Ok, Mr Jenkins, get hold of Staff and tell him what we know, he can brief the MLO himself, I will call the CO of the North York's Rifles, the unit who supplied the manpower and request a meeting as soon as can be arranged, Russ get hold of your counterpart in the Military Police and arrange a visit to sound out how we go about this. In the meantime get those photographic boys working on that picture, I want to know as much as we can about that photographer." Tommy was with Terry, Al and Bob when his secure phone rang, excusing himself he quickly answered the call, "what's Up Tommy asked Al, seeing Tommy's face had taken on a serious look on his return. Tommy quickly filled both Officers in on what he had just learned from Andy. "Christ" whispered Bob, "one of your own kind, setting you up", "He is not one of us" said Tommy grimly, "Ok Ok I know he is not bomb disposal, but he is still Army", Bob said by way of explanation. "What will happen now", asked Terry, "not sure, the Boss will go and have a word with their Boss and I guess the monkeys will have to get involved", "Monkeys?" Asked Bob, "Military Police" explained Terry.

The surveillance team were settling down for the night when Al came back saying that all Zulus had returned from the Mosque in Loughborough, and were now all accounted for at the target. The team had planned to stage another operation on the lock up that night. The plan had been for a smaller entry party, just Bob and Tommy actually going into the unit, Tommy to take his x ray equipment with him in case the parcel that Salim had taken there, had not been opened. Earlier that day the team had been briefed on what had been found on the various hard drives and computer discs they had found in Elmhurst Rd. It seemed that someone at the house, had been a regular visitor to the Tehrik—e-Taliban website, known simply as TeT it was an on line forum where subscribers could log on and pass comment on any number of Islamic issues, it was however primarily a website where users extolled the bravery of the warriors and martyrs fighting the jihads, it was also used for individuals to post details of the various methods in which explosive devices could be made. Another search had revealed that a message to an individual named only as M had been dropped into a draft box on a hotmail account.

For Tommy's benefit, Al explained that to avoid electronic eavesdropping of sent and received emails, criminal and terrorist group would sometimes set up an email account on hotmail or yahoo and everyone in the group would use the same log on and password details. That way a message could be written by one member dropped into the draft box without being sent, a second member could then go to any computer, log on, open the draft document, read the message and delete it if necessary. A reply could then be written, and again saved as a draft, allowing messages to be sent back and forth without ever actually being sent. This particular message had read that the donations had been received and that we will be sending the flowers to the family later, it was signed S.

It was also evident that the same computer had been used to research suppliers of medical equipment, hairdressing suppliers and store that specialised in cooking utensils. More detailed interrogation was now being conducted on the software, looking to recover all deleted correspondence and more information of regularly visited websites. The Surveillance team had reported that Zulu 2, Imran, had gone into Loughborough and Leicester on a shopping expedition, he had gone into a number of stores and in each one had bought glass storage jars totalling twenty in all, he had then gone into a hardware store and asked for twenty kilograms of nails to be delivered to his home address, he had seemingly told the assistant that he was planning to re insulate the loft space and wanted to lay boards down first. He had then gone in to yet another hardware store and bought two sets of replacement headlight bulbs, which was unusual added the Officer as his lights are all working fine, and this was the second set he has bought this week. He had then returned to the lock up and had left all the items there. Mahood Atcha's photograph had been circulated to the team members in the observation post, and another team had been tasked with keeping an over watch on Pankhurst road in the hope he would be sighted at his last known address. As a precaution an arrest Warrant was being drawn up to allow police to question Said Malik regarding the connection between himself as the registered owner of the house where the components ordered from easy build had been delivered to and the receipt found in the compound.

It was felt that as it stood right now there was nothing conclusive to warrant detaining the other individuals, Mahood Atcha had paid for a lock up, and had ordered some medical equipment, and while it was possibly odd was not illegal.

Someone at Elmhurst Rd had been logging onto a jihadist website, and utilising a draft box but police did not who, and it could be claimed that the message was as yet unfinished hence it being found where it was. Imran had recently been on a very strange shopping trip, but it could be argued he had bought nothing that could not have perfectly innocent uses. If they could identify who had taken possession of the photographs, then it was possible charges could be preferred under existing anti terrorist legislation or even under the official secrets act if it could be proven that they were to be used for illicit purposes. The police and Tommy were under the impression that something was going on, and that somehow it was linked to events unfolding thousands of miles away, but as yet could not say what it was or who was doing it. Al said "we just need something that ties them all in, something that we can say categorically is related to that compound or to a planned attack somewhere else". "Right now a bloody parking ticket would be a start" said Bob with feeling.

The armed response unit had arrived and had been present at the pre task briefing, they were to be on call, in a nearby police station, able to respond at short notice if required, it was not expected that their presence would be needed at the lock up, but it paid to keep all options open. The drill was to replicate the one conducted when they first visited the unit, with one or two minor differences, and as far as Tommy was concerned one pretty big one, he was to go in with Bob and would be required to be Bob's eyes and ears whilst he was working on the padlock. Once inside Bob would again take the lead, his initial tasking was to locate the newly delivered items and then to confirm that the lock up contained nothing else that they had not yet identified. Tommy would be on hand to assist Bob in this search and to x ray the package should that be necessary. The walk onto target followed a similar pattern, with operators clearing their way in, Tommy and Bob soon found themselves outside the unit, Whilst Tommy kept watch, Bob made sure there were no tell tale signs on the door or the lock, which may have been placed there by the suspects in order to allow them to see if someone had tried to gain access to the unit in their absence., before beginning to open it. At first Tommy thought this was all a bit "James Bond" but he figured if it could work for 007 it would certainly work for him. Once inside the lock up, Bob again placed the mat by the door and they both stood silently for a few minutes to allow their eyes to adjust to the gloom, and to orientate themselves to the layout of the room. The first thing they noticed was that the newly purchased glass jars had been laid out on the workbench in groups of five, four groups in total, the recently purchased headlamps had also been placed on the bench next to the jars, Tommy began to get a very bad feeling about all this. This was starting to look like some kind of manufacturing process and he was struggling to find an innocent plausible reason for what he was seeing. Bob soon found the parcel, and to Tommy's surprise it had been opened, on looking inside, they found three more of the human organ transportation boxes, identical to the one they had seen on their last visit. Tommy looked at the internal dimensions and gauged that each box would hold five glass jars with room to spare. Once Bob was satisfied that he had recorded everything of interest, he spent a little time photographing and measuring the roof structure paying particular attention to the eaves and to the brick work, he then photographed the light switches and electrical sockets, before informing control that they were ready to extract. Walking back to the pickup point, Tommy asked why Bob had shown such an interest in the switches and roof layout. Bob said simply that they had on occasions used specialist listening devices and hidden cameras to record everything that went on inside a room, and that he had been asked to identify a number of suitable locations for these devices should they get permission to deploy them, now thought Tommy, this really is James Bond territory.

CHAPTER SEVEN

A few hours before Tommy and Bob were preparing to search the lock up, Colonel Wilson was being shown into a comfortable looking ante room in the Officer's mess of the North York's regiment in Ripon, a white gloved waiter brought coffee and left the room carefully closing the door as he left. Opposite him sat Colonel Hugh Willoughby Commanding Officer of the Regiment, after the formalities of the introductions and the almost obligatory small talk, Colonel Willoughby asked how he and his Regiment could be of assistance," well Hugh it's a bit sensitive" began Colonel Wilson, "hence my asking you to meet as such short notice and in private, for which by the way I am extremely grateful", "no bother at all old chap, what's on your mind" replied Hugh sipping his coffee. On the drive over, Colonel Wilson had received a phone call telling him that the best the analysts could come up with was that the photographer was white, and that he wore glasses. Colonel Wilson explained the situation, leaving out how he had come to be in possession of the pictures, and finished off by saying to his host that he was convinced that whoever took the pictures came from within this barracks. Colonel Willoughby sat back and looked across the table, "I find it most distasteful that you are accusing one of my men of breaching the official secrets act David; I believe you will find that you are mistaken and when you do, I shall demand a full apology" he said with some degree of arrogance. David Wilson looked at his counterpart and simply replied in slow measured tones that he would be more than happy to do but Hugh, should prove him wrong first, adding that "there were no other military personnel on the exercise, and all my men have accounted for their movements"." Ok" said Hugh, "let me find out which white bespectacled men we sent on your little exercise", with that he walked to an internal phone and punched in a number, talking quietly for a few minutes he returned to the table, saying his Operation Officer and Regimental Sergeant Major would be arriving shortly with a full list of who was there and where they were now. Four hours, and many phone calls later Colonel Wilson had said farewell to a very embarrassed looking Colonel Willoughby, as he made his way towards his car the North York's RSM who was escorting him said quietly, "do you think it could be arranged for a few of my guys to be part of the arrest party when you track down this bastard, excuse my language Sir", "I rather think RSM, there would be a long list of volunteers for that job, and I shall be top of the pile", replied Colonel Wilson."

Colonel Wilson, Captain Harris, Andy Jenkins and Terry were seated in the secure briefing room at seven thirty the following morning having received a late night phone call from the regimental adjutant informing them that the CO required their presence to discuss an issue of utmost importance. "Good morning Gentlemen, thank you for making the effort to get here so early", began the Colonel. "I believe the photographer is a Private George Peters, formerly of the Adjutant Generals Corps, three years ago Peters was posted to 321 Squadron, for your benefit Terry that is the bomb disposal unit in Northern Ireland, Peters served with them for two years as a clerk; in his role he was responsible for dissemination of all task reports to the various departments and as such had access to all files, codes and of course the reports. During his tour with 321 he spent two months as a stand in driver for the Belfast team. On completion of his tour he returned to England and was posted to Ripon Barracks, again as orderly room clerk, when the North York's were earmarked to be deployed to Afghanistan, Peters asked to not deploy on conscientious grounds, when that was refused, he went absent without leave. He managed to go on the run for six months, returning to the Ripon voluntarily with a counsellor for the Muslim Youth UK, a charity organisation aimed at promoting the Islamic faith within the UK and helping young Muslims find employment and to fight prejudice, in tow. Peters claimed he had converted to Islam and could not now be ordered to deploy to Afghanistan. The Muslim Youth UK had been to a local newspaper in Loughborough and they had run an article about how this brave soldier had been part of a bomb disposal unit in Northern Ireland, but was now forced to flee the army rather than fight his fellow believers. He had become a regular attendee at Loughborough Mosque and it was there a fellow member of Muslim Youth had convinced him to return to the Army. On his return he was confined to barracks and put to work in the guardroom, it was decided that Private Peters would be subject to a court martial, but that the proceedings be deferred to allow the publicity caused by the newspaper articles to die down. The RSM decided that Peters should be used on fatigue duty on any exercise the North York's were involved in, one of these being our validation one. He was sent there primarily to act as a driver, but asked if he could be used as a witness, stating that his knowledge of bomb disposal tasks would stand him in good stead, as he knew what type of information the teams would want. When he returned to Ripon, he was court martialled and dishonourably discharged from the army effective immediately". The colonel finished his summing up of his visit to Ripon by adding that he had spoken with Records and they would be sending across everything they had on Peters file, including past known addresses".

"How much would he have been able to learn about the mechanics of bomb disposal, procedures, equipments, rules that sort of thing" asked Terry. "Pretty much most of it", answered Andy, "he would have seen a lot of jobs at first hand in Belfast, he would have seen every report detailing how every job in the two years he spent in Ireland was carried out, and by being a witness on tasks during the exercise he would have seen how the latest devices are being dealt with by operators in Afghanistan". "Jesus", breathed Terry and do you think he has given this to the Taliban? "We don't know who he has told anything to, we do know that the photos he took have ended up in a house we know is involved somehow with electronic components that we believe have been sent to Afghanistan" said Russ. "True enough" agreed Terry, "can you arrest him?" asked Andy, "Not easily", said Terry, "we only know of those pictures because we were able to search the house by way of a diversionary tactic, We can ask him to come in to answer some questions voluntarily of course, see if he has some sort of reasonable excuse for the photos' being in Elmhurst Rd". Terry was interrupted by the sudden bleeping of the Colonels pager, which was followed almost immediately by the similar tone of his Operations Officer's, the message on both pagers was the same and was prefixed by the number 111, the two men looked at each other, both realising the significance of the triple one message, "another triple one Mr Jenkins" said Russ, packing away his folder, The CO excused himself and walked briskly out of the briefing room, what's a triple one?, asked Terry, an urgent message from theatre explained Andy, the last three triple ones have been used when we have had guys killed or badly injured.

Tommy had just finished telling Al and the rest of search team, how he thought the items they had found and what they had learnt could be used, his assessment could in no way be used in a court of law, but, given what they had, it made sense. The glass jars could easily accommodate 2kg of explosives each, the headlamps could be modified to be used as homemade detonators, the nails that had been ordered would make for some serious shrapnel, the workbench had sufficient tools to make any number of firing switches, the electrical items required could be bought almost anywhere. The presence of the fridges and grinders all pointed towards the manufacture of homemade explosives as did the thermometers and mixing bowls. One such device detonated in a cafe or bar would certainly cause fatalities, and they were looking at possibly twenty of these devices. All in all it was a depressing picture, no one in the room could come up with any other explanations for the presence of all these items, but having them was not a crime, making a bomb was a crime, having the precursors to manufacture explosives was a crime, getting sufficient proof that they had bought these things in the pursuit of committing or planning to commit a terrorist act was proving to be the difficulty. The briefing ended with a plan to keep each of the suspects under observation, and as soon as they had reason to, one or all would be hauled in for questioning. The team responsible for watching Pankhurst Rd, the last known address of Mahood Atcha, had reported that a middle aged couple had been seen entering and leaving the premises' as had two younger females, but no one matching Atcha's description had been sighted. The team however did report that on one occasion all four had left the house, the man, the last to leave, had been spotted possibly arming an intruder alarm control box in the hallway, before exiting the building, which on his return he walked straight to and disarmed, this would seem to indicate that there was no one else in the property. Tommy looked up as the briefing room door opened and was shocked to see Terry with an ashen looking Andy just behind him, his heart sank as Andy beckoned him over, as he moved towards the door, he passed Terry who silently walked to the centre of the room.

Staff Sergeant Ian King had been in Helmand for just over a month, he had already dealt with in excess of a dozen live and in some cases multiple devices, he had been preparing for lunch when the shout came in, a suspect vehicle borne IED, a car bomb, had been reported being placed outside a police station. His team had responded and as soon as all the necessary attachments searchers, protective security platoons and explosive detector dogs had been assembled, the convoy had set off. On arrival at the Incident Control Point, ICP for short, Ian had gone straight into the usual questioning routine, trying to ascertain the type of device, likely target and therefore likely perpetrators; this would in turn lead him to develop an effective and hopefully safe render safe option. Whilst he was doing that his team, led by his Number two, Corporal Bob Fadden, busied themselves preparing the necessary equipment, in this case, the remote controlled robot, known in the close knit circles of bomb disposal as the "wheelbarrow" so named after the every first prototype that had used parts of the gardening equipment that had been incorporated into its design. Ian shouted across to Bob, to "send it", which was the green light for the wheelbarrow to be manoeuvred out of the ICP and to be driven down to the suspect vehicle, the wheelbarrow could be fitted with a wide variety of weapon systems depending on the task, and came with a number of cameras that allowed Bob to steer the machine towards that target from the relative safety of the Bomb van. As the barrow approached the target area, Ian advised the guys on the cordon that were responsible for ensuring that interested bystanders were kept safely out of harm's way, that there would soon be a controlled explosion, which was actually one of the wheelbarrow weapon systems being fired at the vehicle in order to disrupt the bomb if I could be seen, or if not to gain access to the vehicle to allow it to be thoroughly and remotely searched.

The reasons for the advance warning were simple enough, a sudden loud unexpected explosive noise in the vicinity of a suspected bomb was never a good thing, by warning the cordon troops, this was going to happen they were prepared for the noise themselves and could also ease the worries of the locals who would gather at the perimeters of the cordon to observe the goings on. Establishing anything like a full cordon and evacuation in these parts was nigh on impossible, there were numerous areas where locals could, if they so desired approach the suspect car, and there were always people stood on the flat roofs of the huts and on hilltops overlooking the incident sites that the best you could hope for was that you had most avenues covered. Bob had positioned the barrow at the rear of the vehicle and Ian, satisfied with the results gave the order for the weapon to be fired, "Stand by . . . . Firing "yelled Bob as he pressed the fire button, immediately there was a dull muted sound and the rear hatch of the car flew open, Bob had aimed to take out the locking mechanism of the boot and in doing so open the rear of the car to allow the extending arm of the robot to search the boot and rear seats. After a full and fruitless search of the vehicle, and having driven around the immediate area of the car, again finding nothing of any interest, Ian told his number two to park the barrow off to one side and get him prepared to make a manual approach to the vehicle.

Laden down with weapons and tools, not to mention the weightiness of the bomb suit, Ian approached the suspect car, he laid down his tools and approached the back of the car, the vehicle had been parked directly opposite a small police station, and adjacent to a dilapidated wooden shack with a cracked window in its single window frame, the door of the shack had been broken in two and hung lopsidedly on its one remaining hinge. Ian had told Bob take a look inside the shack, which he had but he had been unable to enter due to the position of the door being jammed tight against the framework. Ian looked into the boot of the car and slowly walked around the outside stopping at the passenger window he peered through the glass looking for any signs of an IED, as he walked around the front of the car, he made his way to the wooden shack determining that this was a real area of concern for him and needed to be checked out before he could safely carry on.

Bob was stood at the back of the bomb van, as he always did when the boss was on a manual approach; he had placed the first aid kit, fire extinguishers next to the back door within easy reach. From off to the left flank there came the unmistakable sound of a rifle shot followed almost immediately by the dreaded sound of a huge explosion coming from the where the boss was working, "Contact" he and several other guys yelled and he immediately grabbed the, hoped for never to be used first aid kit set off at a run towards the car. This was a routine he and Ian had spoken about, and between them they had developed a system of talking through every stage of what the boss would be doing, so that in the event of an accident Bob could with some degree of confidence have a pretty good idea of safe routes, of course he could never know for sure what was safe and what was not. What he did know was that his mate was most likely hurt and needed to be gotten out of a very nasty situation and looked after as soon as possible. With that his only conscious thought, he sprinted out of the ICP and ran the hundred metres to where he knew Ian would need him.

Ian never heard the shot; he was stood at the door of the shack, when the bullet, fired from a hill top some two hundred meters away broke the single remaining window, the window shattered and a single small motion switch, the type often found in car alarms, fell to the ground and in doing so initiated an explosive chain of events that resulted in one hundred pounds of high explosive that had been buried in the floor of the shack detonating at supersonic speed, throwing Ian back towards the car, the searing heat instantly scorched the exposed skin, the blast wave that hit Ian at the same time was powerful enough to destroy a house, Ian's fragile human form never stood a chance, mercifully he was dead before he even hit the ground.

Bob turned a corner and stopped dead in his tracks, it was that sudden halt that probably saved his life, the vision from hell he was looking at would haunt him for many years afterwards, the shack had all but disappeared and the car was ablaze as was the barely recognisable as human form next to it. Bob, Bob, stop! The warning screams of the infantry escort scarcely registered, but Bob could go no further, he knew that nothing he could do would help Ian now, the escort reached Bob and grabbed his arm, slow down Bob look out for secondary's. Secondary's were second, third, and even forth devices that were placed to target first responders following a bombing, that threat plus the shot that had been heard just before the explosion raised the odds of something very nasty waiting for anyone who approached the scene, and as such, some degree of caution was necessary. Bob, closely followed by the escort, walked carefully towards the body on floor, as they neared the heat became more and more intense. From a distance of three feet Bob aimed the extinguisher at Ian and his escort a fire suppressant blanket in his hands began to beat out the still smouldering shape that a few seconds earlier had been a human being. It was immediately apparent that no amount of medical care would do anything for Ian, and Bob placed the blanket over Ian's face. As the two men looked about them, the incident commander arrived looking with barely disguised horror at the shape on the floor. The wave that had torn Ian's limbs from his body had moved the car, still ablaze some three feet from its original position and there, roughly, where the front wheel would have been was the unmistakable shape of a pressure plate, anyone rushing to the operator's aid would have almost certainly stood on it, Bob grabbed the incident commander, and pointed out the new threat, we need another ATO here he managed to say before his body, pumped full of adrenalin, gave up and began to shake violently as the shock of what he had been forced to witness overtook him.

Tommy simply stared at Andy, barely able to grasp what he had heard, "Jesus when will this stop" he whispered almost to himself, the door to the briefing room opened and Al, who had just been told the news by Terry, walked over to where Tommy sat still unable to believe what was going on, we will get this bastard Tommy, and everyone who is involved with this, he said, with that he placed a hand on Tommy's shoulders and walked out into the sunshine, the sunshine that Ian would never see again.

CHAPTER EIGHT

The last known address of George Peters was visited by two uniformed police Officers later that day, and having identified themselves at the door were invited in. The Officers were told the George had gone to the mosque, again, he spent too much time there complained his father, mixing with all sorts of weirdo's, George Peters when not at the Mosque spent most of his time in his room browsing the internet, and keeping in touch with old Army mates his Mother told the police. The Officers took a chance and asked if they may be allowed to have a peek into his room, the senior Officer had told the parents that, a former army colleague had reported to them that George may have in his possession photographs of new equipments and they were concerned that he may have forgot to declare these and hand them in for destruction when he left the army. It was, they said a very common occurrence and nothing to be alarmed about, but these days we have to make sure our secrets stay that way he said. George's room was like any other, a single bed, neatly made up, an open copy of a Koran on the bedside table, his laptop and a bunch of computer discs and hard drives lay on a small wooden desk below the window. There were no posters on the walls, nothing to indicate he was involved in anything illegal or subversive. As they were about to leave, the front door opened, and George Peters walked in, on seeing the two policemen he stopped and suddenly looked about him as if searching for a way out. "George", his mum said "these two men want to ask you some questions about a photograph you took", with that, Peters turned and yanked the front door open slamming it behind him he sped off, the two Officers immediately followed him and were just in time to see him run into the road, not bothering to look as he crossed the road, George never saw the red Ford Fiesta that hit him at thirty miles an hour, breaking his leg and effectively stopping his escape bid. He eventually woke up; in the ambulance that was taking him to Leicester General Hospital, he saw the paramedic leaning across him and at the foot of the stretcher was a policeman looking at him with undisguised disgust. The same policeman, as soon as the ambulance arrived at the hospital, managed a quick word with the consultant surgeon on duty, and stressed the need to have Peters kept in isolation and was not to be allowed visitors, a police Officer would be outside his room until he could be questioned.

"We got Peters"!, Al said as he joined the team who were sitting quietly killing time in the motel lobby, immediately the mood around the table lifted, "what's he saying?", asked Tommy, "nothing yet, he broke his leg whilst trying to escape the two Officers who were sent to question him", "wow, your guys don't mess about Al", joked Bob.

George Peters lay in a hospital bed, the broken leg had been reset and was now encased in plaster keeping him immobile, he had complained of headaches and feeling dizzy, however doctors were satisfied he was fit enough to be questioned by the police who had not left the hospital since his arrival yesterday afternoon. On both side of his bed were men in police uniform and at the door stood a big man who had introduced himself as Al, Al had seemed decent enough, asking if he was ok and did he need anything. "Why did you run George?" he asked once he had pulled up a chair. "I don't know" he answered weakly, "I was scared". "What of", pressed Al, "My Mum said you had the pictures, and I didn't know what to do". "What Pictures George?" continued Al, wanting to let Peters tell it all himself. "The ones of the bomb squad, the ones Mo wanted for his book. I thought . . . , I thought . . . ." his voice trailed off as he slumped back on to his pillow, "oh shit" he whispered. "Who is Mo?", asked Al, George looked around him, it dawned on him that the police hadn't know anything, but they did now, he had told him, and they would not let him stop now. His voice broke, "I'm sorry" he said "it's not my fault. I gave the pictures to Mo", he had seen the recent news coverage of the bomb disposal operator being killed whilst defusing a bomb, some of the young lads at the mosque had been praising the brave warriors who had killed him, and were saying that more should die. "I never knew he would tell you about the photos, I only did it because he said he was writing a book to tell the world the real story of the bomb squad, how brave they were, how the world should know that it was the whole team that were the heroes, not just the operator who got all the glory". Al said nothing, instead he got to his feet and walked to the door, he opened it and beckoned two more men inside, Tommy and Bob walked in, the two men had agreed to say nothing but wanted to hear firsthand what was going on. Al turned once more; "Go on George" he murmured softly. Peters lay on his bed, tears of self pity coursed down his face, "I am not feeling well, would you please get me the nurse?" He asked. "Later George, tell us what happened with the pictures", one of the uniformed Officers said.

As Tommy and Bob drove back to the motel, the full impact of what they had heard slowly sunk in. Peters had converted to Islam whist on the run from the army; he had been a regular attendee at the same Mosque that Atcha and Salim attended. Peters had told one of the elders who were teaching him the Koran, about his time in Northern Ireland and how he had not wanted to go to Afghanistan. This was then passed quietly among the more radical members of the mosque. It was agreed that some of this knowledge about bomb disposal work could be used to target the very men who were currently thwarting the terrorist's aims. The teams in Helmand were starting to have some success against the bombers, defusing bombs before they could function, developing sophisticated jammers that stopped the radio controlled devices from operating, the American and British special forces stopping devices before they even got to be emplaced. A new strategy was called for, and who better to bomb than the bomb squads themselves. The difficulty had always been, how to identify what they did, what equipment they used, what were there procedures for dealing with devices.

Peters was at the mosque one day when a serious looking man approached him and suggested they go for a coffee, the man who introduced himself as Mo, told George that he had seen him around the mosque recently and wanted to congratulate him on seeing the true light and converting to the one true God. Mo told Peters that he too had come to the Mosque quite late in life and although born and raised in an Islamic household never really understood what it was all about. Peters had never been an outgoing sort of man, kept himself to himself, the few relationships he had had seldom lasted more than two or three dates, even the supposed camaraderie of the army seemed to have bypassed him and he had few friends he had call on. Yet here he was sitting drinking coffee with a man who understood what he had been missing all his life, Mo was at ease chatting with George about all sorts of things, he expressed complete admiration when he heard how George had been on the bomb squad, laughingly calling him a hero. As the weeks passed George and Mo spent more and more time together. It was Mo who suggested the newspaper articles saying that once they were published he could never be sent to fight their brothers in Afghanistan. Eventually a counsellor for the Muslim Youth UK began to join them for coffee and the process of convincing George to go back to barracks was begun. Initially George was adamant he could never go back, Mo and the counsellor convinced him day by day, he would be a figure head for all converted Muslims in the UK, and his case would be heard on all the worlds' media. One day Mo produced a printed copy of an email, he said he had received from an Uncle in Pakistan who had asked Mo to pass on his very best regards and spoke of his family's profound respect for the brave bomb disposal man who had found the light.

As the day to return to the army life dawned George and Mo spent more and more time together, Mo had told George he was planning to write a book, entitled The True Heroes of Bomb Disposal, and could George help with some of the facts, nothing secret, nothing sensitive just some anecdotes really. George told of how the Bomb Squads Robot was called wheelbarrow, about the bomb suit, how heavy it was, all the time Mo seemed fascinated copying these titbits down word for word, the questions got more probing as the days wore on, where did they train, for how long, initially Peters said he couldn't tell anyone that type of information, so George would hold off for a few days only to return to asking about how did they deal with car bombs, how did they stop suicide devices from working. Little by little George told Mo everything, about coded reports, procedures; after all he figured theses were old stories now, things will have moved on since he was in Belfast. Once George was back in barracks, Mo kept up the friendship with phone calls and emails almost every day asking how he was doing, and all the time getting more and more detail for his book, which Mo promised George would be heavily featured in. One day Peters told his friend that he was going away on a bomb disposal exercise, all the latest kit would be there, the newest devices everything, Mo was immediately impressed, saying how high the army must hold George in regard if he was being sent on that exercise. I wish I could be there, said Mo wistfully, just to see one real life job that would be great for my book, even just a picture would help. He then went on to say he could visit George in Ripon if he wanted him to next weekend, maybe go out for a coffee and visit the local mosque together, would that be good? He asked. That would be great Mo answered George eagerly. They met in a small coffee shop in town on Saturday afternoon, Mo looked delighted to see George again, but his glad demeanour soon dropped when he told George that his book was dead in the water, all the stuff he had, although great, was old, he needed to get new facts, he said that all this work was now wasted and that he may go to Pakistan to work for his uncle. George was devastated, the first real friend he had ever had was thinking of leaving him, they spent the whole day together just talking about religion and how Mo had moved in with some friends from the Mosque, how he had been trying to get a job, but it was no good in Leicestershire. That night George lay in his barracks mourning the loss of a friend, wishing he could find a way to change Mo's mind about leaving the country. What if he could sneak some photographs back from the exercise he thought, that couldn't hurt anyone could it, he phoned

Mo the next day and suggested he could help possibly, but he begged don't go to Pakistan, stay here write your book, and that he would help. Mo instantly changed, his mood once again upbeat, get as much as you can George he asked, I need details of the latest jobs these brave men are dealing with, how they do it, what equipment they use, what rules they have to follow, I want to know who does what in the team, so I can explain how everyone is a hero. With this stuff George I can stay here and carry on writing, I shall call my Uncle and tell him I have changed my mind, I shall tell him I am writing a book with my best friend. George was delighted he had been able to help his friend, and doubly pleased that he would be staying in England now.

George had told the Officers he had originally been a designated driver, responsible for delivering packed lunches and picking up the trash at the end of each day. Instead he convinced the corporal who was in charge of the fatigue party, that his specialist knowledge would be better served as a witness, this way he reckoned he would see lots of jobs, he would be able to watch exactly how each task was dealt with. Mo had bought him a digital camera and George promised to take as many pictures as he could. The fatigue party leader had been very impressed with Private Peters, he was, he told his sergeant, really keen and had volunteered to work on far more tasks that anybody else. George spent the whole two weeks watching, listening and each night he would make notes on what he had seen, convinced that Mo would be able to finish his book in record time now. Once back at Ripon he had called Mo, who came down the next weekend, he was delighted with the package that George had put together, aside from the notes and photographs he had taken, George had been able to get hold of a copy of the exercise folder which detailed the pass fail criteria the assessors used which listed all the things the operator should be asking and doing on each job. Mo told George he had been brilliant, he had everything he needed to complete his book now, and once George could get away they would take a well deserved holiday somewhere, lots of sea and sand and maybe a chance for some fun for two men about town, he added with a wink, George was thrilled, he had, at last a friend, a real friend who wanted to do things like going out, maybe meet girls who knows.

George's court martial had eventually been heard and he had been sentenced as being unsuitable for military life and dishonourably discharged, he returned to Loughborough. Mo in the meantime had been very busy writing his book, he told George in an email one day that his mobile phone was playing up and he sometimes never got the text and voice messages that people sent. Mo was that busy he even stopped going to the mosque every day. Peters had told the police everything he knew about his friend convinced that this could all be explained, he lived with some friends on Elmhurst Rd he had said, Mo's parents had complained about the number of friends he had phoning him at all hours of the night and he had moved out. He said he had never learnt Mo's full name, names didn't matter to real friends Mo had said one day. When was the last time he had seen Mo he had been asked, at which point he said he could not remember but it had been a few weeks, but he was busy writing he said defensively. The Officers had left promising to return shortly to take a full statement, He was warned that his actions had almost certainly breached the official secrets act and he could find himself in a world of trouble. George remembered the look on one of the two men who had entered the room late; they had not said a word, but one of them, the one who looked as if he had been burnt or something gave George a look of absolute hatred as he walked out.

Al, had already spoken with his commanders by the time they reached the hospital car park, an arrest Warrant for Mo, whose description fitted perfectly with that of Mahood Atcha had been drafted, the charges initially were being in possession of materials likely to be used by terrorists in the pursuit of a crime. They had Peters story to back this up and the arrest team would then "find" the photographs in the house. The problem being that at this stage, no one had actually seen Atcha, his parents house had been kept under observation and he had not shown, Peters had told Officers he was living in Elmhurst Road and the house there had been watched around the clock and again no show, nor had he or anyone matching his description been seen entering any other houses on Elmhurst road. It was decided that Officers armed with the arrest Warrant would visit the home of Mahood's parents in Pankhurst road and try to find out as much as they could about their son. Mr and Mrs Atcha told the Inspector who had been accompanied the arrest team, that Mahood had been a good boy until he had started university, it was there they claimed that he had changed, he became much more involved in these radical groups, attending rallies and going to a late night Islamic debating group, held after prayers in Loughborough Mosque, where he would listen to other more radical Muslims call for action against the infidels and suchlike. Mr Atcha had tried to make his son see sense, that this was not the way of Islam, but his new friends continually filled his head with their nonsense. His mobile phone would be ringing till late at night, he took to surfing the internet looking for images of martyrdom operations as he liked to call them, "I told him it was plain and simple murder" said his Mother. Eventually he left home and went to stay with friends from university. He would come around every week, and then two months ago he said he was going to go to Pakistan to stay with his Uncle there, he left for Lahore about five weeks ago his father finished. The Officers were allowed to search Mahood's old room, but the search turned up nothing of any real interest. A check with UK Border Control showed that Mahood Atcha flew out of the UK to Pakistan on a six month visa five weeks earlier, he had not since returned, at least not on the same passport as he flew out on, the immigration man added.

The operation had now taken on a new dimension, what had begun as a receipt search had now grown into one where someone was targeting bomb disposal operators, and there was still the possibility of a bomb making facility being uncovered at the lock up. The decision was made to continue surveillance on the house and occupants of Elmhurst road, someone higher up the chain of command was tasked with trying to locate Mahood in Lahore, the family had supplied what details they could, and a frantic phone call to the Mr Atcha's brother in Pakistan revealed that Mahood had indeed turned up five weeks ago, but he has not been at the house for over three weeks now. They had no idea where he had gone to; he had come in one day and told them he was going to visit university friends in Quetta in the North West of the Country, he would be gone for some time and to not worry.

Steve Thompson was going through reports of old tasks, looking at ways in which a new set of operating procedures could be drawn up, he had just considered amending the mandatory requirements for when and when not to wear the bomb suit, when his phone rang. "SAT's office Mr Thompson speaking" he answered, "Sir it's Corporal Turpin from the ops room at Brigade, we have had a tasking message from one of the patrols on the ground, a local has stopped an joint afghan and UK patrol and claims there is a car bomb in the next village". "Wait there, I shall come over" Steve, stopped the flow of information from the excitable clerk and putting on his jacket he made the short journey across camp to the secure operations and communications room. "Ok" he said as he entered the map covered room, "what do we have?" The clerk explained that the patrol were about to enter the village of Urozgan, when a man stopped them, saying that some bad men had placed a car bomb next to his shop, the patrol leader had sent forward a small team to take a look and sure enough, parked outside the man's shop was an old Toyota, it looked weighted down at the back, which the patrol leader knew from his time in Northern Ireland was always a dead giveaway. The patrol had set up a perimeter around the village and was requesting EOD and the QRF, a quick reaction force to assist. Steve had a look at one of the maps that adorned the walls; the village was North East of the main camp, and could be reached via helicopter in less than an hour if needs be. What was worrying Steve, was that this was already starting to feel very similar to the device that had killed Ian. He told the operations clerk to acknowledge the tasking request and to tell the duty team to stand by, but to not move till he had spoken with them. He hurried along the covered walkway to the Colonels office, as he knocked at the door, a plan was starting to formulate in his head, but would the boss authorise such a mission. The colonel looked up as Steve finished outlining his idea, "would this work" he asked "and who did you have in mind for this mad stunt?" "Firstly I have no idea but it has to be better than sending in a team to be set up", said Steve," secondly, Warrant Officer Brian Owens, the Post Blast Warrant Officer, he is one of the few operators in country with the qualifications to take this sort of job on, I am another Boss" added Steve hopefully "and we have Andy Fox in Kabul if we need back up". "Ok I know you would love to do this, but you are not going Mr Thompson, I need you here, Mr Fox is up to his neck in work elsewhere right now, will Brian go for it?", again the ease with which operators of all ranks spoke to each other and allowed for this frank and open discussion became apparent. "I can give him a call", said Steve, "Ok" said the Colonel, "you do that, but this has to happen tonight, I do not want that Patrol out there any longer than necessary. Then, tell the team that I have ordered no move till further notice; I will call Brigade immediately and inform them of this, I will spin a yarn telling them a reliable source has dropped a whisper telling us that we are again being set up. I shall then pop along to task Force twelve, the home of the Special Forces contingent, and let them know of what we want to do, and what we will hopefully be asking them to do, I have no doubt they will relish the prospect. I shall need You, Brian and the Ops Officer to meet me here in thirty minutes. Tell Brian to bring his "black bag""

CHAPTER NINE

Thirty minutes later Brian and Steve knocked at the colonels door, inside was the Ops Officer the boss and two men who wore no badges of rank, but were clearly from the task force., The colonel made the necessary introductions, Brian looked across at one of the two men, nodded his head in recognition and said "we worked together in Herat on a job two weeks ago", Yeah I remember, you doing ok?" replied the man reaching across and shaking Brian's hand. The colonel asked the men to sit and explained that despite some misgivings, Brigade had given the green light for this operation, he said that normally this would take a few days to be fully explored and a full detailed plan drawn up, however time was not on their side and it had to go live tonight, before daylight ideally.

Four helicopters took off from Lashkar Gah later that night, on board the first two were the Duty team and a contingent of the QRF, the third chopper contained Brian, and eight task force twelve operators, none wearing rank slides and all carrying an assortment of weaponry and equipments including, night vision goggles and a miniature surveillance drone fitted with infra red imaging. The last helicopter was for security and would stay airborne whilst the passengers and equipments from the birds that landed were on the ground and defenceless. On reaching the drop off point, the first two helicopters landed, and the teams and equipment were hastily unloaded, once on the ground they immediately began to reinforce the cordon, set up an ICP and conduct the initial arrival drills that all teams carried out on task. The forth helicopter made a big show of circling the landing zone and showing a very overt and menacing presence, once clear all three choppers flew off back to camp. Brian's helicopter had not followed the other three, whilst the equipments and teams were noisily and very obviously disgorging their payloads, the third helicopter, flying without lights, very briefly touched down about one kilometre away from the village, out of sight of the ICP and well away from prying eyes. As soon as the loadmaster signalled that the wheels were down, the men who were stood to on the ramp, which had already been lowered, quickly filed off and disappeared into the swirling dust and the darkness of the night. Brian and two of the men quickly set off for the village, wearing night vision goggles that immediately turned night into day albeit with a green haze allowed them to maintain a steady pace and avoid anything that may warn of their presence. The men who had been left behind at the drop off point were busy setting up the surveillance drone that would form a vital part of the operation.

Brian's team reached the edge of the village, keeping to the shadows they peered around a wall, about two hundred yards away, they could see the suspect car, parked outside a small wooden shop that was presumably owned by the man who had reported his suspicions, it was not yet clear whether these were actual fears about a car bomb or whether he had been coerced into telling the patrol, such nuances very often meant the difference between a regular car bomb and a team or a patrol being set up. Circling back the way they had come from, Brian and his two escorts found their way to the back door of the shop. Brian carefully lowered his bag to the ground and removed a small tool bag, from the bag he pulled out a small handheld drill and began to bore a hole in the base of the door. Once through, he then retrieved a miniature camera on an extendable and flexible probe and inserted that through the hole, using the handheld monitor he could now check that the inside of the door, and the immediate area around was not booby trapped, once happy, he gestured to the two men with him that he was going inside. Brian stepped into the gloom of the shop, he could see a few shelves stocked with an assortment of bottles and cans, he slowly worked his way round the edges of the walls, aiming for the doorway, if there was to be a booby trap it would almost certainly be on an access route, doors windows that sort of thing. The shop front housed two windows, through the smeared panes he could make out the Toyota car parked outside, the likelihood of it being on a timer, programmed to function at night was slim, but somehow the thought wormed its way into Brian's head and he found himself willing to speed up, he fought the urge and concentrated on what he was there to do. Brian edged his way towards the front of the shop and by means of finger tips and a small hand held metal detector he cleared his way to the front door, he had checked the first window on the way round and found nothing that indicated it had been set up in the same way that the earlier device had been. The area around the doorway was also clear, as was the second window, from here he had a clear view of the car, the back was indeed weighted down, but poorly maintained springs or even heavy weights in the back would give the same illusion. Brian worked his way around the rest of the shop and eventually reached the back door, he found his two escorts waiting patiently for him, beckoning them both inside he outlined what he had done and what little he had found. As the two task force men kept watch from the doorway, Brian now took the same drill and camera appliance he had used earlier and crept towards the window opposite the car, one of the advantages of these old shacks was that frames and doors rarely fitted snugly, he was able to feed the flexible probe through a gap between window frame and wall and have a good scan outside the shop. The metal door had been padlocked by the owner as he had left the shop, so there was no way they could exit that way.

The remaining team members had by now, assembled and prepared the surveillance drone for flight, the miniature craft could fly almost silently at a height of two thousand meters above the ground, the infra red camera would detect thermal changes in the terrain and most importantly tonight, someone laying in wait with a rifle or a remote controlled trigger, the team had conducted a thorough map reconnaissance of the village and its surrounding areas, the drones internal mapping system had been programmed and once released would circle pre designated areas of interest beaming back its images to the men waiting patiently below, anyone hiding out in the hills, watching and waiting would then be visited by these rough and ready men who owned the night.

Brian moved the camera through its entire range of movement; he could see the outside of the door was clear; two posters had been stuck to one of the walls of the shop, one advertising an adjacent shop for sale was the newer of the two, and as such it struck Brian as looking out of place. He manoeuvred the camera slightly and was able to see that the edge of the poster had come away from the wall, inching the camera further still, it seemed as if the poster had been stuck onto another one below it, as it looked as if it was raised in the middle. As Brian stared intently through the he glimpsed something that looked as if it had been covered in a black plastic covering underneath the poster. He pulled his head back slightly and tried to align the poster to a spot on the internal wall. Taking a small handheld masonry tool he began to slowly scrape away the hard packed mud that the wall had been constructed from, attempting to peel away the layers underneath the poster. The work was slow, but he had to scrape away the mud piece by piece, thankfully the wall was not overly thick and in less than an hour he had whittled away enough of the wall, and was now able to see that the black plastic covering he had seen was the waterproof covering of a conventional pressure pad. The pad had been stuck to the outside wall and then hidden by the poster, he immediately got onto his secure radio and sent a message to Brigade informing them of what he had found by means of a set of code words, that message was also the one that told the drone team to release their bird. It had been agreed beforehand that any device should be found first before putting the drone into the air, once a target had been identified, then two of the drone team would move silently and swiftly to the spot, the drone would remain on station and would guide the trackers it would also warn them should the target start to move.

Brian continued to scrape away the earth moving from the centre of the pad towards its edges, he had estimated that the most likely area for the connecting cables to be found, was at its lower edges, so that is where he was going. The team wanted the device made safe if that were possible before attempting to apprehend the gunman, the likelihood of him releasing a shot and causing the bomb to function was too great a risk. Brain leant back on his haunches and thought through the method of operation of the IED he was now looking at. The bomb disposal operator would eventually have to approach the car, the gunman would again fire a single round, but this time, not at a glass window this time, teams would be prepared for that possibility and any windows in the area would be subjected to a thorough search before any manual approach. No this time the sniper would fire at a poster that hid a pressure mat, the metal cased bullet would penetrate the black plastic covering and cause the two contact plates inside to come together thus initiating the bomb that had been hidden in a cavity that had been dug into the outer wall of the shop. It was this cavity that Brian was now looking into, he raised his night vision goggles and rubbed his tired eyes, he looked back at the men who were still guarding the back door, if this bomb was going to explode, it would do so as he carried out his next action, no need for three people to be in the firing line he thought. Motioning them across, he explained the layout of the bomb, he did this so if it all went horribly wrong, at least the guys at Brigade would know what type of device it was. He then told the two guys to take up a security position outside the rear of the shop, that way he was still being protected but had minimised the likely casualty count, he also had someone close by to administer first aid.

I hate being so bloody practical he thought to himself with a smile.

Brian replaced the night vision aids, and armed with a small, probe began to uncover the circuitry of the device, he was searching for one of two things, either one would render the device safe. He traced the wires that led to the pressure mat, and eventually found the explosive charge, that if initiated would have certainly killed whoever was stood by the wall. This was not option one of the things he was hoping to find, but it would do as a starting point, slowly he searched his way around the device, finally he could uncover all of the main charge, enough explosive to fit into a hollowed out space approximately thirty by thirty centimetres square, had been packed into a small canvas bag, the detonating chain that began its journey at the pressure mat, ended here, Brian couldn't nor did he want to simply pull the bag out of the wall space, instead taking a small scalpel he cut a hole just about big enough for him to locate the initiator, an innocuous looking silver tube containing a ridiculously small amount of very sensitive high explosive, yet if it were to function whilst you were holding it, would see you losing fingers if not your whole hand. The initiator was inserted into the bulk explosive, and as Brian had explained to hundreds of students could be likened to the kindling you would use to light a fire. Brian continued his search around the device looking for something that would indicate a secondary firing switch or something just not right. He wasn't expecting to find anything but experience and caution prevailed. Finally he was able to remove the initiator, the device was not made safe by him doing this, but it was made safer, in doing so he had reduced the explosive hazard from one that would kill him to one that might make him jump. Brian now concentrated on looking for the power source, this was the key component, no power means no bomb was a mantra he had, had drummed into him, after a few moments further searching he was able to lean back and report over his radio that the device had been found and was safe.

In the meantime the surveillance drone had picked up a heat trace of two men laying prone on a hilltop some two hundred and fifty metres away. The men had not moved for the last thirty minutes, as four black clad figures move steadily towards their position, the drone kept its silent vigil overhead. The covert earpiece of one of the two task force operators clicked into life "Whiskey one, your target is north of your position approx three hundred metres, no change over". The operator simply clicked his transmit button to acknowledge the message; this was not the time for noise. He turned and with a wave of his hand indicated that his team should fan out into their prearranged positions, this was a manoeuvre they had rehearsed and carried out for real on many occasions, each man knew precisely what he had to do, and what his team mate would be doing at the same time. It was this cohesion that allowed them to creep silently and surely to within fifteen metres of the two men laying in wait. "When will they come?" one of them asked his fellow gunman, "soon brother, soon, first they will use the robot, then they will come". The lead operator clicked his transmit button three times indicating that they were in position and ready. The brigade operations Officer immediately gave the signal that the men had been waiting for, the surveillance drone operators, turned off the infra red and instead switched on a conventional camera and video system, at the same time a high powered spotlight suddenly lit up the entire hill top, the two gunmen were instantly blinded by the white light that came from the sky, the task force operators had known this was coming and had closed their eyes as the night turned to day. As one they stood and with undisguised menace in their voices yelled, "Army, stop, stand still, twice and once again in Arabic, the effects of the light and the sudden appearance of these armed men in black completely disorientated the two gunmen, the soldiers were on the two men in a heartbeat, the men were thrown to the floor, weapons cast aside, and were in no time at all searched restrained and most importantly, alive, for this was just phase one of the plan.

"Whiskey one targets secured, all clear, moving out now" with the message sent the operator led his men and the two prisoners off the hill. Brian had packed up the device he had disassembled and with this safely secured, he and his escorts also set off for the pickup point, the drone turned and headed back to the operators, and the bomb team were told by Steve that they had permission to commence the vehicle clearance task, but with caution, the helicopter which had been waiting returned to pick up its passengers, and no one apart from those directly involved was any the wiser. As soon as they landed, the two terrorists were led away to be processed before being questioned, the Colonel was waiting at the helipad, which was quickly turning into one of the busiest heliports anywhere in the world, as Brian stepped down he walked over and shook his hand warmly, "good job Brian, well done", "thank you sir" answered Brian and added in his typical understated way, "it was a bit interesting that job" ", Steve joined the two men with the comment," typical you go all the way to town and you forgot to pick up my laundry". The specialists who would be questioning the suspects had been roused from their beds and were already preparing for the second stage of the nights operation, It was always known that the guy who would be firing the weapon, or pressing the fire button was not the one who had built the bomb, and certainly not the one who had planned the attack. Taking a bomber off the streets was good, but he would be replaced in no time, a bomb maker was harder to recruit, and the planner a lot harder still, but the one they really wanted was the one who briefed the planner, the one who had all the details of how and when bomb teams would deploy. The way to him was through the two men now being fingerprinted, photographed and being dressed in white boiler suits, their own clothes having been taken away to be forensically searched.

CHAPTER TEN

"**S**o then I asked him, did Mary and Joseph stay virgins, is that why some priests can't have sex?, I thought he was going to die, he turned bright red and said he had to visit Mrs Mayer in the next ward, and he was off" Tommy was sat by Marty's bed listening to how she had driven the young hospital chaplain to distraction, to be fair thought Tommy, it was never going to be a fair fight. He had driven across from Leicester, on the way to Oxfordshire for a meeting with Andy and the Colonel. Marty was looking good, she had started her physiotherapy sessions with "some sadistic Australian bitch" according to Marty, she was still having trouble sleeping through the night and was understandably very distressed by all that had happened to her. The Regiment had been great, a visiting roster had been set up by her mates back at camp, and the families Officer came by every week or so. Marty's parents had relatives in the area so where able to come down regularly. Tommy had told her very little about the job he was on, when asked he had said something glib about geeks and electronic components, and the police needing someone who knew how they could be used in a bomb.

Leaving a pile of magazines on her bed he said he had to be off if he was to make it back to Oxford for the meeting, "never mind meeting the SAT, when will you be meeting Mandy" said Marty with a knowing look, "she has been asking about you, you know" "yeah, yeah said Tommy, and anyway she is married", "mmm is she? Are you sure" replied Marty with a smile. "Anyway who was the hunk who was just leaving when I turned up" he asked her. She blushed slightly, and Tommy had never seen her blush, "he is a hunk isn't he? He works here at the hospital, he brings papers and books around, he comes by at least once a day to see if I need anything", "and do you?" said Tommy still amazed at Marty blushing, "Nothing I can get in here" she said with a wicked grin, and then burst into laughter," you are getting better" he said as He stood to leave, she said "look after yourself Tommy, see you soon"

Tommy drove to Oxford, intrigued by what Andy had told him over the phone, something had gone down in Afghanistan last night, and Tommy would want to know. Andy met Tommy in the Sergeants mess and over a coffee, told him of the operation carried out by Brian. The two men had been questioned and were giving very little away just yet, forensics results were not yet in, but one of the men's fingerprints had shown a match, a name and his photograph matched the one on the identification card he had been carrying. "So we have something", said Andy. "The plan, as it is, is to identify who is behind all this, once we have the entire network, task force twelve supported by IEDD teams will conduct an operation to kill or capture the lot in one foul swoop". "Have we been able to pin any of this on Atcha", asked Tommy, "not yet, it is highly unlikely he is not involved in this, given that he has been gathering all the facts about how we deploy, but can we prove it? Not right now". Andy finished his coffee and said that they should be getting over to the Colonels office, he was expecting

Tommy in around fifteen minutes, and it never paid to keep Colonels waiting. Colonel Collins asked Tommy to sit down, and after a few minutes small talk, how was the head? Are the burns healing well? That sort of thing, he got straight down to business. Tell me about Leicester, he asked. Tommy ran through the operation as it stood, the stuff in the lock up, the wrapped clothing, the multiple fridges, grinders, email traffic, finishing off with his suspicions that some sort of manufacturing facility was being established, but they had little idea of what was being made, and none at all as regards why and where it would be used. Tommy explained that the plan was to keep watching the house and the lock up, and hopefully somewhere down the line it would come together, then it can be stopped. The colonel seemed satisfied with that, He had spoken with Terry earlier that day, and Leicestershire Police had requested formally that Tommy remain on task, they felt that something was going to happen sooner rather than later and they wanted Tommy's expertise close at hand, when it did.

"I have spoken again with Manning and Records", went on the colonel, "your move to Nottingham has been approved and you will be getting official notification very soon, you as you well know were selected for promotion and it is in this rank that you assume the position as Troop Warrant Officer. However I feel, and have managed to convince records that your current assignment, taken as it was, when you were officially on medical leave warrants recognition". At that the colonel face took on a look of displeasure, "but the fact that you have arrived here in my office incorrectly dressed has possibly given me cause to reconsider my position". Tommy looked down at his uniform instantly confused, "Sir"? He questioned, "You stand there wearing the rank slide of a Staff Sergeant when as of midday today you are a Warrant Officer, get out and don't come back till you are properly attired, now get out at once". Tommy, knowing the game, saluted smartly and marched out. Once outside he was met by Andy holding his new Warrant Officer badge, thanking all his lucky stars that today's uniforms allowed for rank slides that were simply placed onto epaulettes on the jacket and didn't have to be hand sewn on, Tommy looked at Andy, and said "you knew all along you bastard" Properly dressed, Warrant Officer Class Two Tommy Byrne. Knocked on the Colonels door, "come", a voice boomed out, and he marched in. The colonel, his disapproving look now replaced with a smile, was stood waiting for him, "That is much better, never let me have cause to reprimand you again, many congratulations Q" he said. The Royal Logistic Corps, in common with some other corps in the British Army afforded some ranks, official appointments; these appointments very often had historical or traditional origins and as such were maintained rigorously. In the RLC, Warrant Officer Class Two's were often referred to as SQMS, Squadron Quarter Master Sergeant, and were referred to as Q. "Thank you sir", at that the colonels door opened and in walked the Operations Officer, the Adjutant and Andy, the adjutant was bearing a tray on which stood an opened bottle of champagne and five glasses. Handshakes and congratulations were given as the colonel poured the champagne, once everyone had been given a drink; he raised his glass and formally congratulated Tommy on his well deserved promotion.

Tommy arrived back at the police station in time for the evening briefing, he had been given permission to reveal some of what had gone on the night before many miles away, the team were clearly delighted at the prospect of someone finally getting close to whoever was behind these attacks on the bomb teams, and if it could be proven that they too had played a large part in that, then so much the better. The surveillance team had reported that an unknown male, a white man aged between twenty and twenty five, had turned up at the house, he had delivered a large package, and had been inside for just under an hour, he had arrived in a taxi and had left in the same manner, photographs had of course been taken, but no one could say who he was. The only other occurrence of note was the nails that had been ordered had also been delivered; Salim had come to the door and signed the receipt the delivery man had been brandishing. The five suspects were all at home, and no one had been back to the lock up. Permission had been sought and granted for the deployment of technical tracking and listening devices, the suspect's vehicle was to be fitted with a covert tracking device that would allow the surveillance operators to know where it was at all times, particularly useful if they were to lose the car in traffic, a rare but not unknown occurrence. The lock up was to be revisited and miniature cameras and listening devices were to be installed, these were currently being modified to be hidden in the eaves of the unit. The cameras' would be triggered by a sensor and become live as soon as anybody entered the lock up. The images and sounds would then be sent back via a secure link to a command cell. The briefing over, the team headed off to the motel, Al wanted to know, what would happen if they were able to find out who had been planning the attacks in Helmand, Tommy answered that honestly he didn't know, he was rather hoping a surveillance drone launched hellfire missile would be involved and turn the planner and his team to dust.

Tonight's plan was to visit both the house and the lock up, the house would be done first with a team installing a tracking device underneath the suspect's car parked in the driveway, it was already known that there were no Passive Infra red lights to worry about, and the installation team had been practising the placement on a car of the same make and model, they were very confident that the bug could be placed, hidden and secured in less than fifteen minutes, a number of contingency plans had been put in place in the event of them being compromised by the suspects or any other third party. Tommy was amused and not a little surprised with one of the contingencies which, was to simply throw a crowbar on the ground and run off giving the impression of car thieves being disturbed.

Once the team had finished on the car, the lock up would be paid a visit and the cameras and eavesdropping devices would be put in place, once they were in, then a test run would be carried out to ensure that the images and sounds being received were of a high standard, and that the entire lock up was in the field of view., Tommy would again be in the area, should the specialists come across something in the unit whilst they were carrying out the installation.

The next day Tommy was looking forward to simply mooching around the motel maybe going for a run, but basically being busy doing nothing. This pipedream was shattered by Al banging on his door telling him that Salim and Rahim had left the house ten minutes ago and were heading back towards the lock up. Twenty minutes later Tommy was sitting next to Al heading towards a car park near the storage unit site, the control vehicle into which all the surveillance footage was being beamed was situated at the far end of the parking lot., space inside the converted campervan was minimal, and a lot of that had been taken over by generators, receiver units, recording equipment, and two men who twiddled dials and listened intently to headphones whilst watching every movement on two small colour monitors, the time lag, Tommy was told was minimal, so it was pretty close to being live action. Tommy could see Salim and Rahim, packing five jars into each of the four organ transplant boxes, the wrapped clothing parcel was recovered and placed next to the boxes, from the workbench, Salim was gathering tools and soldering equipment, as well as some, what looked like switches and batteries from a box below the bench. Both men worked oblivious to the cameras recording every move, as they worked Rahim was asking Salim about someone called Khalid, whether he would be able to make it in time. And what would they do, if he couldn't. Salim seemed certain; that Khalid would be on time, and to not worry, if not, Allah would show them the way. The two men had evidently finished what they were there to do, Salim opened the door to the lock up, and between them they placed the boxes, tools and components into the boot of the car, as they were about to leave, Salim also picked up the spare headlamps and placed them in his pocket, with that they walked out, and relocked the door. The control staff immediately alerted the surveillance team that the two Zulus were mobile again in Charlie one. A voice came over the radio net, from call sign Mike 22 informing them that he had Charlie one heading towards the city, with that the controller took over and once again the complicated process of operators, on foot and in vehicles being moved around to ensure coverage was complete and unnoticed by those being followed began.

Charlie one headed into the city centre and eventually parked in the multi story car park of the newly built Shires shopping centre that had been modelled on the shopping malls of America, every conceivable shop under one roof, great for shoppers but bloody awful for surveillance operations, complained Al, as he and Tommy drove into the city. Salim and Rahim left the car and headed off into the mall, once inside the two men stopped briefly and then went separate ways, the surveillance team had obviously planned for this possibility and the two men were picked up by a operators who would routinely switch places, one of the greatest risks in any surveillance job, is that the target would realise he was being followed, the danger was not only of him losing his "tail" but in the fact that he now knew he was being "tailed" and was therefore unlikely to do anything remotely linked to whatever mission he was believed to be involved with.

Officers following Salim, watched him initially wander around the Mall, Al was wondering whether or not he was carrying out a pre mission reconnaissance visit, and was already figuring out the difficulties in evacuating an area the size of the Shires. Salim spent some time looking in a number of mobile phone shops, seemingly browsing, at one point he was observed talking to a customer advisor and being shown a couple of phones from the pay as you go section. Salim however left the shop without making a purchase. Salim continued his wanderings and after a while left the shopping centre and headed into the covered outdoor market area, here he stopped at a stall selling everything from remote controlled cars to low cost pay as you go mobiles, he spent a few minutes talking with the market trader and then bought two of these phones, he paid for his purchases with cash and went on his way. Surveillance operators' although close by and able to watch what it was he bought, were unable to see much more than that, as Salim was followed away from the stall, one of the police man walked across and motioned to the trader that he wanted a few minutes of his time. Rahim had immediately left the shires on separating from Salim, and had made his way to a backstreet novelty joke shop, here he was seen to be talking animatedly to the shop assistant, not sure what he is doing said one Officer as they watched from a doorway across the road, but there is a lot of arm waving, and laughing going on over there. Rahim left clutching a large brown bag under his left arm, again as before one Officer walked into the shop shortly after he had left, and spoke quietly to the girl who had served him. The two suspects were then seen to both enter the same coffee shop within a few minutes of each other, the two swapped stories of their shopping trip and after drinking their coffees headed back together towards the car park, from there they drove back to Elmhurst road, where the boxes and shopping was unloaded and once again, they were lost from view to the ever watchful eyes in the top floor of the hairdressers.

Less than an hour after Salim had returned home, the observers saw an unmarked whit transit van move slowly down Elmhurst Road, the driver seemingly searching for a particular address, the van stopped outside the very house being watched closely. A heavy set white man got out of the van and armed only with a clipboard walked up the drive and knocked on the door. Watchers had already photographed the man and his vehicle, and the registration number had been sent across to the control room to be cross referenced with the vehicle data base in Cardiff to get a registered name and address of the owner, or at least the registered owner. The door was opened by Zulu 3, Said, after a brief conversation the driver returned to his vehicle and from the back door began to offload a number of cardboard boxes, and these again were photographed as they were carried from van to hallway. The man returned twice more to the vehicle the last package was smaller than the previous ones but from the way it was carried and packaged it looked to be more fragile and indeed had a label that marked it as so. The man then asked said to sign for the delivery which he duly did, before closing the door leaving the white man to head back to his van and drive off. "Looked like an awful lot of Pizza" joked one of the surveillance operators as he picked up the phone to inform the control room just what had been delivered and that the van had now left the area. In the meantime a database search had revealed that the van was registered to a Mr Warner with an address in Coventry. A further check had shown that Mr Warner was registered as self employed "man with a van" delivery driver. He had no police record and was seemingly not involved in any terrorist or criminal operations. It was decided that a police unit nearby would attempt to find the van as he drove around town, it was a long shot but they would concentrate on the route back towards Coventry. If the van was seen, police would carry out a routine traffic stop and try to find out what Mr Warner, if it was him driving was doing around these parts. The plan was to simply question without him becoming suspicious that this was anything other than him being hassled by the police for being a white van man. As luck would have it, the van had pulled into a nearby garage and Mr Warner was busy eating a sandwich presumably before driving back home. Traffic Officers were able to watch him pull away and after a couple of miles they pulled up behind the vehicle as it headed towards the M69 motorway, once in place they quickly turned on the siren and blue lights, Mr Warner dutifully pulled over, and as the Police Officer walked across to his van wound down the window, with a look of annoyance asked what was the problem. After a brief conversation during which time Mr Warner showed no sign of being overly concerned or worried as one may expect from someone involved in a terrorist operation, police allowed him to drive on, no caution or tickets were issued and Mr Warner was none the wiser that as he sped off the Police Officers were reporting back to the control room, that he had been contracted to deliver the boxes from an address in Coventry to be delivered to a Mr Malik in Leicester, he had three points for speeding from an offence two years ago, he had been affable and helpful to the police, showing them his documentation for both vehicle and delivery. He had given the Officers the paperwork and while one of the Officers had questioned him the second had had the foresight to record all details of both consignor and consignee.

A few hours later those watching eyes observed Zulu 4 Hussain leaving the house and drive away, the Officers tasked with following him reported that he had driven straight to Loughborough Train Station, where he had parked in the short stay car park and had been seen waiting outside the station, a short while after his arrival a train was seen to pull in, almost at the same time Hussain was seen to answer his phone, it was whilst he was on the phone that a man, approached him also talking on a mobile, both men stopped their individual conversations and shook hands, Hussain almost deferentially took the seconds mans suitcase and led him to the car. The second man, stopped next to the car and as Hussain loaded the case and opened the door for him was clearly looking for anyone paying him too much attention, the police Officers were amongst the very best at their profession and at no time were they in danger of being compromised by such an obvious look around. However what it did prove, Al told Tommy later, that this new man, now being referred to as Zulu 6, knew some counter surveillance procedures, the fact that he alighted at Loughborough and not Leicester was possibly due to the fact the Loughborough was not as well covered by close circuit television security cameras as the major stations were could also be indicative of this careful approach. The two men drove from the train station and within a few minutes were on the A6 towards Leicester and Elmhurst Road, where they were seen to enter the house and once again vanish from view.

CHAPTER ELEVEN

The two men who had been arrested on the hilltop overlooking the shop, had been questioned at length over the previous day and a half, one had said very little, the other, the one who had been carrying identification papers and who was already known to the authorities had been more forthcoming particularly when he realised that his only chance of any leniency was to give as much information as he could. He was able to tell his interrogators of a man who had come to his house one night offering a way in which he could serve Allah. The plan was simple, he was to wait until the bomb disposal man approached the car, when he was between the car and the shop he was to fire at a poster that would be stuck to a wall. The gunman claimed that he never knew the poster was a bomb, he had believed that the intention was to show the invaders that no one was safe and even when it was thought that they had control of an area, we could if we wanted to; kill even men in bomb suits. No one believed his story that this was just a message being sent, but there was no forensic link between the bomb that Brian had recovered and the man being questioned. He told investigators that he and the other man, who he had never met before were collected from the edge of town and driven to Urozgan, they were given two rifles and told where to wait. A little while later they could see two men arrive in a Toyota car and leave it outside the shop, the poster that they had been told to aim at was already on the wall. The men in the Toyota had gone into the shop and the owner had come out and shook their hands before the two men walked off, a little while later the shop keeper had come out of his shop locked it and walked towards the edge of the village. He had heard the helicopters come and still they waited. The next thing they knew was being arrested by men who had appeared from nowhere. The man had been arrested once before when a car he had been a passenger in had been stopped at an army road block and found to contain an AK47. He had claimed he had no knowledge of the weapon and after being processed and interrogated by afghan police was released. He lived in a small village twenty miles from Urozgan, it was decided that a joint afghan and coalition force patrol would go and talk with the elders of the village. The second man had only told them his name and where he lived; his hometown would also be paid a visit, and the elders spoken with. The patrols were welcomed warmly on arrival with offers of sweetened tea and invited to sit in order to discuss how they could be helped. The leaders of the village had said that they just wanted to live in peace, that their people were not terrorists but also did not want their country ruled by outsiders. They told of a man who lived amongst them who was not of their belief, a man who had anger in his heart and hatred in his eyes, a man who travelled a lot, who often had visitors from places many miles from the village. The patrol were told of a compound not far from the village where this man often stayed, a compound protected by men with guns, where visitors were not, unless invited, welcomed. When asked who owned and lived in the compound, the elders shrugged and said they did not know, the compound had been empty for many years, since the man who had lived there died, it had stayed empty until one night men came in cars and had taken over, the elders had gone there the next day to welcome them to the village, they were met by young men with guns who had asked them to leave, no respect was shown by these men, one of the elders had complained only to be pushed to the ground, they had not gone back. The army did not often come here one said or we would have told you about these people. One day a man had been seen, a man who wore glasses, who dressed as a westerner would, he spoke the language but not as an afghan, he had stayed at the compound for three days and had gone.

The patrol leader thanked the elders for their continued support and promised that they would return again soon. On their return to camp this new knowledge set in chain a cycle of events that began with a surveillance satellite being diverted and programmed to send back the latest imagery of the compound. Meanwhile task force twelve were requested to look into the feasibility of mounting an operation on the compound. The two prisoners were asked about the compound and the men who had been there, but neither claimed to have any knowledge of a compound, despite one having lived in the village for many years. The forensics from the "poster bomb" as it was being referred to, had come back with partial fingerprints lifted from the explosives and the power source, as well as DNA from tape that had been used to seal the packaging. These had been loaded onto the terrorist network database but had not come back with any positive matches. Analysis of the specifics of the device had shown remarkably similar characteristics in the workmanship between the poster bomb, the device that had killed Frank

Carter and the one that had killed staff Sergeant Ian King. The particular manner in which the bomb maker had connected these bombs together looked almost identical. Whilst it was accepted that two of those devices had functioned as intended and as such there was not the amount of forensic evidence that Brian had been able to recover, post blast teams had been able to recover enough to state with some confidence that the same man had manufactured, or at least had played a part in manufacturing, all three devices. Satellite imagery of the compound showed that, there were vehicles parked in a courtyard, and thermal signatures indicated that at least two of the buildings were occupied. More information was required, imagery was one thing but what was really needed was hard facts on who was inside the compound, what weaponry they had in there and would the assault team be walking into a heavily booby trapped area. The only way to get that level of detail, was to put boots on the ground, the difficulty lay in that mounting any sort of long term covert observation or intelligence gathering mission in an area where it was immediately obvious you were an outsider was always difficult, the danger of compromise from within the target area or from a third party was always present.

Difficulties and dangers were not things that the men of task force twelve normally shied away from, some tasks were straightforward, others less so, the task still had to be accomplished. Mike and Mark were two of a six man team of CROP, covert rural observation post, specialists; they were given the job of identifying possible positions where the compound could be viewed from whilst remaining undetected, the mission brief they were working to was to achieve complete coverage as far as possible, guide an assault team onto target, identify enemy positions and weaknesses. They had been told that time on ground was to be kept to a minimum thus hopefully alleviating some of the compromise issues. Using the imagery available to them plus information fed back from a goshawk surveillance drone, added to by some state of the art computerised mapping tools, Mike and his partner were able to work from an almost three dimensional template, from there they could see a natural wadi that ran alongside the compounds northern perimeter, the wadi lay approximately four hundred meters from the compound wall, the wadi walls would allow the CROP team to move unseen to a disused sheep or goat herders shelter and from there would afford a view of anybody entering or leaving the area. On the southern side was scrubland but teams could infiltrate under cover of darkness and take up position amongst the sparse fauna that grew wild there, neither hide would survive close scrutiny but would give the occupants a clear view of inside the compound walls. Overhead live imagery would be fed from an unmanned surveillance vehicle flying at twenty thousand feet above the area and transmitted via a secure link to the team leader. Mark had suggested going back to the village elders in order to attempt to use the village as an insertion and extraction point, however the surest way to lose control of a covert mission is to start widening the number of people who know about it. Two CROP teams would go in and take up an over watch position twenty four hours ahead of the main party, they would insert covertly after being dropped off in a valley five kilometres away, close support would be on standby throughout their time on the ground, however, given the topography, that support would take at least fifteen minutes to be with them, "and that Mike is a long time to be in a bad place fighting bad people with only a handful of guys around you", said Mark quietly. The task force commander had sat through the briefings given by the CROP team, the assault team leader and anyone else who would be involved in this operation, including Brian, who was going along to ensure the assault team got on to and through the target area safely. The commander would have the final say whether this mission would go ahead, he had to weigh up the likelihood of success and what that would bring about against the possibility of it all going pear shaped, and there were a number of factors on this mission that if any one went wrong could result in the whole thing collapsing around his ears. "Have we any idea of the number of people inside" he asked the intelligence Officer, "negative sir", he answered quickly, "but we do know there are people inside" went on the Commander, "yes sir, two of the four buildings show hear signatures indicative of human habitation". The assault commander interrupted, "we have hand held thermal intensifiers, would they work from the observation posts?", "tech guy?" barked the commander, a nervous looking man jumped at the voice, "er, no sir, I don't think so he answered, you would need to be fairly close to the buildings to get a complete picture of how many are inside." Ok the commander said, here's what we will do, the men who would be going in on the mission leant forward as the commander began his summary . . . . "and remember we need some of these jokers alive, someone is killing our bomb disposal guys we need to find him because if we don't, we will end up doing that crazy shit ourselves, and I for one am not doing that, now go brief your guys, you know the plan, good luck", the commander finished and as the guys trooped out he watched them go partly wishing he could still be part of these operations and partly remembering his wife's warning of how much grief she would give him if he did purposely put himself in harm's way one more time.

For the want of anywhere else to be, Tommy was sat at the back of the observation post overlooking Elmhurst road, the owner of the hairdressers had been up to offer coffee and biscuits, she seemed to be very impressed at having police Officers upstairs and despite being sworn to secrecy Al and the guys had no doubt that once all this was over, she would dine of this for a long time with her customers downstairs. The details taken by the alert Traffic Officer had been passed through to Police Officers in Coventry following the "Traffic stop" Mr Warner had been checked out and showed no inclination or leaning towards anything subversive, he was just, as he claimed to be a single man business, doing local and Nationwide deliveries out on office in his small semi detached house. The address where the parcels had been picked up from was a rented unit, apparently leased by a Mr Farouk, the unit was currently secured and the landlords claimed that Mr Farouk usually came in once or twice a week and had regular deliveries and just as regular orders being sent out. They had no idea just what he had inside the unit, local rules prohibited dangerous goods and articles being stored inside. They did admit though that they very seldom if ever carried out any checks on what was actually inside the units. Mr Warner had, he freely admitted, been told that one of the packages contained jars of liquid and should be handled carefully.

"Stand by" the quiet voice of one of the watchers broke the stillness of the room, "we have the front door open, I have Zulu 1 and 2 out of the house and mobile towards town" immediately Officers were assigned to cover their targets, "I have Zulu 1 and 2 heading North still towards town" said one of the men following. Tommy looked at Al to see whether or not they would follow, when the front door opened again and Zulus 3 and 5 came out heading towards the car. Al suggested that they stay where they were till they knew just what was going on and where the four men were heading to. Radio transmissions constantly updated the Zulus positions. Zulus 3 and 5, Said and Rahim drove the short distance into town, where they parked the car in a short stay car park and walked into a small coffee shop, where shortly afterwards they were photographed in conversation with a white man wearing what looked like mechanics coveralls. After a brief conversation the three men left the cafe and all headed back to the car park, with Said driving and Rahim now in the back seat the men drove off and headed towards Mount sorrel where they stopped outside a row of corrugated metal garages some bearing for rent signs. The three walked down the row of identical looking units, the only difference being a number stencilled in black paint in the top right hand corner. The white man slipped a key from a large key ring and opened the up and over garage door to one marked number eight, the door was lifted just enough to allow the men to stoop and duck inside, and was immediately closed once all three were inside. Officers used the time they were inside and out of view to take up a position close by where they would be able to look inside the garage as the men exited. After less than five minutes during which time a car was heard to be started and then turned off inside the garage, the men came out blinking into the brightness of the day, Said was then seen to hand over an envelope to the man who in turn locked the garage door and passed him a set of keys. These transactions were all caught on camera and as the door had been opened one of the Officers stated that he had seen what looked like a white van parked inside, although the number plate was obscured by the men leaving. As Said led the men back to his car one Officer stayed behind, to lift latent prints from the door handle of the garage, it had been noted that the man who had opened it had not been wearing gloves. He would then attempt to find out who had rented the garage and for how long. Said then drove the unknown white man back into town, where he was dropped off at the same car park they had used earlier, after which he and Rahim drove to the mosque and went inside, it was impossible for the following Officers to enter the mosque and not be immediately compromised so they settled into a holding and waiting pattern till the two men re-emerged.

Meanwhile Salim and Imran had been seen to head towards the train station where they bought two all day travel passes, the two men seemed to be in no hurry and chatted quietly between themselves at the end of platform one whilst waiting for their train. Matt was stood at the far end of the platform reading a newspaper whilst, another operative Sally was stood near the ticket office both keeping a watchful eye on Salim and his friend, the next train was scheduled to arrive in five minutes, the stopping train to Birmingham, Matt silently cursed their luck, on an express train, he could have simply forward based Officers at the final destination to pick up the two men as they left the train thus avoiding a possible compromise. With stopping trains he either had to have men at each station and leapfrog them ahead of the train or run the risk him and Sally being spotted as they alighted and followed the suspects as they got off. As the men had bought travel passes this also meant that they couldn't simply ask the ticket office what tickets the men had bought. The station tanoy crackled into life announcing the trains' arrival and the two men moved towards the platform edge, Matt and Sally took up positions either side aiming to join adjacent carriages to the one chosen by Salim and Imran. Matt was able by means of sitting in an aisle seat and looking through the partition door, to see the two men take their seats and continue their conversation, to sit in the same carriage would have simply too risky, Sally had removed her jacket whilst approaching the station at Leicester and had it in her bag, she would put it back on as the two men alighted, this would allow her to change her appearance at least a little once she got off. Matt too had a second pack away waterproof jacket in his pocket that he could change into if necessary, the change of appearance was one method of trying to avoid compromise, however anyone trained in counter surveillance knew that it was the shoes that often gave the game away, it was easy to put on a hat or to remove a coat, changing footwear on an operation was a lot more difficult. As the train made its way slowly towards Birmingham surveillance operators in a number of unmarked vehicles were keeping a parallel vigil along the highways and byways that ran alongside the tracks aiming to be in position to pick up the tail as and when it was required.

Al and Tommy had remained in the observation post, the only sign of activity at the house was when someone inside opened up all the downstairs' windows as if airing the house, but no one came out or went in and the only thing to break the monotony was the steady flow of information from the guys conducting the follows. Tommy was considering going along to see how Marty was doing later that day; he had phoned her yesterday only to be told that she was in with the physio, she was doing well the nurse had said although still a sick girl.

Matt's voice came over the radio informing everyone that the train had just left the penultimate station on its journey and Salim and Imran would now be getting off at Birmingham New street, immediately a number of things swung into operation, British Transport Police were requested to ask the ticket collectors to be a touch more methodical in their job giving the team those few extra minutes to get ready, BTP were not to be overtly interested in what was going on or to show the two suspects any untoward attention, surveillance operators took up positions along the station platforms and exit routes, a number of travel passes had already been sourced should the two men simply board another train. Tommy wondered at the simplicity yet complexity of all these things that had to blend together just to allow two men to be followed. Matt and Sally could not afford the risk of continuing the follow, the likelihood of them having been noticed on the train was too great, once they handed over the men to the operators on the ground, they were to catch the next train back to Leicester and await further tasking. As the train pulled in Salim and his friend stood up Sally now wearing a coat and a hat stood at the next doorway, Matt remained seated seemingly engrossed in his book but actually talking quietly to the guys on the ground "Zulu 1 and 2 at door to carriage number four, Zulu 1 first off headed to ticket booth Zulu 2 immediately behind, that's Zulu 1 at ticket office. A voice responded "I have Zulu 1 through ticket point towards concourse" immediately followed by "Zulu 2 now with Zulu 1 at timetables on East side of concourse" With the two men safely handed over and no sign of compromise Matt and Sally headed off to the large shopping area that makes up most of New street to take advantage of the free time to grab a coffee before heading back to Leicester. The two suspects having identified where they wanted to be, set off towards platform eleven with Officers following their every move, the timetable showed that the next train from that platform was due to in ten minutes. Tommy heard the Officers talking about who was where and where the train was due to stop, he was barely half listening when he heard Selly Oak being mentioned, the train was due to stop there, and that was where Marty and many other wounded heroes were recovering, surely it was just coincidental, but deep down Tommy felt something almost primeval warning him that it was more than that. He looked at Al who had seemingly reached a similar conclusion, logic dictated that there was no immediate threat to anyone just now, the two men were not carrying anything suspicious and had not displayed any signs of an impending attack, but

Tommy just knew they were planning something, and he had to put a stop to it.

Said and Rahim had left the Mosque after an hour or so inside, they emerged into the sunlight and headed back to the car, from there they drove back to Elmhurst rd. Officers had been busy attempting to identify the unknown man the two had been talking to, luckily he was no stranger to Leicestershire Police and had been convicted on a number of occasions mainly for motor vehicle theft and forged tax disc offences. The recovered finger prints had shown a positive match, a name and address in Loughborough had revealed the man to be John Sharp, a couple of phone calls to the local station showed John to be someone well known around the area for being able to find you the sort of vehicle, regardless of type you happened to be looking for. He had never been politically motivated his goal was simply cash in hand, no questions asked. The garage owners had said that the rental agreement has been in place for a few months now, rent was paid every month in cash and on time. The name on the agreement said Smith, but the manager admitted that he never really asked for proof of identification, providing the rent was paid he was happy. A decision was made to have someone in uniform pay Mr Sharp a visit, nothing heavy, just a quiet word to see what he had been up to and with whom, he was by nature an old fashioned crook, he knew what he did was illegal and had taken the various punishments his vocation had caused him in the same vein, the adage of not doing the crime if you cannot do the time was one he believed in, he had never been involved anything that had caused him to physically hurt somebody and although not a fan of the police accepted that they had a job to do, just as he had. Officers were confident that a quiet word would at least generate some response particularly when he found out that his rented garage was no longer a secret.

The train pulled into Selly Oak, as it did so Salim and Imran stood and headed towards the exit quickly followed by an undercover Officer who had reported their departure to fellow Officers further up the train, as the train slowed Imran opened the door and the two men jumped lightly onto the platform, making their way to the unmanned exit barrier they were unaware of the three men one ahead and two behind who would be shadowing their every move. The two made their way out of the station and headed off towards the centre of town, crossing the main road they walked directly to the town library, on the way Salim was seen to make a couple of phone calls, during which he checked his watch and spoke to Imran who apparently agreed with what was being said as he nodded his assent. As they approached the library a man was walking in just ahead of them, the two made their way to the natural history section where Salim picked up the first book he came across, within a few minutes the man who had entered the library at the same time walked over and also removed a book from the shelves, he was then seen to replace the book returning it to the bookshelf, but this time, upside down, at that Imran walked over to the man and spoke quietly to him, he nodded and the three moved towards one of the study tables that dotted the library floor, they took their seats and leaning in towards the centre of the table whispered furtively with each other, Officers wearing covert body cameras were able to record imagery of the meet, but were unable to hear what was being said. As the three reached the end of their conversation the unknown man pushed a small package across the table towards Salim who checked the contents and satisfied placed it into his jacket pocket. Shortly afterwards the three left the library, Officers were left with little option to follow Salim and Imran, leaving the third man, still to be identified for another time.

CHAPTER TWELVE

Mike and Mark had assembled their two CROP teams and the necessary equipment to support their time on the ground, there was no room for luxuries, each man, dressed in dark blue one piece ghilley suits, which would blend in with background in each hide location, would carry his own rations, water, night vision goggles, personal radios, ammunition and weapons, in addition each team were equipped with thermal imagery cameras, encrypted radios to allow communication with the assault teams and air support, and an array of cameras, and concealment measures. The plan was to insert roughly four kilometres from the compound and using cover of the night make their way on foot to the two pre determined hides, they wanted to be dug in and hidden from view a good couple of hours before sunrise, from then they would be the eyes and ears on the ground reporting back to the command cell just who and what was in the compound. They would be in position throughout the day and into the night; the assault team would follow their route and be in position to mount an offensive strike against the compound by dawn the following day. Each member of CROP, was handpicked for the role they were asked to do, selection was as tough as any of the special forces selection processes, very often they were alone and many miles from a friendly face, it required a special blend of skill, and courage to sit a few hundred yards from a enemy stronghold knowing that discovery and capture was often a very real possibility, yet without them assault teams would end up going into action blind. It was these traits that Mick and Mark as well as the men they were leading would be relying on in the hours ahead, to not only give the assaulters a chance to grab the bomb makers but once finished get out of the area alive and still unseen. It was one of the often not seen results of the covert surveillance operations that the enemy would have no idea how they could have been compromised and would usually look inwards suspecting a mole from within resulting in witch-hunt's and mistrust in their own rank and file.

The blacked out helicopters lifted off from Bastion as the sun was about to set, on board were the CROP teams and a small group of heavily armed QRF who would be the first on the scene in the event of the CROP being compromised, they would be equipped with two all terrain quad bikes that had been converted to carry a team of four complete with their equipment, this gave Mike and his team at least some degree of support until the main cavalry arrived to extract or support them depending on the situation. As the birds flew low and swiftly to the drop off point the men as usual went through their own pre mission routines some were silent and contemplative others would chat quietly with the neighbours, one or two would pass the time reading, but all knew just how dangerous their task was. The load master gave the five minutes out signal and the teams as one stood to prepare to leave the relative safety of the helicopter, as the chopper touched down rotors still turning the quad bikes rolled off the ramp quickly followed by the men who would be on the ground preparing the way for the assault party. Within a couple of minutes the team were on the ground and the helo's lifted off into the night.

The QRF had identified a small cave at the foot of a valley that would serve as their holding area, it was close enough to allow them to support the CROP, albeit a very hasty ten minute quad bike ride away, but much better than having no immediate support, it was tucked out of sight so they should not encounter any civilians in the area, the same drop off point was to used by the main assault party, and the secondary role of the QRF would be secure the area for the teams that would form part of the assault force. The assault plan was to be a joint top down and bottom up approach, with special forces fast roping onto the roof of the compound supported by their colleagues coming from the outside the compound through and over the walls, this called for the ground force to be in a position as the choppers arrived, and not a little in the way of close communication between the two forces to prevent any blue on blue incidents. The CROP teams moved off in a file formation heading towards their predetermined layup points, they moved swiftly and without incident and the two teams took up positions a little after four am, reporting back to the headquarters with their precise positions and an update on what they could see within the target area, which was, as was to be expected all quiet.

The evening briefing took place at the police headquarters, Tommy sat at the back listening to the surveillance operators describe what their respective targets had been up to during the day, the discovery of the rented garage and the subsequent questioning of Mr Sharp had proved to be of interest as had the photographs taken of the unknown man in the Selly Oak library, John Sharp had initially been very convincing in his denial of any rented garage, however when shown surveillance photographs taken earlier that day he suddenly remembered how he had tucked away a small unit for storage of household furniture and such like, when asked about the white vehicle inside he again attempted to persuade Officers that they were mistaken until they offered to drive him there and check for themselves, at which point he confessed to storing a van for a couple of guys who had been introduced through a friend of a friend, he didn't know the two men, he had been approached and asked if he could source and secure a white unmarked van, he had gotten the van from another mate of his for a couple of hundred pounds, the two men had offered to pay twice that as long as he could store the van for a few days, the van was a white Peugeot van with blacked out windows. As far as he knew the two guys were looking to rescue one of their cousins from an abusive marriage, they wanted to drive to Birmingham one night and use the van to load the girls belongings and her and then whisk away to a safe place, they didn't want to use their own vehicles and didn't want to leave a trail involving rental cars etc hence the need for the subterfuge. He had taken the two men to the lock up that day, been paid his fee and had handed over the keys to the vehicle, they has asked if they could keep it there till their cousin was ready to leave, her husband would be going away on a business trip in a few days and they would move it out then, he had given them a spare key to the garage padlock and as far as he was concerned once the van left that would be the end of the story. He had however offered to let Officers have a key to the garage as long as they would remember his cooperation when he was next in front of the magistrates.

The man in the library had been photographed but as yet he remained unknown, library staff had been approached and had handed over the days CCTV footage, which was being analysed by specialists, all suspects had returned home, the windows to the house had remained fully open all day despite there being a typical east Midlands chill in the air, one suspicion, that Tommy raised tentatively, was that the man referred to as Zulu 6 was either demonstrating how to manufacture or actually making homemade explosives, the chemical released during such procedures were often highly dangerous and the windows being opened may have been to prevent these gasses staying within the confines of the house, he was however quick to add, the occupants could have simply been cleaning and airing the property. What was agreed by all present, was that something was happening and it was starting to get to the dangerous stage, Officers at senior level were beginning to get just a little agitated but had agreed to let this operation run a little longer but wanted assurances that everyone and everything, suspects vehicles and properties was under control at all times.

Officers had arranged to visit the white van in the garage unit that night, they had two objectives in mind, one to get a good luck at the vehicle and to deploy a small covert tracking device and secondly to ensure that there was nothing sinister stored inside it, it was with this second purpose of the mission in mind that Tommy was asked to go along with the team, he agreed readily but would talk with his commanding Officer first to keep in him fully up to speed with the events to date, the team wanted to leave shortly after closing time, in order to keep the chance of compromise to a minimum, and reckoned that providing everything went to plan they would be on the ground for a little over an hour. The briefing over Tommy walked away to call the Colonel agreeing to meet the team in the Police station car park at 2300hours.

Mark's team call sign Echo 1 were holed up in the derelict shelter having used the old wadi that the teams had identified earlier to make their way there, they were approximately three hundred metres from the Northern edge of the compound, and from their vantage position they had a clear view of the entrance and the two outer buildings that had been seen on the satellite imagery, hovering above them unseen and silent was a surveillance drone that was beaming images back to the command post via a secure link, as dawn broke the compound started to show signs of life a man appeared at the door to the main building and made his way to one of the smaller outbuildings, which presumably housed a small well as he reappeared a few moments later carrying a water container, he re-entered the main house and was lost from view, he was immediately given the target designation Tango 1 and his new name and identifying features were radioed back to command, his photograph almost at the same time being transmitted back from the eye in the sky, slowly the compound came to life, it appeared as if there were six men as well as the one originally designated tango 1 all now with a moniker Tango 2-7, the teams had, had to cross reference and de-conflict to ensure that the men were not being identified twice and effectively doubling the opposition. all of the men had been carrying AK variant rifles over their shoulders and at all times during the day, a two man rotational guard mount was in operation, one man would stand watching the front gate of the compound, he would then be relieved of his duty after roughly two hours by a second man, he would in turn be on watch for two hours before the first man relieved him, this cycle then continued. Two women had been seen, but these seemed to be cooks and bottle washers. There were however added to the growing list of possible aggressors.

The main activity centred on a small single story building to one side of the main living accommodation, the four men not employed as gate watchers, had spent most of the day thus far in and around that building, from the two observation posts it was impossible to see just what was going on inside, the only window was shuttered, it did however have power lines running into it, and a possible satellite dish on its flat roof. This building was designated Hotel 2 with the main building being Hotel 1, Three saloon type cars were parked inside the compound, to date these had not moved nor had anyone been inside them, so it was not known what state they were in or what possible dangers they possessed. The teams had seen no other signs of habitation in the area, there was little traffic on the track that led to the village where the elders had been so co-operative and no one had entered or left the compound. All this detail was reported back to the central command cell as well as regular "we're all ok" reports, and the final plans to the assault planned for that night were drawn up, as yet there had been no sightings of the man described by the elders, as not of their belief with hatred in his eyes, nor of the bespectacled foreigner.

Towards late morning one of the men left hotel 2 and headed to a small outhouse, which to Marks eyes resembled an old fashioned outdoor toilet, at the rear of the compound, as he approached the building he stopped just short of the door and, very carefully knelt down as if checking the ground for something, none of the CROP team could make out exactly what he was doing but after less than a minute he stood up again and opened the door, after a few minutes he reappeared carrying a small package, he closed the door behind him took a pace and again knelt down, after which he made his way back to hotel 2. Mark immediately reported what he had seen and the outhouse now became hotel 3.

Tommy got off the phone having briefed Andy back at Headquarters, Andy had intimated that Brian was about to get close and personal with some "mutual friends overseas" and that he would be sure to pass on Tommy's best wishes should they meet. Tommy then phoned the hospital and managed to grab a few minutes with Marty, she was in good spirits, the physio was coming along nicely, her librarian friend had been in to see her, and although Mandy was now no longer assigned to her ward, she too popped in every now and then to say hello and to see how she was doing. Marty suggested that her real reason for visiting was to bump into Tommy. Part of Tommy wanted to warn Marty of his concerns regarding the hospital but he knew that to do so would not only cause her to worry but would possibly compromise the whole operation, he promised himself that should anything put the hospital or her in jeopardy he would somehow be there to do whatever he could to prevent the situation getting out of hand. Just how he would do that, right now he didn't know, but he knew that he would be in the right place at the right time should his and the police suspicions prove to be correct.

He met up with Bob at the Police station shortly after ten pm having made use of the hotel gym for a work out followed by a bite to eat, the team was to be three men, Bob Tommy and one other, supported by a team of watchers to ensure they could get in and get out quietly. The plan was very simple, they wanted to deploy a small tracking device underneath the vehicle which could then be followed at a distance should the car be driven away, a second objective was to allow Tommy a look at the car and to ensure its safety. One drawback of deploying tracking devices was not only the risk of discovery should the owners search the underneath of the car but from a police perspective it tied up another resource. It was no good having a beacon on a car if there was nobody detailed to monitor the signal being received and to be in a position to follow the vehicle once mobile, so once the tracker had been emplaced another surveillance car would be parked up out of sight ready to pick up the tail when necessary. The teams set out as planned at 2330hrs and before too long Tommy found himself heading towards the rented garage unit, True to his word John Sharp had produced a key, and the Officers watching the house on Elmhurst road had reported no movement. The risk of Sharp phoning Said and telling him that he had been questioned by the police could not be discounted, Sharp had been very forcibly warned that he should not even consider this but aside from having him detained there was little the police could do to prevent him doing so, should he wish.

The men stopped outside the garage and after a quick check of the doorway opened the lock and stepped inside, the garage was small and mostly filled with a white two door van. The tracking specialist immediately moved to the rear of the vehicle and began to deploy his device underneath the rear bumper. Tommy and Bob began to search the vehicle, the doors were unlocked and there were no signs of any car alarms fitted. Before touching the car, Bob produced a small forensics kit and swabbed the door handles for prints; the van was empty apart from two detachable blue flashing lights that had been put in the passenger foot well, the rest of the garage contained a few cardboard boxes with old number plates, and some tools, paint tins and brushes and set of oil stained overalls hanging on a nail, but nothing to cause Tommy any real concerns, but also nothing to give Bob and his team any real clue as to what was being planned and more importantly when.

The white van, the blue lights, a reconnaissance, possibly, of Selly Oak, even the human transplant boxes all pointed towards something being planned for the hospital but precisely what, remained a mystery, all they could hope for, was that whenever it did happen, they would have all the players under control and be in position to thwart the terrorists aims, and most importantly prevent the loss of life and injury. With the beacon placed, Bob radioed the tracking vehicle to ensure that the signal was being received, the specialist carried out last minute checks tweaked the transmitting device slightly as the control car called in the signal strength, once set, the device was switched off, it had a small motion switch inside that would turn on the system once the car moved, and would turn it off once the car had been stationary for thirty minutes, thus reducing battery drain. After a quick check that the team had left nothing behind to indicate their presence, Bob informed Control that were ready to leave, once satisfied that the area was clear, he opened the door and led his team back to their pick up vehicle.

The assault team leader, a hardened veteran of numerous compound assaults who everyone simply called Boss, or to those who were allowed Sean, had been receiving regular updates from the CROP teams and had assembled his men to finalise, as best they could, the assault planned for later that night. The original notion of a top down and bottom up approach was still the preferred option with the ground forces being dropped off at the same spot as the CROP teams, this being first secured by the waiting QRF, from there they would make their way on foot to the compound, where they would get themselves in position to strike. The assault team on the ground would split into two waves, one over the compound wall on the North side the second breaching the wall on the opposite side, from there they would, make their way to the front and back of Hotel 1, if the CROP team reported that any other of the buildings were occupied then the assault force would further split and one team would make their way to that building. They would remain hidden and would not go loud till the helicopters arrived and disgorged their load of twelve heavily armed men via fast ropes on to the roof of Hotel 1. The fast ropers would be aiming for the upper story windows were they would deploy the flash bangs, small pyrotechnic grenades that emitted a deafening sound and blinding white light that would stun anyone inside immediately, the grenades would be almost instantly followed by a team of deadly professional and highly motivated assaulters intent on one thing, killing or capturing everyone inside the building

At this point the front and rear doors would be explosively opened and the assault force would follow their well practiced routine of kinetic clearance operations, the idea being to leave the occupants completely dazed and disorientated by the sudden and rude awakening leaving them little time to organise themselves and mount any form of counter attack, the assaulters would be attempting to have the building secured in as short a time as possible, under normal circumstances they would have had a floor plan to work from and teams would have been allocated areas of responsibility, this operation did not allow for such luxuries so it was essential that the commanders on the scene were able to think rapidly and to be in almost constant communication with other teams. The main attack would initially focus on this building with designated teams being assigned Hotel 2 and 3, the idea being that any building showing signs of occupation be hit simultaneously. From what Mark and Mike had seen, hotel 2 appeared to be a workshop of some sort, and hotel 3 possibly a storage area. Brian had stood up at this point and pointed out that the unusual behaviour of the tango when entering and leaving hotel 3 could well be indicative of him disarming and then re arming a safety switch, which may well mean that the door or the area around the door to hotel 3 is booby trapped. Sean told the team designated hotel 3 to await the ATO before entering the building, Brian was to initially go with the main assault force and clear the way into the compound, from there he was to be available as and when to respond to any calls for ATO assistance. No worries Boss said the hotel 3 team lead, and gave Brian quick thumbs up. Sean reminded everyone that although it was the Commanders intent that prisoners were taken if possible, no one was to take unnecessary risks to capture these guys alive, if the choices were take one alive but risk being killed in the process, or simply shoot the guy, then shoot him! He reminded them that all the men seen so far had been armed and were therefore regarded as dangerous, unarmed civilians were not to be attacked unless they showed themselves to be hostile, and then appropriate force was to be used. Once the compound was secured, and the prisoners detained then a search of the area would be carried out, once complete Helicopters would fly in and extract everyone. As soon as all friendlies had left the compound the CROP teams would pack up their hides and move back under cover of darkness to the initial drop off point, still being secured by elements of the QRF to be picked up by another chopper and flown home. One helicopter with an assault team would remain in the area until the CROP team and QRF were airborne. The mission was not over till everyone was back at Bastion he concluded.

The assault had been planned to go in at 0330hrs that morning, the time when the body was at its lowest ebb, rehearsals were planned for 2000hrs. The first wave would be "wheels up" at 2300hrs which would give them sufficient time to be at the compound in time for the second wave of fast ropers. Once the first wave was on their way into danger then the second wave would be on immediate notice to move in case of them requiring assistance or extraction. Brian left the briefing with Sean, who pulled him to one side and asked about the likelihood of his men running into booby traps inside the compound, Brian answered that the fact that the CROP team and surveillance footage from the drone had seen no obvious signs of access areas being avoided, apart from the area around Hotel 3, and that the occupants seemed to be roaming around the compound without skirting around or stepping over certain areas, then it would appear unlikely, but we have no way of knowing what is inside the various buildings. He reassured Sean that he would personally check out the area's leading up to the entry points and would if required get his men past any obstacles they encountered. If we have to split assets and attack two buildings at the same time, Brian had said he would check out all doors before entry was attempted if time permitted, if not the he would stay with the main force at Hotel 1. As the two men went their separate ways, Sean said to Brian, "you know I am not sure you can do what my guys can do, and I damn sure know I cannot do what you do, but tonight we have, simply both got to do it, good luck ATO, look after my men for me and we will look after you, see you later" with those words he headed off to make sure his team were as ready as it were possible to be going into the unknown. Brian had his gear already packed, he, as was his habit, rechecked that the batteries were charged, and the items he would be most likely needing first were easily to hand, a couple of items he had attached small pieces of coloured card too, he had learnt that asking someone to dig into his bag and get his x ray machine or his explosive detector kit was far easier if he simply said get me the thing with the orange tag on it. Once satisfied he made his way to the chow hall and although not hungry, forced himself to eat something knowing that the next 24 hours were going to be long, challenging and not a little worrying.

CHAPTER THIRTEEN

A ctivity at Elmhurst Road had began at eight that morning with Hussain and the as yet unrecognised Zulu 6 leaving the house, as they left Officers watching could see that all the occupants had gathered in the hall to say goodbye and there was much hugging and embracing. Zulu 6 again took a good look around him as he walked towards the car. Hussain again drove him to Loughborough railway station where 6 got out alone and walked towards the platforms without a backward glance. Surveillance Officers had been supplemented by specialists from neighbouring forces and one of these had been detailed to pick up Zulu 6 if and when he went mobile. Hussain immediately drove back to Elmhurst Road where almost as soon as he pulled up outside the house Rahim had come out and got into the car, where they headed once more into the city, the two drove straight towards the area where the lock up was, surveillance operators knowing that as soon as the lock up door was opened the concealed cameras would be "woken up" and would record everything as well as beam live footage into a command cell that had been set up and manned continuously since the night the devices had been installed, could afford to sit back a few car lengths allowing other motorists to act as unknowing shields, the car also being tracked was at no times in danger of being lost either. The two men pulled up and from their position could see the two men enter the lock up, again they seemed to have no idea they were being watched and showed none of the normal counter surveillance drills that Zulu 6 had demonstrated. The door of the lock up closed and they were lost from physical view, almost immediately a small screen flickered into life nearby and a man drinking from a flask of tea watched the two make their way towards the workbench, Rahim removed his jacket and from the pocket pulled out the headlights that had been bought only a few days ago, he opened one of the drawers and pulled out what looked like a sheet of sandpaper which he placed on the bench and began to rub one of the glass bulbs along the paper stopping every few minutes to check his handiwork. It seemed to the watchers that he was attempting to rub a hole through the glass part of the bulb. After several minutes he seemingly achieved his aim and as Hussain watched he poured a small amount of what looked like black sand from a bottle he had also taken from his pockets into the bulb and then dabbed a blob of superglue onto the bulb effectively resealing the headlight. He followed this routine for each of the four headlights he had brought with him.

Once all four were done he told Hussain to bring him the soldering iron, which he duly did, as they waited for iron to reach operating temperature, Rahim cut eight lengths of electrical cable each approximately twelve inches in length after stripping back the plastic sheathing from both ends of each piece he placed the first bulb into the set of helping hands, a small weighted multi handed and multi position clamping set, that had been placed on the bench, he then soldered two of the cut lengths of wire to each of the bulbs. The whole operation took about an hour and throughout that time the two men spoke little, but they did once again mention the name of Khalid saying how clever he was and that how sure they were, that the work he had done yesterday would meet with Allah's approval. Rahim in particular seemed to be very impressed with Khalid saying how he had taught him how do adapt the bulbs like this and showed him the way to make the white crystals.

The surveillance operator although not completely certain what he was watching being made, had no doubt it was something that deserved some form of higher command input immediately called his superiors and informed them what he was currently watching. Tommy's mobile phone burst into life with a text message marked meet in lobby urgent and signed Al. He grabbed his always packed "go bag" and ran down the steps forsaking the lift and was in the lobby within a minute of his text message, on his arrival he saw Al talking earnestly on the phone, Bob was stood to one side so Tommy walked over and asked him "what was going on, why the urgency?" "Not sure Tommy" Bob answered; "Al has called everyone involved downstairs". Phone call finished Al called his men to him and told them what was going on in the lock up. "Shit" breathed Tommy as it dawned on him just what the two men were doing; they were making initiators, homemade detonators. Or at least that's what it appeared to be. Al finished his briefing and immediately asked Tommy, what he thought was going on. Tommy took a deep breath and told Al that he believed the men were in the process of making the initiators that when put into contact with some types of homemade explosives would cause them to detonate once sufficient power was applied to the two cables now attached to the headlights. "Are they dangerous?", Al asked immediately, "only in so far as they could cause injury to your hand if you were holding them and they functioned", said Tommy, "but once they are placed inside or next to the explosives then yes, you are have two of the five components you need to make a bomb, and as such become a lot more hazardous. If we assume that the man who arrived recently was someone who knew how to manufacture explosives and, if we further assume that the delivery man who arrived shortly after Zulu 6 was, albeit unwittingly, bringing them the precursors needed to make the explosive, and the open windows in Elmhurst were indeed evidence of the actual process taking place then it's a good bet that these guys now have explosives and although not in the same area the means to initiate them".

Al's phone rang again he listened briefly, "thanks" he said "keep on them", hanging up, he told the team that the two men had left the lock up, leaving the now modified bulbs on the bench and were heading back to Elmhurst Road. He then told the men that Zulu 6 had been followed to a flat in a suburb of Nottingham, electoral rolls gad been requested and DNA lifted from a cup he had left on his table when he went to the toilet had been taken and results would be sent across as soon as they had them. Al went on to say that if the men in the house showed even the slightest signs of moving the explosives then the armed response unit on standby would be called in to take them out. As Al was talking, a thought came into Tommy's head, maybe there was something that could be done, that would allow Operation Vanguard to run but at the same time reduce the hazards and carry out an action that would ensure that the bombs would not function as intended. The operation was not without risk and would need sign off from both senior military and police Officers. The first thing was to have a quiet word with Al and then a fast car to Oxfordshire to get permission and the necessary equipments. Al seemed at first unsure when Tommy explained the procedure, when asked had this been done before Tommy had to admit that although not by him on a live operation he had exercised the skills many times and other operators had indeed carried out similar actions and as a direct result devices had not exploded, terrorists had been arrested and more importantly lives had been saved. Tommy stressed that the decision was not his to make, and indeed nor Al's, but with his permission he would get back to headquarters and talk to the Colonel, in the meantime Al could go to his commanders, Tommy would be happy to brief them himself on the technical aspects if it were necessary. Al shrugged and said "why not" get one of the team to drive you there I will request a "chat" with my boss and we will see what they say. What's the plan if they say no? He asked, "I guess we let the Armed response unit take them out we have a full Bomb Disposal team on standby and once the bad guys are safely accounted for the team make safe whatever they find, of course we will need to ensure we get everyone at the same time", Tommy replied, With that they went their separate ways, Tommy pressed the speed dial number for Andy Jenkins to tell him he was coming in and would need to talk with the Commanding Officer and that it was important.

A few hours before Brian had lifted off into the Afghanistan night, Tommy had walked into Andy's office to find the SAT poring over the latest reports from Afghanistan, "these guys are getting good Tommy" he said as he waved his mate into a chair, "I know" said Tommy "how is Brian doing with his op over there?" "Going in tonight" Andy answered, "let's hope he gets to catch the bastards behind all this, What's going Tommy, why the urgency to see the boss?", Tommy quickly filled Andy in on the events that were starting to unfurl in the East Midlands and finished off by telling him what he had in mind. "What do the police say?" Andy asked, Tommy replied with a shrug, "they may need convincing at the higher level, but the guys on the ground think its got legs, I have asked Al to speak to his bosses to scope out their likely reactions, but I have told them at this stage it's all dependent on getting the necessary permissions." "Are we sure that these are the only initiators" Andy asked, "No, not totally but we know that they have bought two sets of headlamp bulbs, two bulbs per pack, we know we have four bulbs in the garage, of course they may have some more at home but if so why take four to the lock up to modify and do the others somewhere else?, it's not an exact science Andy, you know that, but everything points to the four bulbs being the only four initiators". "I agree" said Andy" but the Boss will be asking the same questions and more. Shall we go and talk to him", "Will you back me?" Asked Tommy as they stood to leave, Andy paused, and looked at Tommy seriously, "Tommy if this goes wrong we all stand to lose, none more so that the poor sods who will get hurt in the chaos these guys are planning, but to answer your question, yes, yes I will".

An hour later Tommy was once again heading back towards Leicester, the Commanding Officer had accepted Tommy's plan, technically it was sound and providing that all suspects were still under control then he agreed that the operation could continue. Before he had left Tommy had paid a visit to the stores and picked up one or two additional tools he would need to carry out the planned task. He was just passing through Banbury when mobile rang, Al had been in with his bosses who wanted Tommy or someone from the Bomb Squad to explain just what would happen and how they could give a guarantee that the bombs would not explode. Tommy had foreseen this and had asked the Colonel if he would, should the need arise step in and explain at the higher level, he told Al that he would get his CO to talk with Al's boss and hopefully that should sort out that side of the problem, Al had said that the Police commander would not give his approval till he had spoken with the experts, so could Tommy respectfully ask his Colonel to be a good chap and hurry along. Tommy took Al's boss's name and office number and then immediately called Andy and explained what was required, Andy promised to go and talk with the Colonel straight away.

On the other side of the world, It seemed strange to Brian as he stood alongside some of the most professional soldiers he had ever worked alongside, that at a time when most of his civilian mates would be staggering out of pubs, he was about to board a helicopter to be dropped off miles from anywhere to walk a few miles carrying a load of equipment to capture or kill the very people who were responsible for killing and maiming a bunch of his fellow operators. Rehearsals had gone well and everyone was now ready and keen to get on with the job in hand. The load masters gave the signal and the men trooped off into their respective seats, unlike conventional air force flights no one bothered buckling seatbelts and the "loadies" wisely refrained from trying to insist that their passengers did so, falling out of a door was the least of anyone's concerns just now and besides seatbelts had a very disturbing habit of getting tangled around web straps and preventing you from exiting the aircraft when you needed to. One by one the helo's lifted into the night sky, pilots flying without lights swiftly gained altitude and sped off towards the secured drop zone where the QRF stood to ready and waiting. With the one minute warning issued the men stood and watched the night sky loom into view as the rear doors opened, as soon as the wheels were down the teams surged forwards and ran to take an all round defensive position until all the helicopters had delivered their payloads and once again lifted off to head back to camp. The QRF commander had quickly identified the assault team lead and the two of them had a brief discussion about the current state of play.

Whilst they were busy doing that the assaulters had gotten themselves organised along with the elements of the QRF who would accompany them on the assault. Sean ran across to his position at the head of the pack, and after a quick radio check to command and one to the CROP team to tell them to expect company sometime soon they turned towards the North and set off, Brian in his position in the middle of the squad quickly fell into his usual routine patrol mode. Surprisingly silent the attack force made good progress towards their target, the only sound the occasional radio chatter from control or the CROP to update on the activity or more welcoming the lack of it at the compound. As they neared the compound the attackers halted, split into three distinct groups and as they prepared themselves for their respective missions, Sean and his deputy moved off to have quick face to face with the CROP leader. The purpose of which was to get a first real look at the compound and to ensure that everyone involved not only knew who were the good guys, but also where they would be both on the insert and extraction phase of the operation. One of the secondary roles of the CROP team was to watch out for would be "squirters" people fleeing the compound and attempting to escape, the CROP would be responsible with the aid of the eye in the sky for spotting and ultimately stopping these individuals, rules of engagement prevented these simply being shot as they escaped unless they posed an immediate threat to life, so pursuit and capture would be the order of the day.

As the time ticked down to zero hour Brian had found himself being part of a team that had clambered over the Northern wall of the compound and had then he had led the team covertly searching his way up to around the front door of Hotel one, once Sean was happy that he and his men were in position, Brian was immediately dispatched under escort around the house to assist the team on the rear door who were unhappy with a patch of earth that showed signs of being recently dug up near the very door they were planning on using. Brian arrived to find a team of eight heavily armed guys stood alongside a wall, the leader pointed out the questionable ground to Brian, who agreed that it did indeed look disturbed. He moved forwards armed with a silenced metal detector and began to search around the area, his detector vibrated in his hand as some form of metal was located, not big enough to be a pressure mat but certainly metal thought Brian to himself, he slowly began to pick away the loose earth around the area of concern looking for any wiring or evidence of an anti access type device, stopping every few seconds to reconfirm the metal detector was still picking up a metallic source, as he got deeper he found a couple of old and fairly rusty screws, after removing these from the ground and putting them to one side he again waved his detector over the area, it was not unheard of for terrorists to camouflage a device by laying something innocuous over the top of it to be found by a metal detector, and hoping to fool an unsuspecting operator into thinking that, that was what had caused his detector to alarm, when the real threat lay buried below the screws. Finding nothing to cause him concern Brian continued searching up to and around the back door, once the team were happily in the start position he moved back, again under escort, to his position at the front door. It had been decided that Hotel two and three, showing no signs of habitation would be cleared after the main building had been secured. The lead entry pair had placed an explosive door opening charge on the front door, and Brian knew the back door would by now being prepared in the same manner, the rest of the team had their weapons our, night vision goggles on and were ready to launch themselves into the hallway almost as soon as the controlled explosion tore the door from its framework. The time was now 0310hrs everyone was in place, Sean had received confirmation that the fast ropers were in bound and would be over the target in fifteen minutes, nothing to do but wait, but prepared to move early should the occupants now silent, start to show any signs of movement.

At 0325hrs Sean signalled to his guys to stand by, almost imperceptibly everyone tensed their muscles the plan was as soon as the helicopters dropped the ropes the doors would be blown quickly followed by the windows of the upper story at which point, Sean would unleash his men. The seconds passed quickly and Brian felt the air above his head become electrified by the rotor induced static as two Blackhawk helicopters dropped out of the sky and came to a hover about fifty feet above the roof almost immediately the sky was full of men sliding down rope towards pre designated target areas, Sean gave the "Go, Go, Go" signal, on the second "go" Brian closed one eye to preserve his night vision, and on the third and final "go" both front and back doors vanished in a wave of light and noise that assaulted the ears of all who were nearby. Brian found himself hurrying to catch up with the man in front as the teams split into pairs clearing room by room, upstairs he could hear yelled commands, followed by a short controlled round of gunfire, "room clear" came a shout from his left as two men ran out to move onto their next target, Brian had positioned himself close to Sean, not for any sense of protection, although there was plenty to be found around Sean, but more so he was immediately on hand should his services be needed. From upstairs came more gunfire and shouting, although the temptation to rush upstairs was almost uncontrollable, Sean was talking to the guys up there to find out what was going on and before he committed his men up the narrow stairway had told the assaulters they had friendlies joining them from the downstairs, in the confusion of an assault it was too easy to mistake someone coming from an unexpected source to be an enemy.

Within a few minutes quietness descended on the compound building broken only by the sound of a women crying and the soft moaning of a man who had been hurt but was alive. Sean quickly established that all his men were accounted for, two had received slight injuries one had been shot in the arm and the second had miscalculated the leap from rope to window had had possibly broken a leg in the ensuing fall. Medics were already dealing with the two men and with one of the captives, who had been shot during the assault, as for the others three were dead and the rest were now bound, blindfolded and probably feeling very confused. Sean satisfied that he had control over the building sent out the two teams responsible for Hotel 2 and 3. Brian, as suggested had joined the team that would go into Hotel 3, he met them at the now destroyed front door and they set off, from the CROP reports they knew roughly were the man had stopped before entering the building, Brian had briefed the team leader to stop a few meters short of the target and he would take over from there. Brian knew that although his body was pumped full of adrenalin he had to take control of himself, the adage of dealing with the different types of devices, drummed into him during countless hours of training sprang to mind, if its time—react, if its command-take control, victim operated-take your time. This was almost certainly the latter variant, a device designed to function as someone unsuspectingly walked towards the door or opened the door to Hotel 3. He knelt down and began to very carefully finger tip search his way around the area using a combination of metal detector, and threat assessment he came across a length of two core wire with the ends bared and twisted together. A very simple yet effective way of completing a circuit and by untwisting the wires making the circuit safe and allow the door to be approached and opened. Brian reached into his bag and selected the appropriate tool for the job in hand, once set and ready he backed off a few meters and set in train the sequence that would safely and remotely cut the wire. He could of course simply untwist the wires, however experience had taught him to not place trust in a terrorist device and secondly forensically, the last person to touch those wires was one of the bad guys so why destroy potential evidence needlessly. Moving back to confirm the cut, he traced the wires down to where they went into an improvised pressure plate and from there he could find the explosive charge and detonator, after a few minutes he was as happy as it was to be in the circumstances that he had control of the device, but to be absolutely certain he attached a line of rope he had brought with specifically for this purpose to the door handle and taking up a position some thirty metres away he tugged on the line and opened the door, quickly he dashed forward and confirmed that there was nothing else rigged inside the doorway before allowing the team to enter.

From the door Brian could see that the building consisted of two small rooms neither of them had doors, and inside at least one of them was a row of shelving, a shout from one room had Brian moving in that direction, a trapdoor leading down to a small makeshift chamber had been found and inside was a wooden box showing a red diamond shaped warning sign that indicated explosives. Brian lowered himself into the chamber and having checked for signs of tampering opened the box, inside were approximately twenty five sticks of commercial plastic explosive, next to the wooden box and out of sight from initial viewing was another smaller box, this was one was metal and closely resembled the type of ammunition box he would expect to find in most western military ammunition stores, again after a thorough check he opened the container to discover a load of electric detonators some still in their commercial wrappings. He removed the two boxes and passed them up to the guys stood at the opening; these would be taken back to Bastion and exploited for intelligence purposes. The remainder of the building revealed a number of boxes containing various bomb making equipments and one large padded envelope with parts of electronic circuitry and components inside.

Hotel 2 had proven to be a workshop with assorted tools and the paraphernalia involved in any small scale manufacturing process, again a forensic collection operation was underway to recover as much evidence as was possible to collect in a short a time as possible. Less than two hours after the first shot had been fired, the sky above the compound was full of noise as helicopter after helicopter touched down and prisoners, wounded and assaulters either climbed or were helped aboard to head back to base. From the hide locations the CROP team had had a change of plan forced upon them from higher command, they were to stay where they were for the rest of the day to observe if anybody came to the compound, the reason for this was explained away as an opportunity to capture more of the network involved, however Mark and his fellow teammates felt that there was something else afoot. That said they had sufficient cover and provisions for another eighteen hours or more so it was no real hardship, they would move out after dark and then head back to the initial drop off point to be picked up. Brian climbed aboard and sat next to Sean as they lifted off Sean looked across at him gave him a wink and a slow nod, a real token of approval from a man who was rightly hard to impress. Brian looked through the side door of the chopper at the one ferrying the prisoners back to Bastion for interrogation and wondered whether one of them was the man referred to as Atcha.

CHAPTER FOURTEEN

A t about the same time, allowing for the time differences, as his friend was boarding a helicopter, Tommy arrived at the hotel and immediately went to find Al, who was in his room deep in conversation with his team leaders; the tension in the air was palpable as Tommy walked in. Al looked up and motioned for him to join them, as he sat down he quickly caught up on the ongoing conversation All Zulus were still inside Elmhurst Road, the lock up was under constant surveillance and the armed response unit had been fully briefed and had notched up their readiness state, already high, by a couple of degrees. The talk turned to planning another visit to both the house if possible and the lock up, the lock up was the easy one to plan they had been there a number of times now, they knew the layout and of course it was not occupied. Al told the assembled operators that Tommy's commanding Officer had called police headquarters to briefly explain what it was that Tommy could do, the decision had gone all the way to the Deputy Commissioners desk where it currently sat waiting approval, in the meantime Al had decided that they should at least plan the operation even if it never came to fruition. As before Bob would lead the operation backed up by the usual contingent of controller's surveillance operators' et al. Tommy would now, of course be going in with the main team to do whatever it was he was going to do, at this point Al asked if Tommy could maybe shed some light on just what he planned to do and was dangers to the entry team, and himself did the task involve, and more importantly how safe would it make the bombs if they were ever built. Tommy leant across and from a desk grabbed a piece of paper and drew a basic circuit explaining just how an improvised explosive device worked, he then drew the improvised headlight and showed them how he would attack it, but leave it is such a manner that it would appear to look untouched. It was critical, he said that none of the Zulus know what he had done; this would allow them to carry on with their planned operation and may lead to the police being able to identify and capture more of the cells involved rather than just the two guys they had on film modifying the bulbs. As Tommy was giving the surveillance team leaders his basic how to make a bomb course, Al who had left the room to take a phone call returned with a satisfied look on his face. Well guys he said, it would look like the DCC has some bottle, he has given us the go ahead, with caveats he added, if Tommy is in any doubt that his actions have not made the device safe then we move straight into an arrest and detain operation complete with the armed response unit, at all times while we are in the lock up, a unit will be parked on Elmhurst road and will swoop as soon as we give them the word. The DCC is not and he stressed not, prepared to have a live device being driven around his patch. Al looked at Tommy with a serious look on his face, Tom he said I know you are a good operator, and while I have no doubt about your skills and courage, this is not Afghanistan, this gets played by the book, straight down the line, if this cannot be done, you have got to let me know, I know we have a laugh and take the Mickey out of each other, but this is serious. Can you do it? Will you do it? Tommy knew that the time for laughing was gone for the time being at least, he looked at Al and said quite seriously, I have not done this before, at least not for real, but I know what to do and how to do it, I also know what will happen if I fuck it up, if I get stuck I will tell you, that I promise you. Satisfied, Al looked at his team and said we go in tonight, Bob you know the drill, get your men organised, we will aim to have the doors open at 0100hrs. This, although Tommy didn't know at the time, was about the same that Brian would be getting back on board a chopper to head back to base with prisoners in tow.

Later that night Tommy was seated next to Bob in the back of a specially adapted minivan, Bob had already opened the sliding door a fraction, the interior lights as had the brake lights been disconnected to avoid any flash of light as the door opened or the van stopped to offload its passengers, one of the team who would not be getting out would be on hand to hold the door as they alighted and would only close it fully once they were away from the drop off area, again with the intention of minimising any signal that would indicate just what had happened. Once out of the van they moved away from the immediate area and stopped, the team then carried out drop off drills, ostensibly laying low, keeping silent, looking and listening for any tell tale signs that they had been seen or heard. Hearing nothing Bob clicked the send button of his radio the single click, a message to the listening controllers that the team were on the ground, safe and moving towards the target.

As before Bob checked out the exterior of the lock up before making entry, although to be fair surveillance operators had had the unit under observation all day, but old habits die hard and it never paid to cut corners even when you knew you could. Once inside they again carried out the listening and looking drills, before venturing off the drop mat they had stepped onto to avoid leaving footprints. Immediately Tommy and Bob moved towards the workbench, the modified headlamps were neatly laid at one end, bits of cut off wire littered the floor and a few grains of the black powder that had been poured into the bulb lay on the bench. Before they began work Bob carefully recorded the positioning of all the items so as to be able to accurately replace them afterwards. From his backpack Tommy pulled out a small tool roll and began to lay out what was needed. He had warned Bob that this particular task did pose some small degree of risk and anything that could spark or induce static had to be avoided at all costs. The task in hand, by Tommy's estimation would take less than an hour but that was allowing for nothing going wrong, what he could not afford to do was to rush into it and damage the bulbs, well, at least visibly damage the bulbs, from his roll he removed a small scalpel, a long thin metal rod with a tiny hook on the end of it, a bottle of glue, a multi meter and a roll of tissue paper, Bob looked on seemingly amazed at the simplicity and scarcity of the tools Tommy would be using, "what happened to just cutting the red wire" he said jokingly, "I never passed that part of the training" answered Tommy, "they only trusted me with the simple tools" he added laughing.

Tommy took the first bulb and began to carefully remove the glue that had been placed over the hole made by Rahim, once the glue had been removed Tommy carefully placed it on to the tissue paper, he then slowly poured out the black powder from inside the bulb, once empty he then inserted the thin rod inside and by carefully twisting and pulling gently he broke the filament, and then removed it from the glass, he then tested the bulb with the multi meter. Tommy recognised that this was a rough and ready fix, but he also knew that the bulb would now not function, however the only way the terrorists would know this, was if they tested the bulbs before placing them into the complete device, this was possible but there was nothing he could do about that. Once the filament had been removed he poured the black powder back into the bulb and taking a bottle of super glue he had brought with him resealed the opening. He placed the bulb off to one side and after the glue had dried inspected it minutely for signs of his tampering, satisfied he showed it to Bob who just nodded in silent approval, putting it to one side Tommy tackled the second bulb planning to carry out exactly the same actions. The second bulb completed Tommy passed it to Bob asking him to replace it as it was when they came in and pass him the third one in line.

Neither Tommy nor Bob could tell anyone exactly what happened next but somehow the third bulb fell from Bob's grip as he handed it to Tommy, whatever the cause the resultant fall broke the fragile glass of the bulb spilling the black powder over the floor, "fuck" whispered Bob anxiously, "mmm my thoughts exactly" answered Tommy equally worried. "What can we do?" Said Bob now suddenly aware that what was a relative routine task now had developed into a possible situation where compromise and the sudden ending of the operation now a real possibility. Tommy knew that the time for calculated rational thinking was right now and right here, this was not a place for those who could not remain calm and capable of clear thought, all the years of psychometric testing, training and carrying out operations all over the world now came into play. Kneeling down, he firstly and carefully scooped up the spilt powder, and the pieces of the now shattered bulb, once there was no trace of the broken initiator left to be found on the ground, he looked at whether the bulb could somehow be patched up, but it was very quickly apparent that no amount of glue and prayer could hide the breakage. Bob had called into control, saying simply that the task would take a little longer to complete, and he would get back with a better timeline as soon as he could. Tommy glanced at his watch, he looked at Bob, "are there any all night supermarkets or garages around here?" he asked, "Now is not the time to thinking of doing your Christmas shopping, what are you thinking of buying?" Bob asked. "Can you get your guys outside to do a drive around and find somewhere that sells headlamp bulbs, we need a pack of P45T 12V 45/40W" said Tommy reading off the identification details from the body of an intact bulb, "and we need it soon" he added, "actually get them to get a few packs so we can ensure we have a matching set, and some sand paper also."

Not wishing to reveal just what had happened inside the lock up to the entire team, Bob called Al on the radio and simply said one word "switchblade" this was the signal for Al and Bob to switch the channel on the radio, they had recognised from the very onset of Operation vanguard that at some point they may have need for a quick chat away from the team, they had arranged this simple yet effective way of doing that without having to resort to insecure mobile phones. Tommy couldn't hear what Al said in response to Bob's quick summary of what had just happened and the sudden need to go late night shopping, but he could guess it was both worried and expletive laden. At one point Al had clearly asked the question of Tommy, was this still a viable option, Bob looked across at Tommy as he relayed the message, Tommy looked up from his work on the forth headlamp, and simply said "get me the bulbs and then I can give you an honest answer, if we can't get bulbs, then, the answer is no, the op is blown.", with that Bob ended the conversation with Al and returned the radio to the working channel. "what did he say" asked Tommy, "he will send two teams one to trawl garages and one to go to the nearby 24 hour Tesco supermarket, we will get you the bulbs" promised Bob.

Once the last bulb had been completed, there was little to do but wait and hope that the shopping trips proved a success, whilst they waited they inspected the lock up again to ensure that nothing unseen had entered or been taken away. They knew that the four organ boxes and glass jars had been taken back to the house, it was hard to gauge just what switches and other components had also been removed. To Tommy it made some sense to keep the initiators away from the explosives but he also knew that the usable shelf life of some of the more commonly used homemade explosives were quite short, after which time they became very unstable and hazardous to transport without exercising extreme caution and using specialised equipment and then by experts in ammunition management and transportation. This limited life span most likely meant that whatever was being planned was due to happen within days as opposed to weeks.

The message came across the radio net that one of the crews had found a whole rack of headlamp bulbs in the nearby supermarket and that they had bought a whole bunch, the bulbs would be at the lock up in fifteen minutes, once again the chain of events that allowed the men to enter and leave the lock unobserved moved into gear. Bob was stood next to the door as the countdown indicated that the drop off man was less than two hundred meters from the lock up, as he got closer, Bob Knelt down and having first ensured there was no lights on, he opened the door just enough for him to slide a hand through and withdraw it again this time clutching a small plastic bag with the necessary purchases. Passing the bag to Tommy, Bob closed the door quietly and moved towards the work bench, Tommy had emptied the bag and was selecting the right set of bulbs, the sets were probably serial numbered but that detail would be on the packing and not the bulb itself, so providing the bulb was the same model then it should pass any scrutiny. Having got the right bulb, he opened the packet of sandpaper and placed a sheet of rough grain on to a sheet of paper he had ripped from a note book he had in his bag so to avoid leaving a mess on the workbench. He then took one of the bulbs and copying the procedure Rahim had carried out he began to rub a hole in the glass, once through he then followed the same steps with the filament that the three original bulbs had been subjected to. He then replaced the black powder they had salvaged off the floor and sealed the hole with glue. He then took out a gas powered soldering iron from his tool roll and having de soldered and removed the two lengths of electrical wires from the broken bulb he simply reattached them to the new bulb. He finally tested the circuit and satisfied that it was broken, he passed the replacement to Bob, to be returned whence it came. All that remained was to clean up their equipment, while they were doing that, Bob again had the cover teams move into position, before long he and Tommy had left the lock up and were heading towards the pickup point, as they turned a corner the minivan pulled up next to them and without it actually stopping the two men got inside, not fully closing the door until they were away from the immediate area.

Al was waiting for them as they returned to the police station, he immediately came across and asked Tommy how it went, Tommy gave him the reassurance he was looking for, saying that "the bulbs would now not work and that although we cannot say hand on heart, we have control of the bomb, largely because we haven't seen the bomb, we do have control of the key part of the bomb." Al then turned to Bob asking what had happened that necessitated the late night shopping trip, Tommy quickly butted in saying that one of the bulbs had been done in such a way that we couldn't get the glue off without cracking the glass and that we took a call that the best way, and the safest option was to simply swap it out completely. Al was happy with that and excusing himself he left the two saying he had to call the DCC who had been badgering him all night for updates. As he walked away Bob turned to Tommy and said "thanks for that mate, I owe you one", "no worries" replied Tommy "it can happen, we were most likely both to blame, if any blame is to be apportioned. The important thing is, we didn't panic and we got the job done, now I am off to bed, give us a lift back to the hotel would you?" on the drive back to the hotel, Tommy phoned the Operational tasking room at Regimental Headquarters in Oxfordshire and asked them to contact the SAT first thing in the morning with a message from Warrant Officer Byrne, the message was simply, job done, no problems will call you mid morning. Tommy stressed the importance of the message and was promised faithfully that it would be delivered as soon as he came into the office.

The debriefing and interrogation of the prisoners captured at the compound had begun as a soon as they were escorted off the helicopters. A team of trained specialists had been brought in and once the necessary in processing had been completed they had been led to individual cells were the questioning could begin, this after the wounded had been taken to a nearby medical facility and the dead also removed from the compound taken to a makeshift morgue. The first priority was to identify all those captured or killed; fingerprints from a corpse are as useful as those taken form a live captive, in the hope that one of them was the man behind the wave of targeted attacks against the bomb disposal operators. None of the men resembled the man who was known as Atcha, but that was no guarantee that he wasn't amongst them, if he wasn't, then it was almost certain that at least one of them would know him and hopefully where to find him. The questioning followed a set routine, and none of the treatments often claimed, by the radical websites and forums, to be visited upon prisoners, beatings, deprivations or humiliations was hinted at leave alone actually carried out. These cruelties very rarely resulted in success, men, under enough pain, will say anything they think their torturers want to hear just to stop the hurting, even for a short time. Give a man hope and he will eventually learn to believe in you, take away any hope and he has nothing to lose. This directive followed the embarrassing and damaging fallout from the photographs that came out of Abu Ghraib prison in Iraq, and by the Commanders learning's from Nietzsche, who had said that "generally speaking, punishment hardens and numbs, it serves to strengthen the power of resistance "The fingerprints, DNA and photographs taken as they were brought in, had been quickly loaded onto a terrorist database and as a means to cover all bases, sent across to National databases in Washington and London. Technicians were now eagerly waiting for any "hit" with instructions that any positives were to be immediately flagged up to the Task Force Commander and that details passed to the interrogators.

In the time it took for the first positive hit to come in, the first real breakthrough had been made by the interrogators' A match had been made from a latent thumb print taken from the "poster bomb" and one of the sets of prints taken earlier that day from one of the captives, thankfully one of the ones who was still alive. This information was, as had been requested passed immediately to one of the specialised debriefers, a kindly looking man who went by the name of John, despite his appearances was as tough as they came when it came to extracting usable intelligence from captured insurgents. John thanked the database technician and armed with the printed out match re entered cell number four. Inside the cell, sat on a hard backed chair, a man who had called himself Hakim who had thought his interrogator a decent man had confessed, that he and another man, whose name he claimed to not know had helped a third man who, when asked, said he used the name Mohamad, to make a bomb, he had said that he never knew where the bomb was to be placed, but that it had been hidden inside a battery. Hakim had claimed that he was there to protect the others and only helped with the bomb because there was no one else available. When questioned he had told his guards that a man had come to the compound and had told them just how to make the bombs and what they should look like. This man did not stay long at the compound but he would come every few weeks, sometimes Mohamad would go to a nearby town and meet him there, he would then come back with diagrams and they would then make more bombs, when Mohamad went to the city, Hakim would drive him there and act as his bodyguard. The interrogators had shown Hakim photographs of all those captured or killed at the compound and asked him to identify all those he was able to, he was assured that his cooperation and willingness to help would not be forgotten. Hakim had looked at each photo in turn, putting a name to some and to others he had said what role they had carried out. He turned the last photo over which showed the bloodied face of one of those who had been killed, he looked up and said "This is the man I know as Mohamad" before adding "may Allah grant him peace"

As the interrogation continued John learnt that Hakim had been recruited from a small village having been promised a better life in this world and the next if he helped to throw the invaders out of his land, faced with a lifetime of poverty and hardship, the choice had been easy. Every now and then John would steer the conversation back to the compound, to

Mohamad, and to the visitor who came every so often. When was the last time he was there, when did they meet and where, how were the meetings arranged and by whom. Every word spoken was both written down by a dutiful stenographer and captured on video from a camera placed high in the corner of the cell. John stopped the interview after three hours having gotten as much out of Hakim, for now as he was able to. John promised Hakim he would be well looked after and that he would not be treated badly whilst he was under his care. He told Hakim that if at any time he wanted to talk with John he need only ask, and that he would come. Meanwhile in the other cells similar promises were being made, the interrogation team had agreed beforehand that they would curtail the first round of questions at the three hour mark to allow prisoners some rest and respite but also to compare notes and to agree on the next strategic move when they began again later that day. A few hours later the head of the interrogation team was with the Task Force Commander outlining what they had learnt so far. "So, we have a dead bomb maker, a bomb maker helper cum bodyguard, a cook and a cleaner, someone who claimed to be visiting a friend and the rest either dead, too hurt to talk or simply saying nothing at all" summed up the Commander after listening to the report. "As it stands sir, yes that is about it, but I must stress that it is still very early in the process and to have this much is quite an achievement if you ask me" said the interrogator by way of explanation. "Yes, Yes I know and I am not criticizing you, your techniques or your men, but we need answers and we need them soon" said the Commander. We will be having another crack at them in a few hours maybe we can get something else out of them then.

The bomb making materials and other items collected had been taken directly to the department that exploited all explosive devices found and rendered safe and any evidence recovered from bomb scenes across the Southern part of the Country. This unit peopled by highly trained bomb disposal operators backed up by forensic scientists and Intelligence analysts, had for now put all other tasks on hold and were focussed entirely on what had been recovered from the compound, it was to this secluded and secured enclave tucked away from prying eyes within Camp Bastion that Brian had headed after, grabbing a few hours rest, showering and sorting out his kit. As Brian entered the makeshift Laboratory where the evidence recovered had been brought to, he saw that three distinct areas had been set up, as he walked over to where the resident IEDD Operator was working, he could see that one part of the lab had been earmarked for the exploitation of all documents, and the laptops and computer discs that had been found during the search operation, the second team had moved into another but closed area of the workshop where they were gathering as much forensic evidence from the recovered components as possible and then they would photograph every single item meticulously recording every detail. This would then be used to identify likely sources whether they were hardware stores, electronic suppliers or as was commonly found "friendly Nations" supporting the insurgency. The evidence had been triaged as it arrived, the first priority, after being booked in to the department, was to preserve and collect as much forensic evidence as possible, once that had been done then the items were moved to whatever workstation they would be worked on, as a priority it had been decided that the IED components would be treated first.

The third area at which Brian now stood was dedicated to the bomb making materials and explosives that had been found. At its head was Captain Hood, known to his friends obviously as Robin, Robin had been through the ranks as an operator and had recently been commissioned to his current rank, Brian had served with him on many occasions and it was with this familiarity he greeted him, "what have we got Rob" "We have only just started to be fair Bri", he answered, "but it looks straight away as the guy who made your poster bomb also made the anti access device you found by the front door to the store". Robin showed Brian a photograph of the soldered wires that had led to a battery, he had last seen in the village, Robin then handed Brian a set of forensic gloves telling him to put them on and take a look at the battery connections from last night's job. Brian could clearly see what Robin had already identified; the wires had been wound together in a particular way and then soldered together, on both devices, the bomb maker had left a small piece of wire unsoldered, this would make no difference to its operational ability but showed a unique style of workmanship, that was unlikely to be carried out by two different people. "OK so we know that the two devices were made by the same man", said Brian, "do we know who?", "The forensic team lifted all available prints and DNA that will be cross matched with the samples collected off the captives you so thoughtfully didn't kill last night" Robin added with a grin, "maybe we will then be able to say with certainty who made these, if not we will look at the wider database".

The Task Force Commander had ordered a collective debriefing session where the interrogators, scientists and analysts would give him a quick look report based on their initial findings; from there they would decide on the next step. He called the meeting to order with his usual curt and straight to the point manner, first to speak was the lead interrogator who informed them that some leads had been generated, we have one man, who has called himself Hakim, who seems willing to talk, it would appear that the bomb maker, who he referred to as Mohamad, would receive detailed instructions from a man who either came to the compound or was met in a nearby town. His prints have been flagged as being found on the poster bomb, although he claims he was only involved in a device hidden inside a battery. Hakim has identified one of the killed in action insurgents as Mohamad, now he could be doing this just to pin the blame on a dead man, he also claims to know what this mystery man looks like and is willing to assist us with an e picture. The rest are not saying much, one woman has pretty much backed up Hakim's version of an unknown man who would visit every so often, but not much else. We have fed them and they have had a few hours rest we will be talking again very shortly. Thanking the interrogator, the Commander invited the chief scientist to speak. Forensically we have a match between the devices found in the village of Urozgan and one found last night in the compound, we also matched set of finger prints from this man, he held up a photograph of one of the dead insurgents, and the same device. The picture showed the man Hakim had referred to as Mohamad. Documents recovered show detailed wiring diagrams, in English he added, showing various IED firing circuits and receipts from an electronic supplier in the United Kingdom. The rest of the findings are still being worked, and the captives details are being cross matched as we speak. Sean was next to take to the floor, he briefly explained just how the raid had been conducted, he gave an update on the wounded both his men and the insurgents, the CROP team were still on the ground, to date nobody had gone near the compound and a routine patrol had gone into the nearby township that morning and had not received any feedback, verbal or otherwise, that the locals were aware of the operation having taken place. He asked the question, how often did this mystery man show up, how often did they meet and how were these meetings arranged. The commander looked thoughtfully at his assault leader and said, "Just what are you thinking Sean?", "nothing yet" came the reply, "just running through some options in my head", "Would you care to share them with us?" the Commander ventured. "Not yet Sir" Sean said, "but if we can find out how often they met, where and how, then, yes I think we should talk". The Commander nodded at his man, and then thanked everyone for their attendance and hard work to date, but added that they needed to keep at their tasks, this was time critical, priorities were issued, more information on the meetings with the mystery man, how many devices had been built and moved out and to where. Forensic specialists were to keep up the efforts, database analysts told to pull in as many favours as they could to hasten the search. The CROP team were to keep eyes on the compound, and Sean was to pull whatever plan he was hatching, together and be prepared to talk it through at the next scheduled meeting. He was, he reminded them to be kept aware of any and all developments. An hour later the door to cell number four was suddenly opened, Hakim who again had been seated on the single chair saw a determined looking John walk into the room, John had been given a clear directive, pump Hakim for all information regarding the mystery man, he had already admitted his part in one device and we now have his prints on a second. He talks to us or he goes away for a very long time.

CHAPTER FIFTEEN

Tommy woke feeling refreshed and almost certain that whatever was going to happen was going to happen very soon, he made two phone calls, the first to Andy to give him the lowdown on last night's task, Andy had, as had been promised told of his message and had already briefed the Colonel. Like Tommy, Andy was pretty sure that this was going to come to a head very soon, when it did, Tommy was not to go "lone wolf" on him. He reminded Tommy that the Regiment had many assets around the Country and they were to be tasked and used when necessary. The second call was to Selly Oak hospital, he hadn't actually spoke with Marty for a while and was pleased to hear that not only was she up and about but that a nurse would go and tell her that Tommy had called, she would hopefully be in the nurses' station in five minutes if he would either hold or call back then. Tommy rang off promising to call again five minutes, he checked his watch and headed to the shower, one benefit of being a bloke was the ability to shower and dry in less than five minutes he thought turning the mixer taps on. As promised he was on the phone five minutes later, he recognised the voice of the nurse he had spoken to earlier and likewise her, his." Hello stranger", Marty said with a smile in her voice, they spent the next fifteen minutes chatting away like the trusted friends they were. Tommy learnt that Marty was to be allowed home in a couple of weeks; she still had to undergo Physio, but could do that at a local hospital. The Regimental families Officer was in regular contact and she had been assured that she still had not only a career in the Army but with the Regiment if she wanted it. He told her a little of what he was involved with but clearly not the whole story, He said he would try to get to see her real soon but he was a little busy just now, "too busy for me?", she said but he could tell he was being teased. He asked about her librarian hunk, Marty retorted by asking whether he had asked Mandy out yet. He rung off reminding her he still had the number of the chaplain, and if necessary could contact all manner of religious organisations that would be only too willing to convert a war hero lying in a hospital bed. Marty reminded him that she had access to a shed load of nurses who would just as happily supply her with as many laxatives as she wanted to convert a war hero into a gibbering wreck. Ouch! He thought to himself, promising to call again soon, "stay safe Tommy" she told him, and finding herself wishing she could tell him that to his face.

Tommy came downstairs to find Al and the team gathered around a table, "morning" he said pulling up a chair and joining them, "'what's going on?" "Hi Tommy" Al said, "not a lot, our guys are safely tucked away in Elmhurst; the Lock up is as we left it, and the white van is still in its garage". "Good" answered Tommy, "what we got planned for today then?", "we sit and wait" Bob replied, "if they head back to the lock up and remove the flashbulbs, we let them, if they put anything into the car and make as if to move out or leave the house carrying anything more than a small purse, we follow, and if necessary stop them". Sounds like a plan Tommy thought to himself. He reached across to the coffee pot and as he did so, his mobile rang, looking at the screen he recognised the number as being Andy's. "Hello Mate" he answered "what's up?" "Can you talk?" Andy asked, the usual euphemism for can you talk without being overheard, "wait one", Tommy replied and moved away to a quite area in the corner of the room, go on he told Andy sitting down at an empty table. He listened intently as Andy told him as much as he could about the raid and what had been learned so far, Tommy despite the trouble he had falling and staying asleep some nights, nights he woke to memories of compounds, broken bodies and a myriad of other less than pleasant sights and sounds he and many others had been forced to witness, wished he was part of that operation, he reckoned just a few minutes alone with Atcha, or anyone of those involved in targeting operators would be worth the pain and difficulties going back to Afghanistan would bring him. Andy told him that the questioning as was the exploitation still in its infancy and that more would undoubtedly follow, but he guessed rightly that Tommy would be keen to hear just what was known so far. "Thanks mate, I appreciate it, keep me in the loop will you? He said hanging up the phone with a thoughtful faraway look in his eyes. "Everything alright mate?" asked Bob as Tommy rejoined the group having been watching his reaction to the phone call closely, "yeah just some work stuff" replied Tommy quickly, respecting Andy's instructions to not divulge what little they knew just yet.

Hakim had initially, as was expected, denied any involvement in the device in Urozgan, John let him exhaust himself saying he had never heard of a poster bomb, he was a bodyguard who had helped build one device, the litany of how he was not involved went on, John sat back, having done this a thousand times before knowing that sometimes the best way to get information is to say nothing, the guilty will usually fill the silence for you and in doing so, find themselves deeper and deeper in trouble." I never told you the poster was stuck to a wall outside a shop Hakim, now how would you know that then?" John said after Hakim's latest plea of innocence. Hakim realising his mistake tried to backtrack saying that he had heard it somewhere, "from who and where Hakim?" Asked John and then dropped the bombshell. "We have your fingerprints on the bomb, we have a diagram of the bomb found in a compound you were living in, we know that the same man built the bomb and another bomb that we found last night in the same compound, we have your confession that you have helped build bombs before, now put yourself in my place Hakim, what would you believe to be the truth?" Hakim sank back in his chair looking defeated, John moved closer and spoke quietly, "we don't really want you Hakim, we want the man who comes to the compound, and he is the man behind these attacks, who is he Hakim? How do we find him? Help me, Hakim and I can help you, my Commander wants to hand you over to the Americans, I don't want that Hakim, but I have to tell my Commander that you can help us" Hakim looked around as a cornered animal would, looking for a way out of the situation he now found himself in, he had heard about people who had been captured by the Americans who were sent away and never came back, he had seen the footage of prisoners in orange jump suits being led away to a foreign land shackled and blindfolded.

John and the lead interrogator stood together as the Commanders aide knocked at his boss's door after a very brief conversation, the two were escorted in, the commander stood to greet them telling his aide that they were not to be disturbed. I believe we have some developments he asked the two civilians, beckoning them to sit down. John began by telling the commander of Hakim, his initial protestations of innocence, his unintended slip about the poster bomb and finally how he had told John about a man called Mahood, a man from the West who had supplied them with details and plans, who had shown them how to kill bomb disposal men. John then explained how Hakim had told him how they met, and more importantly how these meetings were arranged. The Commander listened, interrupting only to ask a question occasionally, as he finished, The Commander asked John the one question he knew was coming but which he was dreading. "Do you trust this guy, is he telling us the truth," John leant back, "look sir" he began, "he is an insurgent, a terrorist just a few days ago he was planning on spending the rest of his days killing and attacking the likes of you, me and everyone in this camp. Do I trust him . . . ? Not one little bit, do I like him . . . ? No, is he telling me the truth . . . ? I believe he is, he does not want to be passed on to the Americans, he knows we have enough to put him away, which we will, but he thinks by helping us he stands a better chance of at least one day seeing his children again." "Thanks guys" the Commander said, "keep at him, find out what else he knows, find out who amongst the other prisoners will also know Mahood, and then start on them, we have a name, we have an idea how they meet, let's get more, I want this man and I want him alive". John headed back to cell number four with the intention of finding out as much about Mahood as his prisoner knew, on the way the Forensic scientist in charge of the computer hard drive exploitation came hurrying across the open square that separated the holding cells and the laboratory," have you got a minute he asked breathlessly"?. "Of course" replied John, "what's on your mind"? "We have cracked some email traffic that was encoded", the scientist said, "That's great" replied John, "anything we can use?" "Well that's just it, there is", said the man, "but you will need to be quick".

At roughly the same time as the scientist and john were talking, Brian's duty phone rang; he looked at the caller ID and was surprised to see the SAT's name illuminated. "Hello mate I was about to come and see you", he answered, "Can you come across to the office Bri, right now?" Said a grim sounding Steve, He rung off without waiting for a reply. Brian looked at the phone puzzled but his immediate reaction was that something had gone wrong somewhere. He immediately headed across to the home of the bomb disposal command cell, as Brian turned the corner, he saw Steve and the Colonel talking to the Operations Officer, all three looked ashen. Steve looked up as Brian arrived, with a nod of his head he beckoned him to the office, once inside he closed the door. "What's going on Steve?" asked Brian now convinced that whatever it was, was almost certainly bad. "Andy Fox was killed this morning", Steve said, "I am sorry Bri; I know you two were close". Immediately memories of two mates howling with laughter racing headlong down a white water canoe course in Wales, images of drunken nights in Andy's hometown of Newcastle and a million others sprang to Brian's mind, Andy and Brian had formed a close friendship, the two had followed very similar career paths, they had served together on more than one occasion, Andy had asked Brian to be his best man at his wedding, with a promise that he would be his first child's Godfather also. "Fuck off Steve, that's not funny" said Brian dismissing the idea that Andy could be dead. "He is Bri, I am so sorry"; Brian slumped on to the chair behind him, "what happened?" He asked. "We don't know yet, he went out with one of the task forces who were raiding a house outside of Kabul following a tip off, from the assault leader it seems that Andy found a pressure plate near to a doorway, from what we know, he had cleared it, he had certainly removed a main charge because he had passed that to the team leader who was behind him. The device that killed him was small, not enough to catch anybody else, just Andy. Medics were there immediately Brian, but he was killed instantly, he never felt a thing, and to cap it all, the house was empty; someone wanted that task force there, or somebody wanted an operator there." I have tasked the local Post blast team to the scene, with instructions that we are to be told immediately they have anything. "Has Jo been told?" Brian pictured Andy's wife Jo opening a door to see two solemn faced men in uniform outside, "the Boss has been on to Regiment this morning Brian, it will be done, and it will be done properly" Steve said, "and if you want, we will get you back for the service, I will make sure of that Bri" Thanks mate", Brian answered, "I think I need to get outside for a while, tell the boss I will be back later to talk to him about last night, will you?" "Yeah, no worries, look, take it easy eh"? Steve replied as Brian walked out of the office.

"What is it then" asked John," we think there are some more devices out there, some type of booby trapped booby trap or something, the email chain refers to the plates that went out last week, it would seem some of them have been planted and if they work more will be needed, the message went on to say the bombs would need to be made quickly before the invaders learn what we are doing. The email comes from an IP address in Kabul, but it seems to be routed through half the country before it reaches its target. All the incoming messages are either signed by someone who refers to himself as M, or from someone named Zayeed. M has apparently agreed to a meeting with Zayeed in the market place in Urozgan, the massage refers to the meeting and says that Zayeed will visit the compound afterwards". "Have you told the commander this" asked John, "Not yet said the scientist but I am on way to talk to him now". "Good work, I will throw this at Hakim and we will see what falls out of it, thanks".

"Who is Zayeed, Hakim? . . . Is M the same man you call Mahood? . . . What happens when anyone visits the compound?, John had been at Hakim for twenty minutes, all he had was that Hakim had met Mahood once but did not know whether he was M who had sent emails, he never looked at the messages, the only one who did was the leader, the leader, a man referred to by Hakim as Najir, was one of the captives being held in the medical facility and was at present not fit enough to be questioned, he had been kept isolated in a secure part of the facility, local nationals who, by necessity and as a means to win hearts and minds, formed a large part of the civilian workforce, were prohibited from entering the area where he was being held. Visitors to the compound normally arrived after dark and never unannounced, when one was expected, the guards would be at the gate, they would check the vehicle and only if they were happy, would they let someone in. "We always knew when someone was coming", went on Hakim, "the women would make fresh breads and the leader was always checking to make sure things were in the right place". "what does Mahood look like Hakim" asked John for the tenth time, "he looks normal" replied Hakim "he wears glasses, he had dark hair, it's hard to tell you" he protested, "if I saw him here I would know it was him but I cannot tell you what he looks like, he looks like everyone and like no one" "Hakim" said John suddenly, "if you saw him would you tell me?" "I would, I swear, but how can I tell you I am here and he is not" John said he had to go now, he asked whether Hakim needed anything whilst he was gone, and once again re reassured him that no harm would come to him whilst he was under his protection, this for the benefit of both Hakim and as a reminder to the guards who were responsible for the daily welfare of their charges. Leaving the cell, John made his way to his superior's room before heading across to the commander's block with an idea that was forming in his head; he had no idea if it was tactically viable, stupid or just plain suicidal, but he felt it may just work. As John left the Commanders room he heard him yelling at his aide to find Sean and get him across here as soon as possible.

Tommy took the phone call from Andy Jenkins later that day, he was numb, like Brian, he had known Andy Fox well, he and Andy were not as close as Brian had been, but in this small community in which he lived, it was a given that at some stage you would work alongside most people. Andy promised to keep Tommy informed of what developed in terms of the type of device and also what Brian and his team were able to produce form what was recovered at the compound. Activity at Elmhurst Road was almost nil; the suspects had not been since except for when Said had opened the door to a delivery man who had a small package in his hand that required a signature. Since then no one had entered or left the property, teams had both the lock up and the rented garage under control, the police were as happy as circumstances allowed that they had things as they wanted them just now.

Sean and his Colonel spent half an hour discussing what the interrogator had told them, the plan seemed like a simple one but one that had the potential to go wrong very quickly, Sean was confident he had the men with the right skills and aptitude for the job, but he would have no control over almost everything else, including civilians who would be packed into the area, all they could do was to plan for every eventuality, and when the opportunity arose strike quickly and strike surgically.

The plan was in two parts and for one to work the other had to be carefully executed. Sean had decided that he would have four strike teams in Urozgan, and two at the compound. In the towns blending in and remaining out of sight was the difficulty, but they had a strategy that had worked before albeit in Kabul so it should work again. The plan was leave Bastion in a convoy of vehicles on the morning of the meeting, with the second team flying out to meet up with the still watching CROP teams. John and Hakim would be travelling with Sean, Sean had no intentions of being set up on this operation and if it looked like that was the case he wanted Hakim close by. The strike teams would be at pre determined positions around the market place when Mahood was spotted by Hakim, he would relay that information to the closest team who would carry out a follow and snatch operation. if Mahood was alone they would let him walk to the meeting place Ideally they would catch both Zayeed and Mahood, if that was not possible they would grab Mahood as he left leaving Zayeed to head towards the compound where another team would be waiting. Sean went off to talk to his teams and to set in motion the necessary sequences that would allow the operation to be conducted.

In the meantime John had gone back to the cells and was convincing Hakim his best chance of seeing his children again at least while they were still young was to work with the Army on this job. He was told that he would be in no danger providing he stuck to his part of the deal; no one would ever know that he had been involved. Hakim understandably was unsure, but over time John worked on his doubts, his sense of loyalty and eventually it was agreed that Hakim would finger Mahood, and allow him to be captured. Hakim sat, with his head in his hands, a beaten man yet no one had lifted a finger to hurt him he had been defeated by his reluctance to face up to the punishment his crimes deserved. John felt no sympathy for Hakim, he had chosen his path and now he had to walk it, and deal with whatever obstacles lay upon it, he had seen too many good decent Afghan's who lived a hard yet honest life, Hakim and the others who followed the paths of violence promised nothing but death and hurt, the Afghan people had suffered enough of that to last them a dozen lifetimes. John was simply doing a job, a job he was good at and one that often saved lives. John told Hakim that he would be sent back to his cell and no one would be any the wiser, he would be brought back to be questioned as was everyone else, to not do so would raise suspicions.

While Hakim was being convinced to turn against those he had supported, and Sean was setting out his plans to capture Mahood, Brian sat with his back to a Hesco barrier, he often thought if he had the benefit of a crystal ball in 2001 he would have bought shares in the company that manufactured these wire framed barriers that now were to be found in NATO bases all over Afghanistan and Iraq, someone somewhere had made their fortune in the war against terror, yet the real cost was borne by people like Andy, and in equal measure by those who were left behind. Brain had lost friends before; he had seen the injuries that left young people to live without legs and arms, he knew why he was here in this Country far from home, he knew what he was doing had a purpose, he even knew what would happen should he and the likes of Andy left for good. What he didn't know, was how to get rid of the hurt and the sense of desperate loss he felt. It was there, by the barriers that Steve found him, he had gone first to the hut where Brian lived, then to the "bomb shop" the name given to the home of the bomb disposal teams, till finally he simply walked the perimeter till he came across his mate. Steve sat down next to Brian, he sat there silent knowing that Brian simply needed to know he was not alone, eventually Brian looked up, "anything from the post blast team yet?" he asked. Some answered Steve, there was a second anti handling device beneath the mat, no metal, and a battery buried way below detection range, Andy never stood a chance, the main charge was hidden in the door frame at head height of anyone who was kneeling down to clear the pressure mat. Whoever put this there knew exactly what we would be doing.

As the day wore on Tommy was wishing more and more that whatever was being planned behind the closed curtains in Elmhurst Road would be put into action sometime soon, he and Al were sitting down to dinner when Al's phone rang he listened for a few minutes. "Any idea what they are up to" Al asked, his eyes revealed the answer to Tommy, "Ok" said Al "keep me informed, what are the others up to"?, "ok, ok" he said "see you later", and with that he hung up. "Seems that two of the men have left the house and driven to the rented garage unit in Loughborough, Officers were currently sat less than two hundred meters away with eyes on", "and we have no idea what they are doing there?", asked Tommy, knowing the answer, "Not a clue" said Al. Later that evening the two men left the garage and were followed to the lock up, once there, they parked the car and one of them went inside returning to the car after only a few minutes carrying a small box, they both then returned to the house and once again all went quite. The camera team were able to report that from their covert camera's vantage point it seemed as if the man had gone into a drawer removed a box and then placed the four headlight bulbs inside before leaving the lock up and heading back to the car. Tommy spent a restless night, and eventually gave up trying to sleep at four thirty, he threw on a pair of trainers and figured a few miles hard slog may be just what he needed. At six 'o' clock, after a decent run and a circuit of trim trail nearby, he was showered and shaved and walking along the high street towards the petrol station that sold a decent cup of coffee, sleep he thought ruefully was overrated. He was walking back into the lobby when he saw Al and Bob in conversation; he walked over to the two men to hear Bob, saying "they did what?""I tell you they are having a bonfire in the garden at half six in the morning""what's going on" asked Tommy, "our lads in the ranch saw smoke rising out of the back of the house this morning", said Al, "one of them went out for a quick look and Salim and Hussain are out there burning stuff in an old oil drum", "what are they burning" asked Bob, "not sure the guy reckoned it was clothing and sheets or something, whatever it is we will not get to see it, but it is bloody odd to say the least. They must be destroying the stuff they don't want us or anyone else to find, which can only mean one thing", "Yeah whatever it is, it's soon, real soon" said Tommy. The three men were having breakfast together when it was decided that they would move everyone up to a higher state of readiness, things were looking ominous and it seemed to Tommy a wise decision, the entire team would move to the local police station, all surveillance vehicles would be positioned to allow for a quick deployment, the armed response unit would be boosted by a second car and Al had requested helicopter support be on standby. Tommy phoned Regiment and spoke with both the Operations Officer and the SAT, a full bomb team would be pre positioned also at the police station in case they were needed, they were however not to take part in any follow or surveillance roles. Tommy was reminded, if time permitted, that he was to call the SAT before any positive actions against a device, if indeed any were found, were carried out.

They had just about got themselves organised at the station when word came in that a motorbike had pulled up outside the house and the rider had gone inside, the rider was wearing a full face helmet so could not be recognised but was also carrying a second helmet as he entered. Al's attempts to secure a police motorbike unit were being hampered by a motorbike rally that was taking place later that day where a number of motorcycle chapters had arranged a protest ride through town aimed at highlighting the increasing number of deaths caused by reckless car drivers. They were attempting to change the driving test to make it mandatory that a number of motorcycle awareness questions were included in the theory test portion, which at present was not the case. The protest had gathered large support and Police were expecting in excess of two hundred bikes to ride through the city, necessitating a large number of police outriders. In an attempt to see into the future, and having no other viable target, Al had a unit move to Selly Oak Hospital, at least that way they had some elements of a welcoming party should the suspects be heading that way. Al, Tommy and Bob had rigged themselves up with their covert earpieces in order to hear immediately what was being said by the operators on the ground, so at eleven thirty, all three heard one of the static teams report that the front door to the house had been opened, and having placed two large boxes into the boot, four of the Zulus, one carrying a black rucksack got into the car, they were followed by the motorbike rider but behind him was a second man identified as Zulu one Salim wearing a similar black rucksack, the rider jumped onto the bike, his pillion passenger climbed up behind him with some difficulty, once he was secure the rider gunned the engine and they sped off, the car with four men inside drove away more sedately. Immediately a flurry of radio transmissions and activity kicked in, throughout it all, the calm voice of the controller moved teams and personal around as if on a huge chessboard. Two teams were dispatched to follow the bike, no mean feat, the rest of the team were either following the car or being positioned at strategic points to pick up the tail if it came their way. The car, keeping to the speed limits drove from the house straight to the rented garage unit they had last visited the night before. Stopping outside the two rear passengers got out one carrying the black rucksack, they went to the back of the car and removed one of the large boxes, they then opened the garage door and moved inside, as they did so the first car drove away. After only a few minutes the white van appeared however it now sported two newly painted red crosses one on either side and had a set of blue emergency lights attached to the roof, the men, both of whom, who were in the front appeared to be in some sort of green medical style uniform. Stopping only to shut the garage door, they too drove away.

The surveillance cars following the motorbike hit St Nicholas's Circle at the same time as hundreds of motorbikes were converging on the city centre, screaming abuse at the helmeted masses they had no choice but to stop, allowing the swifter and far more mobile bike to pull further and further away, by the time they had manoeuvred their way around the traffic circle the bike was nowhere to be seen, the number of possible routes the bike could have taken were too numerous to attempt any sort of follow up operation. Tango one lost contact last seen heading onto St Nicholas Circle, a forlorn sounding voice said over the radio system. Tango one move towards Selly Oak said the controller hoping they could re-establish contact en route. Meanwhile the cars following the white van and the car were faring slightly better, both vehicles were heading towards the motorway system that would eventually lead them into Birmingham.

Lunchtime traffic on the M42 was light and the surveillance cars confident that they had both physical and technical coverage were able to sit a few hundred meters behind the two suspect vehicles, due to them leaving at different times from the rented garage unit the two vehicles referred to as Charlie one and two were not travelling together, resulting in a split surveillance operation. The controller had to retain control of all cars involved in order to not have the second team interfere with the team following Charlie one. Al, Tommy and Bob were travelling slightly behind the last surveillance car, taking no actual part in the leapfrog game that was being played out whereby cars would routinely switch positions even going so far as to overtake the suspect car to come off the motorway only to rejoin behind the fleet of vehicles wending their way to the Nations second city. As the convoy approached the M6 junction Al tensed, he had banked on the suspect cars heading towards Selly Oak, he had people in place to cover that eventuality, and if they decided to go elsewhere then he would need to play catch up whilst on the move. "Charlie one from lane two to lane one" came a voice over the radio telling all those listening that the suspect car had moved from the centre lane to the inside lane, "I have indicators on signalling left that's Charlie one off off off onto M6". Al breathed a sigh of relief, all he needed now was the second vehicle the white van which was not that far behind to follow the same procedure. As Charlie one moved onto the M6 and surveillance teams followed Charlie two approached the same junction again tailed by an invisible convoy that was eagerly tracking every move." Charlie two off off off onto M6" came a voice calmly. The cat and mouse game continued along the M6, traffic now heavier meant that surveillance Officers had to keep closer to the two suspect vehicles not wanting to rely on the tracking devices solely. Tommy had time to call Andy during the pursuit, once connected and secure, he told him that they had three vehicles, two cars, one bike heading towards Birmingham, possibly to the hospital at Selly oak, The Bomb team complete with an electronic jamming capability were following at a safe distance well out of sight of the suspects. Tommy had with him his bag of tools, and as it stood would be arriving not that far behind the suspects, he went on to say, that the Police position was such that they would stop at all costs the suspects heading into the hospital buildings. Andy thanked him for the update and informed him that he, the Ops Officer and the colonel would all be heading towards Birmingham very shortly, not to take over but to act as top cover and to counter any media interest should the situation develop. "Thanks for that Andy, that's just what I needed" said Tommy sarcastically, "come on mate you know the score, what can I do?" protested Andy before adding that he would catch up with him later.

Meanwhile two uniformed Officers from Birmingham Constabulary were stationed at the entrance to Selly Oak with orders to be watching out a blue Suzuki SV650cc motorbike with a rider and pillion carrying a black rucksack, their instructions were to report any sightings, if the rider and/or his passenger made as if to enter the buildings they were to be stopped and questioned by Officers chasing up a report of a stolen motorbike matching the description of theirs. This would hopefully allow enough time for more Officers to arrive and contain or control the situation. "Charlie one approaching junction six, off off off that's Charlie one off M6 on to A38M towards Birmingham" as happened before the second vehicle a few miles behind followed his fellow suspects off the M6 and onto the trunk road leading towards Birmingham. As Charlie one was heading along the A38 a blue motorbike pulled to a stop three hundred yards from the hospital entrance a pillion passenger got off, removed his helmet and jacket and placed them both into the bikes back box, hoisting a black rucksack more comfortably onto his shoulders he said a goodbye to the driver of the bike and walked off towards the hospital, the biker turned his powerful machine around and drove off unaware that the man he thought was simply visiting a relative, he had been approached in the mosque and asked if he would give a fellow believer a ride to Birmingham, was in actual fact planning on killing and maiming a large number of innocent people. He would later go to the police and tell them everything he knew about the man and who had approached him. The two policemen were too busy watching the car parks and looking for the suspect motorbike to notice the young man in a blue t shirt with a backpack heading towards the main entrance to the hospital. He passed within a few feet of the two Officers; if they had listened closely he was convinced they would have almost certainly heard the beating of his heart, so loud it seemed to him. Once inside he quickly found out where he wanted to be, however his time was not now, he would have to wait, to kill the time he followed the signs for the multi faith prayer room and once inside he sat down and bowed his head in silence. Charlie one pulled into the main car park at one forty five, Officers nearby watched the car park neatly between two other vehicles and almost opposite the glass fronted administrative block which formed part of the newly modernised hospital frontage. The two men inside, having switched off the engine sat as if waiting, one unmarked police car secured a parking spot nearby and the Officer in the passenger seat walked across to the ticket machine, walking almost right behind Charlie one, once at the machine he spent some time looking at the tariff and then searched hi s pockets slowly for change, at all times keeping the two men under observation, eventually he had no choice, if he wanted to avoid attracting attention to himself to select a handful of coins and feed them into the machine, taking his ticket he walked back to his car, where the other Officer sat waiting. What do you reckon? He asked as he got in, they're just sat there he said, couldn't see much in the back seat, and nothing obviously out of place with the car. They stuck the ticket on the dashboard and then the two of them having told control they were going "foxtrot" meaning on foot, left the vehicle and headed towards the entrance block.

Charlie two having taken on the appearance of an emergency vehicle drove straight to the "ambulance only" parking areas, the guard in the booth opening the barriers automatically and then immediately lowering them again, Officers in their unmarked cars were unable to follow and had to wait while the guard after initially waving them towards the public parking areas, then realising what a Warrant card being brandished by a very angry policeman looked and sounded like opened the barrier. Cursing to himself the lead car passenger alighted and ran after the van on foot, he was just in time to see two men wearing green medical uniforms carrying two human organ transplant boxes walking through the doors that led to the accident and emergency unit He immediately broke into a sprint to try to catch up with them,. On hearing this Al swore violently they were a few seconds behind, "fuck this" he yelled "put the lights on now! Get us as close to those doors as possible", as the car screeched to a halt and Al, Tommy and Bob leapt out in unison, they headed at a run for the doors ignoring the confused stares of the onlookers, thumbing his talk button of his radio, Al gave the order, "get uniform in here now and start moving people out but quietly, let's not spook them just yet, I also need armed Officers up here immediately, secure all doors, those two jokers in the car", he paused, "get them out and hold them, any pretence will do, illegal parking I don't care". Bob had caught up with the first Officer giving pursuit, "they have taken the lift, to the", with this he stopped, as the indicator lights above the lift door revealed its destination, "The third floor", as a group they ran to the stairs, passing a security guard on the way, "get security up to the third floor" yelled Bob showing the man his Warrant card, "Now!" He commanded as he took after the others up the stairs.

CHAPTER SIXTEEN

Tommy burst through the double doors to see a security guard, his name tag showed him to be Karl, hurrying down the wide corridors, "two men carrying organ boxes" shouted Al breathlessly, "have you seen them?", "hey just passed me heading that way", the guard said pointing back the way he had come from, his American accent somehow incongruous in the situation, "Come with us" Al said setting off at a run along the passageway, Tommy followed close behind, he knew this corridor well, he had walked it a few times when visiting Marty. As they turned a corner they saw the two men not more than twenty meters away kneeling on the floor with one of the box lids raised, "stop" yelled Al, as the four of them rushed towards the two men one stood and reaching into his green uniform, pulled out a handgun aiming at the onrushes, the second had picked up his box and was attempting to get into the doors of the ward, The security guard flew at the would be gunman hitting him with such a force that he was knocked backwards both gun and organ box falling to the floor, the noise of the impact was lost however in the unmistakable sound of a shot being fired, Tommy could not make out who if anyone was hit, all he could see was two bodies struggling on the ground, whilst Bob joined the melee attempting to get a hold of the suspect, Tommy and Al had followed the second man and had managed to corner him in the Nurses station. Al had his arms outstretched, one hand holding a Warrant card, towards the man, "Salim" he said, "you have nowhere to go, put the box down, we have your mate outside and we know about the car" Al gambled on the strategy of keeping his suspect confused and disorientated, and by using his name letting him believe that the police knew everything. Tommy could see Salim struggling, he was staring at the box in his hand; Tommy could not see any switches on the outside could see nothing that would tell him how the bomb functioned. Bob came into the room, still breathing hard from his exertions. "We got Hussain cuffed, the guard suffered a slight gunshot wound to his arm, more of a graze than anything else, and a doctor is with him now". "Where is the box?" asked Tommy quickly. "Still on the floor" replied Bob "the lid fell off, but I haven't approached it yet". "Get onto Uniform" said Al not taking his eyes off Salim "we need this place evacuated", Tommy stepped out of the room and back into the corridor, more Officers had arrived, and were standing over Hussain who was laying on his front hands cuffed behind him, "have you searched him?" he asked the closest Officer, "yes nothing apart from a wallet and some keys", "thanks said" Tommy walking towards the box laying a few feet away, on the way he passed the guard being treated by the doctor, "you going to be ok Karl?" He asked, "Sure man just a scratch" the American replied. As Tommy approached the box he told the police that he was part of the bomb squad and could they give him some room, which they were only too happy to do, the doctor however said that he could not move the guard till he had stabilised the wound, to do so would only increase the likelihood of worsening the situation. Tommy kneeling down next to the open container, looked inside, he saw four of the glass jars each one filled with an off white granular powder the jars had been surrounded by a number of plastic bags containing nails making for a snug fit inside, into the void in between the four jars a plastic bag had been placed again with a white looking powder inside and with a car headlamp bulb inserted into it, the leads of the headlamp then connected to a circuit board onto which a number of components had been soldered this was attached to a battery and a mobile phone that at present was turned off.

Tommy now had a dilemma, he had already "made safe" four initiators, but he had no way of knowing whether the one he was now looking at was one of those or one that was still capable of functioning. He really had little choice but to treat it as potentially "live" and deal with it accordingly. Looking around Tommy could see that the doctor was still treating the wounded guard, the police had begun to evacuate the floor but it would take some time before it was complete. He took off his backpack and removed his tool roll pulling on a pair of forensic gloves he selected the tool he needed and with a steadying breath he reached into the box.

Officers and security staff had swung a well rehearsed evacuation plan into place, all those who could were being asked to leave the building and make their way to one of three assembly points, the main area was the car park to the front of the building it was towards, this that most of the initial evacuees were now heading as the numbers swelled no one noticed a young man in a blue tee shirt wearing a backpack amongst their ranks, placing his hand into his pocket he extracted a mobile phone, he knew the number he had to dial off heart but he had also added it to his speed dial list, taking care not to attract attention he allowed himself to be stewarded to a place of safety, they will soon have cause to rethink that he thought to himself. Marty limping along with the aid of her crutches, her damaged leg still giving her some grief despite the physio she was having, joked with the young nurse who was walking besides, that this was some type of drill or maybe someone had burnt the toast again and pressed the fire alarm inadvertently, it was only when she saw the familiar sight of a white Royal Logistic Corp liveried Bomb van did she think, that maybe this was something else.

Tommy stood up, his knees aching from the cramped position he had been in whilst removing the initiator from the device, the bomb disposal team would be needed to safely deal with the main charge and forensics would be working long hours on everything else, but for now it was safe. He returned to the Nurses Station, Al and Bob between them had convinced Salim to put the box down and empty his pockets, as before Tommy was looking for any indication of a firing switch, finding none he asked if Salim could be taken outside and again could they give him some room in which to work. Once again he put on his gloves and once again began the methodical task of searching and making safe, at least for now the bomb, he knew that this type of thing contradicted all the known laid down procedures but he also knew that there were a number of people in the danger area who could not be safely moved so he had little choice but to do what he did by hand. Walking out of the ward he passed Al, who looked at him questioningly, "safe as houses" said Tommy glibly, "at least for now" he added, "we will need the bomb squad up here though at some point." He walked across to Karl who was now sitting up his arm swathed in bandages, noticing a familiar looking tattoo with the words "Semper Fi" written below, "Ex marine?" he asked him "Former Marine sir" Karl corrected him with a smile, "sorry Former marine" said Tommy accepting the correct American terminology US Marines were never ex anything, "Well Karl you are a brave man said Tommy thanks" The two suspects were now securely handcuffed and being led away by a throng of police Officers, Al Tommy and Bob followed, leaving behind them three uniformed Officers who would escort the remaining patients down when it was safe for them to be moved. Al got onto the radio "what's the story with the two men in the car?" he asked, after a short delay he was told that Zulus three and two, Said and Imran had been arrested on suspicion of terrorist offences, they had got out of the car when asked to do so, in their possession they had a rental car agreement suggesting that they were to collect a car from the local Avis dealership later that afternoon. Officers had conducted a quick look around the car and had seen nothing on the back seat but had not yet opened the boot. On hearing this Al told then to put a cordon around the car let no one approach it and leave it for the bomb squad, "we know they put a box into the boot already" he said by way of explanation. "Any word on the bike" he then asked, "negative not seen a thing I have had all the car parks checked and nothing found" came back the reply. "OK keep looking we are heading over to you now". The Officers who had been checking the car suddenly realised that they were standing in the middle of assembly area one and within a few seconds almost a hundred people would be crowded into the area they had been instructed to clear and cordon. It was like trying to stem the tide, we need more manpower one Officer yelled into his radio trying desperately to turn the masses around, and get them to another part of the car park at least two hundred metres away.

Marty was towards the back of the crowd, slowed down by her injuries and the throngs of people around her, she was able to see the confusion ahead, three police men seemed to be trying to move the crowds away from the assembly area, they had formed a ring around a car that was parked some two hundred meters from where she currently stood and were yelling and pointing to an area on the far side of the parking lot. She noticed a young man wearing backpack who had stopped and he too was looking at the car, he pulled a phone from his pocket and as she watched hit a button on the keypad, unusually he didn't raise the phone to his ear as you would if making a call, instead he was watching the car, a confused look crossed his face, he looked at the phone and again pressed the pad, Marty found herself moving towards the man, her threat antennae was telling her something was most definitely wrong, she watched as the young man began repeatedly hitting the same button over and over, whilst watching the car as if expecting something to happen. Without actually knowing what she was about to do, she raised her metal crutch and with all the might of her one remaining arm struck the man across the back of his neck with a sickening thud he fell to the ground instantly Marty leapt on top of him screaming for help, the man beneath her was slight in build but deceptively strong he swung a hand backwards catching Marty a glancing blow but with a desperation borne of anger and hurt, she held on still screaming for help, within a few seconds she heard yelling and the sound of running footsteps and two men jumped onto the man securing him whilst one set of arms lifted her gently up a voice, telling her," it's ok, we got him we got him", it was a voice she instantly recognised. "Oh Tommy she cried what have I done, what have I done?" Al looked up from the floor, one hand firmly placed on the back of the young man being searched by Bob, "Miss you have just saved the lives of all these people here, that is what you have done," before adding "I take it you know this man" nodding at Tommy. "Tommy here quick", Bob yelled, drowning out her reply, Bob had opened the backpack and was looking inside, Tommy let go of Marty who was immediately held by the nurse by her side, Tommy glanced inside the bag, without raising his eyes he said softly and urgently, "get everyone away from here, now, Al keep hold of this joker if he so much as twitches, break his neck, Bob can you get my bag off my bag for me and pass me the tool roll, it's got an orange band around it",. Tommy felt rather than saw the crowds around dispersing, "Got it, what do you need?" Bob said, "Thanks can you open it and place it next to me, then I need you to help Al I don't want this guy moving a muscle, kneel on his hands for me will you?" Acting quickly, not knowing what sort of firing switches were incorporated in the device Bob had found in the bag, Tommy located the same type initiator he had seen earlier, the bomb was similar two glass jars, and the rest of the backpack stuffed with nails, Tommy removed the initiating system and placed it to one side, after a quick check he then cut the straps of the bag and removed it from the man's back, once done he had Al and Bob turn the man onto his back, "Hello Rahim" said Al, "we've been waiting for you to show up" Rahim was searched his mobile phone was placed on to one side next to the backpack, with that he was manhandled into an upright position handcuffed and led away. Tommy looked across to where Marty was standing, white faced with shock at what she had just seen. He gave her a thumb up sign and shouted he would be back soon, with that he headed over to where the Bomb disposal team had set up their incident post.

It was many hours later that Tommy, Al Bob and the Colonel sat in the Chief Constables office in Leicestershire Constabulary, going over the day's events, the bomb team had found a large device in the boot of Charlie one linked to a mobile phone, the operator had been confused when it became apparent that the phone had received at least two incoming calls which should have caused the device to function, for some reason though the initiator had failed to work as intended to. "With permission Chief Constable" the Colonel said "I would prefer it if the exact mechanics of why the initiators failed were not reported. We do need to keep some secrets to ourselves" he added. "No problem" answered the senior policeman, "I understand that for reasons of explosive safety all the initiators have been removed by the army, anyway, I would not be at all surprised to learn that your experts have already disposed of them in a suitable manner after of course photographing them for evidential purposes". "Indeed sir" said the colonel with a smile. The two organ boxes had contained mobile phones that had been rigged to function when a pre set alarm automatically turned on the phone. The backpack was intended to function once Rahim connected a 9volt battery that he had placed in his pocket to the battery connector that was tucked away in purpose built pouch on the straps of the bag. "The plan seems to have been", continued Al, "that the two devices Tommy made safe in the hospital would function causing untold damage in the hospital ward, a ward that was set aside for wounded service personnel" he added grimly, or they would be found either way the patients would be evacuated to the main assembly area where the car bomb would then be initiated by Rahim, after a short while he would then move amongst the survivors and rescuers and initiate the suicide device. All in all the four devices would have possibly killed or wounded hundreds of people, as it is we only have one minor casualty, the security guard who risked his life to bring down Hussain. There is still a load of work to do, searching homes, picking up some others most notably the man referred to as Khalid the explosive expert. But we have the major players safely locked away downstairs. The conversation ranged on for a while longer, talk about court cases and the use of military experts as witnesses and then onto the possibility of the police wanting to award certain individuals with something to recognise their involvement in the operation. As they left the Colonel asked Tommy how he was getting back to the hotel, "I will get a lift with Al" he said, "do you think you could get a report to me by close of play tomorrow" the colonel asked, "I will need to go and talk to the Brigade Commander he will want to know just what happened today, and do not be at all surprised if he wishes to talk with you personally" he added. "Will do sir, I will drive down to headquarters tomorrow and deliver it myself" "Ok and Tommy", "yes sir?" "Well done, that was a brave thing you did today" "to be fair Sir, there were a few brave people out there today" replied Tommy; he never did sit too well with praise.

The next morning Tommy drove back to the scene of yesterday planned attacks, there were a number of media vans and reporters gathered around the front entrance, secure in his anonymity he made his way to Marty's ward. He was instantly recognised by a number of the Nursing Staff who greeted him with undisguised affection and gratitude, he apologised for coming outside of visiting hours but he had to get back to camp, could he have a few minutes with Marty? It seemed he could have asked for and been given the key to the crown jewels so ready were they to accommodate. Marty was propped up in bed, understandably still taken aback by all that had gone on "Hello you big bully" he said as he approached the bed, "fancy picking on people smaller than you, I am ashamed". "Where were you when I needed you hiding behind some nurses back" she fired back at him "you only came when I had him down?" "Hiya you" he said smiling at her," how are you doing?" "Alright" she answered, she then proceeded to give him grief for not telling her what he was up to, and hadn't he had enough getting blown up, and "why is always you Tommy?". He told her how the job had taken on a life of its own but that it was over now, at least on this side of the world He then gave her some of her own medicine back, what did she think she was doing fighting terrorists in her condition, but finished by saying he was bloody glad she had and that lots of people, him most of all, were very proud of her. Now would she just concentrate on getting fit again? After thirty minutes a nurse came in and told him that the doctor would be doing his rounds now, and he would have to leave. He said goodbye to Marty, promising to come again as soon as he could, this time with a proper present he added. "Goodbye Tommy do try to look after yourself, and please no more heroics eh? at least, for a day or two".

Brian was finishing off a report in his office when Steve walked in, "want some good news?" he asked, "sure why not?" said Brian happy to stop banging away at his keyboard, if only for a few minutes. "You know Tommy got himself involved in an op in Birmingham, well it turns out he did more than that, he managed to prevent four guys blowing up Selly Oak, disarmed a suicide bomber and managed to have some input into defeating a vehicle borne which was parked in the car park." I have just had the word from the Colonel who got it first hand from the Regiment, what's more it's all linked to our guys here", went on Steve "it began with a receipt found here when Tommy and Marty got hit, it led all the way back to Birmingham, and it would seem that it is heading back this way, a mobile phone found in one of the suspects house has a number on it that has been flagged as being one of those found at the compound" "Christ" whispered Brian," the hospital? They were planning on blowing up the hospital?" "It would seem that way, we haven't got the whole story yet, but we will do in time, Tommy is being written up for some award, and rightly so" added Steve before telling Brian that the Colonel had had the Task Force top brass in this morning, "Task Force are planning an op to catch Atcha, given the link between him and everything that has gone on, the boss wants you to go along with the assault force just in case" "when" asked Brian, "tomorrow, not sure of the details, best nip along to their place and talk to them direct mate" "One more thing" with this he turned serious "I have spoken with Andy Jenkins in the UK, Andy Fox's family have requested a military funeral, he is being repatriated later this week and there will be the usual post mortems before he can be released to the family. I have asked the Colonel if you can be given compassionate leave to attend, if you wish to, he of course has agreed, he too will be attending and so will most of the Regiment back home, Andy was a good man, it is only fit we send him off properly" "Thanks Steve I appreciate you doing that, I shall pop along to task force now and see what's going on and get back to you with the details" answered Brian soberly.

CHAPTER SEVENTEEN

Sean was more than happy to have Brian come along on the task, neither expected there to be a need for his specialist skills but it never paid to be over complacent, he was even more pleased to hear that Atcha and friends' latest escapade had resulted in nothing more than mass arrests and no casualties, the choice of target however caused Sean to emit a low whistle and his mouth set in a hard grim fashion as he muttered how he would love to be allowed to remove the shackles of military law just for a day. The planned meeting was scheduled to take place in the market square tomorrow afternoon, Sean had outlined his plan to Brian and it was agreed that Brian would travel with one of the cut off teams, Sean took him across to meet with the team leader Adam, a man Brian had seen around camp but had never actually worked with, Sean made the necessary introductions and added that Brian had more than proved his worth on ops before so Adam need have no fear of having to babysit the ATO. Brian agreed to meet up with Adam later that day to go through some team vehicle exfiltration drills, getting out of a moving vehicle whilst coming under fire and being able to do so whilst sending rounds back towards the enemy was not an easy feat and everyone inside the vehicle had to know precisely what was expected of them, where he should position himself so as to give covering fire and where his mates would go so as to allow him to safely move out. The drills differed slightly, with each vehicle and even more so when you had additions to the team, the plan that Sean and his Colonel had concocted meant that each team would be driving a vehicle very different to ones normally used. Rehearsals had gone well Sean had briefed his men on the importance of getting Atcha, giving some details of the operation recently undertaken in Birmingham, the choice of target he purposely let slip, knowing that even men such as his would harden their already staunch resolve to get their man knowing that the target was capable of attacking wounded soldiers back home, they all knew friends and colleagues who had been treated at the Military wing of Selly Oak and as such it had become untouchable. John had been given the task of ensuring Hakim was ready, he had been brought down to the holding area shortly before the final pre operation brief given by the colonel who simply restated the urgency of this task. At a little after nine thirty in the morning, six armoured land rovers and four recently bought civilian taxis resplendent in their yellow and white livery, with an array of pendants and assorted charms hanging from the rear-view mirrors were driven out of camp each taxi driven by task force operator with a local interpreter in the passenger seat and with passengers, again heavily armed operators dressed in local costume in the rear. Brian was seated in the rear seat of one of the rovers watching with some amusement as the strange convoy raced towards the village of Urozgan, about an hour ride in a helicopter considerably more when driving, even at this pace. The second team had flown out and would meet up with the CROP team in case the target was missed and made it to the compound. As they reached the outskirts of town, the convoy split up with four of the armoured vehicles taking up strategic positions around town effectively cutting off all the arterial routes in and out, a surveillance drone would be used if anyone tried to flee cross country. The four pseudo taxis took up position around the market square, with the windows tinted and the back screen mud smeared the occupants in their civilian dress would pass unnoticed from passersby, anyone paying too much attention would be persuaded not to by the local interpreter. Brian in one of the remaining two land rovers was parked just outside the market areas out of sight. Sean's plan now rested on Hakim recognising Mahood and then giving John the signal, at that point a convergence of vehicles would surround Atcha and he would be lifted, without struggle quickly efficiently and without recourse to violence. The meeting was scheduled for mid afternoon and knowing how the Afghan people were with punctuality Sean and the team settled in for a long wait. Hakim sat in the back of one of the taxis, nervously fiddling with his beads, watching the road which Mahood would surely use. He didn't know what type of car he would be in or if he would be accompanied or not. The team had been sent electronic photographs from the UK of Atcha taken when he was a student, these had been passed among the men although they had little idea how close a resemblance the man they wanted had to the old photograph. The radio net clicked into life, apart from the occasional radio check it had been silent, Whiskey one, one of the taxi call signs had seen a possible sighting of Tango, Atcha, standing next to a shop overlooking the market, he was with an unknown male and they seemed to be nervous, they were certainly being very careful. John, and Hakim's taxi was commanded by a newly arrived operator called Dan, call sign Delta, Sean's voice came on the air, "Delta move up to

Whiskey's location let our fox sight the rabbit", "Roger, out" replied Dan. As the taxi began to move, Whiskey reported that tango was moving again this time headed to the far side of the market, Dan carefully steered his way through the crowded roads to where Tango was headed, once there he found his way blocked by a mass of traders and their carts all shouting and yelling in a cacophony of tongues and dialects. John grabbed Hakim and together they got out of the taxi accompanied by one of the operators, "Fox and Minder Foxtrot to Tango's position", said Dan, informing everyone what had happened. As John with Hakim close behind rounded a corner they saw three men standing together, two were deep in conversation the third, a tall man with a vivid scar that ran along his jaw line was looking around as if scenting danger lurking nearby. That's Mahood whispered Hakim pointing towards the three men, the one with the glasses. As he pointed the watchful third man looked straight at them, quickly he grabbed Atcha's arm and said something, whatever he said had the desired effect, the three men turned and ran into the bustling market place. That's Tango towards Market place yelled the operator into his radio as he set off at a run hoping to head him off, John Grabbed Hakim and manhandled him back to the waiting taxi, simultaneously the other vehicles went into a well rehearsed pattern of movement all but the drivers got out and headed on foot to support the chasing operator, the armoured land rovers had positioned themselves to cut off any runners. Atcha and his minder headed towards the market knowing that any chance they had of evading capture depended on them losing the men chasing them. The man with him, whose role was that of minder and protector had but one aim, to prevent his charge falling into enemy hands, as they ran he pushed Atcha down a narrow alleyway and in an attempt to give his man time to escape he deliberately ran into a market stall sending the sellers wares sprawling across the floor, he then ran off in the opposite direction to Mahood. The chasing operator now supported by three of his comrades had seen the man they wanted being pushed down an alley, and it was him they chased leaving the scarred minder to run unheeded. Atcha ran with a desperation fuelled by fear, he skirted around pedestrians not knowing who was chasing or even how many he had behind him. He burst out of the alleyway and ran for the nearest building trying to get off the street and away from sight. As he tore through the door the land rover in which Sean and Brian were desperately willing the driver to go faster had narrowly missed running over a tall man who turned and stared with undisguised hatred at the occupants of the vehicle, Brian saw the long red scar that disfigured his face, the driver with the skill of a formula one driver had kept the engine running and now gunned it, as he took off heading towards the last known sighting of Atcha, Brian looked behind him and through the dust cloud kicked up by the vehicle he could see the scarred man looking back at the disappearing rover before turning and began running towards the centre of town. The man was heading for some wasteland and the vehicle that would let him escape the trap that had been set. He had arranged with Mahood that should something happen they would attempt to meet back at the car, if one arrived before the other they should wait no more than fifteen minutes before driving off. He was under no illusions that if Mahood had got there first he would have driven of immediately, he reached the wasteland, the two young boys he had paid to watch his car were still there.

Mahood had forced his way into a typical Urozgan house, inside the woman, old beyond her years, who lived there with her daughter, son in law and four children stood as the strange man came into her home, she had lived all her life in this village yet she had never seen this man before, from outside she heard the sound of men running and shouting in English and cars, many cars all stopping outside her house. She had seen many people die in her lifetime, she didn't want to see more, she stepped outside and shielding her eyes from the sun she told the young man dressed in local dress but with western skin, the house was empty, her family were out, he is in there alone. The operators quickly surrounded the house and shouted for Mahood to come out the answer was a quick burst of gunfire followed by a scream of defiance. Sean, who had by now turned up, yelled back, that he was surrounded and he had nowhere to go. The directive was that Mahood was to be taken alive if at all possible, Sean knowing this had just two options he could wait for Mahood to give himself up and come out of his own volition, however that meant he had his men static with no immediate cover in a potentially hostile environment, or he could go for a quick hastily planned assault relying on skill, speed and confusion to achieve his aim, they knew Mahood had a bag with him when he ran, they knew he had at least one weapon and that was most likely a hand gun as opposed to anything larger. On the other hand he had superior firepower numbers and ability at his disposal. Sean quickly reached a decision he had his men throw stun grenades through the windows as four operators, led by Sean stormed into the house, a single gunshot rang out then silence, yelled shouts of "Clear" "Clear" heralded a quick resolution to the standoff, Brian followed the other operators into the small shack to find Mahood, a gunshot wound to his left arm already being treated by the team medic laying on the floor, his hands outstretched pleading to not be shot. A bag lay at his side, as Mahood was searched and then shackled Brian looked inside the bag, a laptop computer and two USB thumb drives were inside, along with two UK passports and various other documents', all of which would be gold dust to the exploitation teams back at Bastion. Brian looked across at the man who was responsible for the deaths and maiming of many of his mates, a sudden red mist descended and he moved as if to strike the man, Sean sensing this, calmly and quietly placed himself between the two, and turning to Brian, said simply "No Bri, he is not worth it, look at him whimpering like a baby, brave when he sits behind others, but not so big now, come on mate, we are better than this" with that he said over his shoulder, "get him patched up and out of here" and then placing a hand on Brian's shoulder led him outside.

From the darkness of a nearby house the man referred to as Zayeed watched Mahood being led away manacled and bundled into the back of an army vehicle, cursing softly he dialled a number long memorised, the man with the vivid scar recognised the number on his phone, answering he simply said "speak", careful to not reveal his name nor the identity of the one who had called him. He is caught; meet me at the home of the old man. Both men cut the connection and headed towards a house on the edge of town, the elderly man who lived there had no loyalty or affiliation to any political or terrorist group, he lived simply and lived alone, he was known as the old man by virtue of his age and the wisdom he imparted for food and small gifts. Zayeed stood silently watching the road outside, presently a car pulled up outside, thank you for your guidance old man, stay in peace he said leaving a handful of coins on the battered wooden table he left the safety of the building and stepped outside. He got into the car and sat quietly as they drove away from town. The two men stopped at a crossroads, and sat in silence, eventually Zayeed turned and said, you were supposed to protect him now he is taken, he will be made to talk, and you know how important he has become. The father will be displeased with your failure. With that he pulled out his phone, thumbing through the contact list he found the number he was searching for and called, in a secure building inside camp Bastion a mobile phone recovered from the compound rang, a technician quickly made a note of the number and name that popped up on the screen and called his commander. After maybe ten unanswered rings, the call was cut, Zayeed cursed again, the phone was always answered within ten rings, that was the agreement, he pressed the redial button after several rings the call was answered but with silence, not the usual coded greeting, it could only mean one thing, that the army or the traitorous police who had taken the American dollar had found the man who should have answered the call. First removing the Sim card and cutting it into many pieces he then took out the battery and threw the remains of the card and phone out of the moving car scattering them over two miles of Afghanistan countryside. This done he turned to the driver and told him to head to the border, they were to cross into Pakistan and go to the man they called the Father. Waiting till nightfall they crossed the porous border using one of the multitude of unmanned crossing points that were supposed to be guarded by the Pakistan border agencies and military, They made their way to Quetta avoiding the few roadblocks that had been set up to show the world that the Pakistani Government took seriously the claims that they were in any way aiding terrorists or their causes. The journey would take many hours but there they would find shelter and a way to make amends for their part in losing Mahood.

The exploitation of the laptop and other documents both paper and electronic began immediately back at Bastion, the actual interrogation of Mahood unfortunately had to wait till the doctors had agreed he was strong enough to be questioned, his laptop however, encrypted as it was, was soon unlocked and being poured over by keen analysts, inside they found an Aladdin's cave of emails, letters, links to other sites where likeminded fanatics and there wannabes swapped ideology amongst other things. The emails proved most informative particularly one received recently which told of a plot to bomb a military hospital which had been thwarted, the email suggested that someone had told the police as they seemed to know just what was going to happen and even knew the names of the brothers involved, a witch-hunt of all those who had information was being set up, the email finished by saying, rest assured Allah, blessed be his name will show our brothers the rat in our midst, your work and your planning would have caused many deaths, the traitor will be found and punished. The email had been read and forwarded to Mahood from an address in Pakistan. The passports recovered were found to be very clever forgeries and almost as good as the genuine documents. Both passports had been used and showed entry and exit stamps for several European Countries including France and the United Kingdom. The analysts were able to put Mahood as being in regular email contact with the people in the compound and with a whole group of contacts based around the United Kingdom as far afield as London, Leicester, Birmingham, Liverpool and Newcastle as well as many smaller provincial towns. It seemed that these followers regularly supplied details of local regiments deploying or returning from tours of Afghanistan as well as a growing number of repatriation parades and military funerals being held around the Country. Once again Mahood's emails were forwarded from addresses in Pakistan. From the information they were able to gleam from his computer files, it became apparent that Mahood had been living in Pakistan but had crossed regularly into the Country, he had been using a number of aliases whilst travelling but had only changed addresses twice, his latest abode a few miles from the border was a small village well off the beaten track and very seldom visited by outsiders. From here it would be an easy task to cross into Afghanistan and make your way almost anywhere you wanted to providing you access to transport.

A string of emails from someone who simply called himself Father had seen Mahood make several trips into around the Country, the Father was clearly some form of leader or maybe a collective term for a leadership group, but whoever it was, had been the driving force behind Mahood's latest travel plans and the planned trips to Urozgan and the compound, as well as previous visits he had made to the village and surrounding areas. In Country he had stayed in a number of places, the last, less than twenty miles outside Urozgan. The Father had arranged for Mahood to meet a man by the name of Massouk who was to be his guard and driver. The emails had given a description of Massouk which spoke of a vivid scar caused by a gunshot wound suffered during the Russian invasion; this clearly showed that Massouk was a veteran warrior and likely to be a dangerous adversary but secondly that Mahood had not met the man before, an address at which Massouk could be found was also given. It was decided that a visit by a combined Army and Afghan Police patrol would be paid to the address given as Massouk's home. There they would try to establish exactly who Massouk was, and what connections he had with both the Father and Mahood. Information was always key during interrogations if you already knew some of the answers to the questions who would ask it served both as a useful honesty gauge but also unnerved the one being questioned if it seemed that your captors already knew a lot more than you would have thought, the spectre of a spy in the terrorists network was always likely to provoke a panicked reaction, and panicky men reveal things they would not normally reveal.

Whilst the analysts were hard at work Brian was busy organising a flight home in time for the funeral of his mate, he had some mid tour leave owing him anyway, although he never expected to be able to take it such was the tempo of operations, but the colonel had pulled a few favours and had almost insisted that Brian take it, see it as a pat on the back for a job well done he said referring to his latest few trips outside the wire accompanying the task force. Andy had been born and raised in a small village just outside Newcastle, it was often a source of amusement to see him react when people called him a plastic Geordie, although he was so attached to everything Newcastle particularly the football team he loved, Andy was convinced that his blood ran black and white, Brian thought back on his mate and was saddened by the thought that Andy's blood as red as everyone else's had ran freely, too freely not that long ago. The funeral, ten days away, was to be held in the village his parents still lived in, he was to be buried with full honours in the small graveyard that adjoined the church in which he had married his childhood sweetheart Jo.

Zayeed and Massouk were ushered into a room immediately upon arriving at the address known to only a handful of trusted men, the immediacy of the meeting showed not only the importance but also the level of displeasure being directed towards them, they were offered none of the customary welcome teas and sweetmeats one would expect upon arrival at the home of a wealthy man. Inside a dimly lit room, a man sat at a desk to his side were his most trusted advisors and bodyguards, once inside he bade Zayeed and Massouk to sit down, "tell me what happened" he said, Massouk began to speak but Zayeed cut him off, "the army were there waiting" he said, "they must have known we were coming to town, the army had a local man with them, I don't know who he was but he pointed at the three of us, that is when we ran, Atcha tried to escape but was quickly caught, I saw him led away and one of the soldiers had the bag he was carrying". "Did he pass any message to you?" asked the man at the desk, "no" answered Zayeed, "he said he had some more information for us, but before he could tell us what it was, the army had arrived". The man looked at Massouk, "you", he said "you were there to protect him, to stop him being taken, why did you fail me?", as he spoke one of the man behind the desk moved silently to a position behind Zayeed and Massouk. "I tried father, but there was no escape", the man at the desk exploded his voice simmering with anger "you should have been caught in his place, you should have fought like the lion you were when the Russians invaded, instead you ran like a young girl". He said then continued in a more conciliatory tone, "I am sorry, forgive me I am tired, you have travelled far, you must be hungry, go with Hassan here he will take you to the kitchen, I shall talk a while longer with Zayeed, do not worry, we will find a way for you to make amends", with that he made a small motion with his hand to the man who know stood behind Massouk and said "Hassan take our guest outside, make sure he is properly looked after" "I understand father" said Hassan and led Massouk to the door. As the two men left, the man, stood and walked to the single window which overlooked a small courtyard, he was slim but tall, Zayeed could see him better now he stood in the light he had recently had his beard cut fashionably short, yet still wore the dress of the mountains from where it was rumoured he had been born although none but the man himself knew for certain, His parents, two brothers and youngest sister had been killed by a missile launched by an American surveillance drone, The Americans had claimed it was a legitimate attack against a known insurgent gathering, the family had claimed they had been celebrating a wedding when the missile struck, he had suffered slight injuries in the explosion but the wounds to his body were of nothing compared to the scars he carried in his mind. "We need to hit back, we need to show the British and the Americans we are strong, I need men who will not let me down", he said turning back towards Zayeed, "Massouk has failed me; he will not do so again", almost as he said this, the unmistakable sound of a gunshot echoed from the courtyard, the man looked once more out of the window, nodded, almost in satisfaction and without turning said to Zayeed, "you will not fail me next time will you"? Almost unable to believe that he had just heard Massouk being killed for failing to prevent Atcha's arrest, Zayeed simply shook his head and replied in the only way he could, "No Father I will not fail you". The door to the room opened and Hassan returned, an AK 47 held loosely in his hands, he crossed the room and once more took up position behind the father. "I need you to go once more to England" the Father said once looking at Zayeed, "Hassan here will go with you. Your passport and tickets' will be arranged, you must leave in two days". "Where am I to go Father and for what purpose" asked Zayeed still shaken by what had happened, "A place called Newcastle in the North", he replied "We have brothers there who will help you to show the British that even in death there is still a time to die. Now go and rest I shall talk with you more once you have eaten".

As two men carried Massouk's body outside to be dumped in a roadside ditch, just one more dead body for the police to find and possibly investigate in a land where violent death was an everyday occurrence, Zayeed found himself being led to a sparsely furnished room which was to be his home until he was driven to the airport to begin an operation he knew that if he failed would see him meeting the same untimely end as

Massouk had. Across the border Brian had just been given his departure details and was busy packing the few essentials' he would need, most of his personal stuff was already in the UK, it was bizarre to think that a plane ride away was actually a world away from where he currently sat, he had had one piece of good news, a couple of the task force guys were also flying back to England at the same time so he would have some company on the way. One who had been christened John, but went by the name JJ, came from the tough but loyal streets of Newcastle that Andy had loved so much. JJ had done some work with Andy when he was in Kabul and would also be going to the funeral, he had told Brian that although he and Andy were not mates in the true sense of the word he would like the opportunity to pay his respects, and did Brian think that the family would object, Brian told him that they would be more than happy to have someone who had worked alongside Andy at the service and he would do the necessary introductions as required.

CHAPTER EIGHTEEN

U nbeknownst to each other Brian, JJ, Zayeed and Hassan all arrived in England within a few days or each other, the soldiers flights were relatively straightforward or as straightforward as the military system allows, a combination of helicopter, Hercules transporter and an Royal Air Force passenger carrier where the seats oddly face the rear of the plane saw them safely landing at Brize Norton. Zayeed and Hassan had flown from Pakistan into Germany and then had been driven to a French ferry terminal by an unnamed and almost totally silent driver, from there they had boarded a mini bus carrying British Muslims back from a wedding party in Paris, their sudden arrival on the bus was greeted by some whispered comments and stares but a word from the driver quickly quietened the mainly female passengers, the few men on board sat silently, no doubt wishing that the trip would soon come to an end and they could be rid of these two men who had joined what had been a joyous journey. The mini bus arrived at Dover at possibly the busiest time of day and was very quickly processed through immigration all passengers had British passports with the necessary documentation to prove who they were and where they professed to live, there was none of the usual alcohol smuggling worries that the customs Officers had to contend with and they were soon on the road out of Dover heading towards London. At a service station on the A20 the mini bus pulled over. Zayeed and Hassan both left the vehicle and were soon heading North in a legally owned taxed and insured vehicle driven by a man who went by the name of Samir, Samir was to take them to a safe house just outside Newcastle, from there they would then be taken to meet the ones who would help them with the Fathers plan. The plan, when Zayeed had been told of it had shocked him to the core; he had always considered himself an honourable man fighting for a cause that he truly believed in, but this went beyond anything he had seen or heard of before. The father had told him that in war there is no place for scruples Zayeed knew this not to be true, but the father had gone on to say that this would strike a blow for all those who had been taken prisoner by the British and Americans, caught thanks to one weak man who hadn't the strength to fight and had gone crawling to the Police and the army informing them of the plans being hatched by the brave brothers who now languished in jails around the world. This would send a message that although you may have found one traitor in our midst we are strong and are still able to come at you and kill you when and where you least expect it. Finally in a cold voice he had told Zayeed that if he wanted no part of this, then just say so, there was always someone else who was willing to do his bidding.

Tommy had spent the days since the attempted attack at the hospital catching up on the holiday he had cut short, he had gone back to Liverpool for a few days, and then once again taken himself off to the peacefulness that could be found in the Brecon's, He had walked up and down the hills and tracks around the Welsh borders and slept the sleep of the exhausted relishing the absolute stillness and quiet of the nights, Marty had managed to undo some of the good work the doctors had done by her life saving heroics that day, she had been readmitted to the military wing but was now once again putting her physiotherapist through all sorts of anguish, Tommy had kept in touch and it would seem that her hunky librarian spent more time with her than actually delivering books, Tommy was happy for her, he had grown very close to Marty, lots of people believed they, if not already, almost certainly would an item to use the old fashioned term, but he knew, in fact they both knew they were always destined to be friends, good friends to be sure but more like brother and sister than lovers. Both Tommy and Marty would be travelling up to Newcastle for Andy's funeral along with many other of his colleagues and friends, The military grapevine had been working overtime and it had arranged that as many as could make it would gather the night before and see Andy off in a manner he would approve of, there were plenty of pubs around the city were a glass would be raised in his memory and to that of absent friends, Brian had been asked by Jo if he would say a few words at the service and Andy's former Commanding Officer would also deliver one of the readings, Neither Andy or Jo were deeply religious and the service was to be more of an opportunity to remember Andy as opposed to talk about God's great plan. As it was a military service Andy was to be carried into the small church by a pall bearer party made up of his closest friends all wearing dress uniform, other serving members in the congregation would also be in similar uniform, it promised to be a very moving occasion and the type of service the small village community had not seen the likes of before. The local British legion had offered the use of its bar and hall immediately afterwards, the usual cost of hiring had of course been waived and members had requested they be allowed to form a guard of honour outside the church, which had immediately reduced Jo to tears, she found herself swaying between almost unbearable sadness and being deeply grateful that so many good people were willing to remember her Andy such a fitting manner.

In a neat terraced house in London a young woman sat nervously next to the telephone her husband was away at work and she had the house to herself, she had spent the day busily unpacking the suitcase she and her husband had used on the trip to France to celebrate her nieces wedding. She had tried to speak to her husband about the two men who had joined them on the bus, but he had forbidden her to talk of it, she had looked at the two men closely and was certain she could remember their faces, she picked up the telephone hesitantly, she had seen the posters asking the good citizens of Britain to be watchful for terrorists and knew the number she should call if she suspected something was wrong. The woman was a devout Muslim and knew that the acts the wild men with their bombs and their guns had carried out in London and elsewhere in the name of her religion was wrong. The phone was answered almost immediately and a kindly sounding female operator asked her how she could help. She told the policewoman of the two men, and how they had joined the wedding party, how they had gotten off the bus and where, how she has suspected they were up to no good, why else would they board a minibus like thieves in the night. The information that the woman gave was noted along with the time of the ferry, the date and type of vehicle, she was asked to describe the men, what she knew of their names anything at all to help the police find them. She answered all these questions, at least, as best as her memory would allow, however, when she was asked for her name, her resolve finally gave up, and she broke the connection. The information would be recorded and port authorities in Dover would be asked to trawl through all the records of mini busses carrying wedding parties back from France, with a cross check on passenger details matching those of the same vehicle on the outward bound journey. The task was huge and with an under staffed workforce would not be completed for a few days, the police would register the information and it would be loaded onto a National database but without further information, would go no further. The woman who had taken the very brave step to contact the police hoped that she had done the right thing and that the two men would be found before they had the chance to perpetrate whatever evil act she believed they were planning. She would never know that despite her best intentions, her willingness to do the right thing and her courage, the police would be too late to stop the men from planting the bomb in the very place that a man called the Father had told them to.

Zayeed and Hassan had eventually been taken to a house outside Newcastle; there they had been allowed to rest. The house was lived in by three men who claimed to have attended a training camp in Pakistan, it was there they said that the Father had told them that they must return to England, they should avoid the radical mosques, they should work hard and arouse no suspicion, they should not be seen to celebrate the deaths of British soldiers rather if asked they should show sympathy and tell those who would listen this was not the way of Islam and that they abhorred those who killed in Allah's name. They were told that the British Government would be monitoring the internet to see who went on line and visited the radical websites and that they should not be tempted to do so. They were to become invisible and that in time they would be called upon. A man would come and utter the words that the father had forbidden them to write down, they were to be committed to memory as was the appropriate response. That call had come a week ago, they had been put in touch with a man who gave them a package and showed them how it worked. The package now lay in a box in a cupboard under the stairs. The three men had been told to expect visitors and what was expected of them. The next day Zayeed and Hassan were driven by one of the men to Heddon a small village a few miles outside the city. They drove past a churchyard with a small cemetery attached to it, as they drove away from the church they passed a British Legion club with the red white and blue of union flag flying at half mast.

On the day before the Funeral service Tommy had driven from Liverpool up to Andy's hometown, the village had opened up its doors and a number of Andy's former neighbours had offered serving soldiers a room for the night, the few pubs in the area had offered reduced rates for bed and breakfast as had the local hotel, the other mourners had either found alternative accommodation in Newcastle or a few of the more hardy souls had brought with them camping gear and would set themselves up in a nearby campsite. Brian had arranged for him and JJ to stay in one of the pubs, Marty had planned to grab a lift of one of her friends and would join them on the day of the funeral, many more had made their way by road rail and air to be able to see off one of their own in fitting style. The evening had gone well, drinks had been raised, toasts had been made and once it became known who these guys were, and why they were in town publicans and locals were very keen to buy them a drink, only one joker had tried to spoil the night, a local hard guy had wanted to prove himself against these tough army boys to show his mates how big and hard he was. Brian laughed to himself as he watched this guy square up to, of all people JJ, he may be tough thought Brian but his threat assessment is bloody shocking. JJ to his credit had shown no willingness at all to fight the man who was by now calling him outside, "you army guys are all talk lets settle this like real men" as he said this, an old man hands scarred and toughened by years of hard physical labour sidled up to the now swaggering tough guy and without a word being spoken slapped him hard across the face, the tough guys mates looked on he was then grabbed by the ear and frogmarched out of the pub like a naughty schoolchild, every step accompanied by a tug on the ear and a reminder that these boys are men, real men who do what they do, so scum like you can sit on your arse and claim benefits, as they reached the door it was opened wide and he was thrown into the street, a couple of men who had been drinking with the old man accompanied by the landlord who had come from behind the bar had by now moved up to stand in front of the would be fighters friends and without a word motioned to the door, go along now lads the landlord said quietly and be thankful we are not letting these boys here loose on you. The rest of the night passed peacefully and Brian, JJ, Tommy and a few others found themselves in an Indian curry house long after last orders had been called. They had eventually called a taxi to drive them back to the pub, as they pulled up outside and paid the driver, Brian had said he felt like a walk, he wasn't going to be able to sleep anyway, he set off towards the churchyard, JJ looked at Tommy asking him was he going to be alright? Tommy shrugged, they were good mates he said, he will not show it but he is pretty cut up about all this, let's go see where he goes make sure he is ok shall we. Brian walked slowly and eventually found himself in the small cemetery; he had recently found himself drawn towards places that offered quietness and peacefulness he guessed it was a direct response to the need to get away from the noise and confusion that current operations seemed to throw up. He sat down with his back to an old tree and suddenly felt very alone.

He sat there in silence and was presently aware of Tommy and JJ who had quietly followed him and had now sat down either side of him. As they sat there watching the day slowly break, they watched two men who were working next to a freshly dug grave, they seemed to be rearranging the pile of earth that would soon cover the earthly remains of Andy, One of the men then pulled a green tarpaulin carefully over the mound. As they watched one man removed the hat he was wearing and mopped his brow, Tommy said, to no one in particular "those guys are keen aren't they, digging at this time of day" "mmm" answered JJ thoughtfully, "that guy on the left looks familiar, did we see him in the pub last night?" "Not sure" replied Tommy "I don't think so". The two men seemed to have finished with their work, one of them pulled a phone out of his pocket and whilst making a call stood looking around him, something must have attracted his attention and he turned to his fellow gravedigger and pointed to whatever it was that caught his eye, his friend nodded in agreement to whatever was being said. The man finished his call and the two of them made their way to the narrow gateway that lead to the road. Brian looked at his watch, four thirty in the morning no way he would sleep now he thought to himself but a coffee would go down well. The landlord of the pub had told them to make themselves at home whist they were staying there; "do you fancy coffee lads?" He said to the other two, "sure why not" said Tommy and the three soldiers heaved themselves to their feet.

They had not gone more than half way to the pub when JJ who had been uncharacteristically quiet suddenly stopped and swore violently. "that guy, the grave digger he was at the village" "what guy, what village" said Tommy thinking that maybe that last pint had been a mistake for JJ, "the village we raided to get Atcha, he was talking to him when they split up, I thought I had seen him before" immediately sobering up

Brian said "are you sure it was him, we have had a few beers", "It was him I was there when they ran, we all raced after Atcha but he was there along with some other guy with a big scar on his face". With that the three turned and ran back to the cemetery, the place was empty apart from the neatly covered mound of earth. JJ moved towards it intent on ripping it apart, "stop, wait" yelled Brian "we don't know what's in there, wait a minute" the three of them stood next to the pile of earth now possibly containing something far more sinister and deadly than simply soil.

Given the high profile military event and the fact that they were burying an operator the duty Bomb Disposal team from the nearby garrison of Catterick had been moved forward from their normal operating base and were housed in a Police Station in Newcastle along with the Officer Commanding and Senior Ammunition Technician of that particular unit. Andy Jenkins was also staying locally, Brian, reverting to the almost automatic role of taking responsibility and decision making that made him such a good operator and perversely put him in the front line more times than those who were blessed with better decision making would strive to avoid, said "Tommy give Andy a call tell him what's happened, I will nip along to the police station and talk to the local coppers see if we can't get hold of the registered grave diggers maybe it was them after all", turning to JJ he asked "are you dead sure you are right?" JJ replied, "I have just spent three years working surveillance, I know my faces and I it was him Brian, I should have put two and two together sooner". Andy, initially drowsy from being awoken from a sleep he had barely started, immediately realised the importance of the phone call, he asked the obvious question regarding JJ, his sobriety and the reliability of his recognition of a man he had seen fleetingly half a world away. "He has had a few beers Andy as have we all, but he is dead certain it is the same man who was with Atcha, I only met him tonight for the first time but Brian knows him and believes him, that's good enough for me". "Ok" answered Andy "where are you know", "stood by the mound Brian has gone to talk with the local coppers trying to get hold of the grave digger, JJ has gone with him". "Ok make your way to the gate", said Andy "and wait there, make sure you keep an eye of the grave if you can, no one goes into the church or the cemetery till the police arrive, I will call the CO now, and we will see what he suggests, in the meantime I will get the Ops room to warn off the duty team". Brian had banged repeatedly on the door of the locked but thankfully manned police station and a sleepy looking constable had eventually opened the door. Once Brian explained who he was and what had been seen coupled with JJ's assessment, the Police man called the vicar and after apologising for waking him at such an early hour, got the names and addresses of the gravediggers. the grave digger lived locally, the policeman accompanied by the two soldiers walked the short distance to an old and rundown house on the edge of the village, the tools of his trade stood neatly outside the front door, after a short delay a man appeared looking as if he has just been woken from a deep sleep, certainly not the appearance of a man who only thirty minutes ago had been hard at work. The gravedigger looked at the young constable as if he were stupid, when asked had he just been digging in the cemetery, "the grave was dug yesterday" he said "and will be filled when the brave young feller is laid to rest later today". "Thanks Albert" said the policeman and again apologised for waking him, "who are these guys" asked Albert, pointing towards JJ and Brian, Brian answered simply "We worked with that brave young feller Sir, thanks for your time", with that they turned and made their way back to the station now seriously worried. Brian phoned Tommy to tell him what they had found out; whoever had been digging wasn't anyone who should have been. JJ was now deeply upset he hadn't twigged beforehand. Tommy in turn called Andy again to tell him the bad news, Andy answered almost immediately, gone was the sleepy tones from before "ok the Colonel is talking to the local police as we speak, I guess this is going to escalate, what time is the service due to start?" "Two this afternoon" answered Tommy "although I expect people will start turning up from one ish." "That doesn't give us much time" said Andy "I will get the team moving, the Colonel will no doubt get the local Police to start the ball rolling from their end, I have asked him and he had agreed to try to get them to keep this as low key as possible. Can you keep an eye on things there I can be with you in less than thirty minutes the team will be with me, by that time the coppers should have at least started the business of putting a cordon in place." As he hung up he was joined by Brian and JJ with a young policeman nervously looking at the now suspect pile of earth in the cemetery, Tommy quickly told them what was happening, as he was doing this the policeman's radio squawked into life, he excused himself and moved away to answer it, Tommy looked at Brian and asked, "what do you think?" Brian looked around him and replied "has to be command, too hit and miss for timed and why on earth put a VO in the heap of earth we won't be touching leave alone moving, yeah I say command but with a possible secondary backup system maybe timed back up in case the RC doesn't work, has to be RC there is no cable running away from the area and they haven't had time to bury one". JJ looked on, and said, "Excuse me for asking but I am just a simple Special Forces guy, what the hell are you two babbling on about"." Sorry mate" answered Brian, "we were talking about likely firing switches, the use of a timer to target a group of people is a bit random, the bad guys would need to know we would be right next to the bomb at a precise time, they may know what time the service starts but not what time it will end and certainly not at what time we will standing by the mound". "VO" went on Tommy "stands for victim operated, or booby trap, for that to work one of us would need to do something to the bomb, step on it move it; whatever, it's not likely that any of the mourners are going to start playing in the dirt is it?" "Which leaves command" finished JJ getting the point quickly, "precisely" said Brian "and most likely radio controlled with, a possible back up timer in case they are discovered or the bomb fails to work." But where would they fire it from?" asked JJ, "It would need to be somewhere they can see the cemetery from and ideally see the pile of earth to know just when is the best time to press the button the green cover over the mound would stand out a mile so they would have no difficulty in spotting that" said Brian in reply, "but If they use a phone, can't they be miles away though?" asked JJ, "yes they can but someone, not necessarily the firer has to have eyes on the target area, and then he, the spotter, must be in contact with the firer". Replied Tommy patiently. JJ looked around him, on one side of the cemetery lay the church which a group of tall trees in tandem with the steeple obstructed any line of sight into the graveyard, the village lay towards the west and it was unlikely that whoever fired the bomb would be wanting to have to escape from the village area immediately after the event, one thing about firing positions was that apart from line of sight they also needed to be able to provide a reliable and effective means of escape. The most likely position was to the South where there was flat ground for approximately half a mile but then the ground rose sharply culminating in a number of wooded areas often used by picnickers and for secret lovers' trysts. "How far away would they need to be?" he asked, "depends on what they are using" answered Tommy "a mobile phone can be fired from a good distance away if you come right down to basics then a wireless doorbell can be rigged to fire a bomb but only has a range of less than two hundred meters". "We will know more when the bleeps arrive with the team" said Brian, "Bleeps?" asked the Policeman who had by now rejoined them, "Signals specialists said Tommy the ones with the kit that can jam radio signals" "That was the Control room" went on the policeman indicating his radio, "they want me to start putting a cordon in place, they are sending a few cars down to help me out but it would seem that your Colonel has been flexing his muscles, they tell me that he says I can talk to you guys about how far the cordon should be and anything else I need to know". No problem said Tommy, let's get started shall we? How far away is the nearest house? We are looking at a cordon and evacuation area of about one hundred meters from the cemetery in all directions and then we will look at what other stuff we need, does your force have a helicopter?" He asked looking at the woods to the South. "A helicopter?" Laughed the Policeman, "Around here we are lucky to be issued pushbikes"

By the time the Bomb team led by Sergeant Joe Riley accompanied by the Major in charge of the squadron to whom the bomb team was attached, the Regimental Colonel and the Senior Warrant Officer, Andy Jenkins, the Police had set up a security cordon, given the isolated location of the church there had been no need to start evacuating people from their homes at such an early hour. The Bomb team commanded by the young sergeant set up in an incident control point about one hundred meters from the cemetery gates. Tommy and Brian both felt an empathetic sympathy for the young operator, Tommy had in fact seen him once before on a revalidation exercise, he had impressed Tommy with his approach to what was always a difficult day being assessed for continued operational ability by a posse of the most senior and experienced operators of the day. It was never easy being tasked to any incident, more so when it possibly had terrorist implications add to that the threat from a remote controlled switch then throw in the obvious emotive issues surrounding this particular task with the additional involvement of an audience of some very experienced and senior Warrant Officers, your immediate Commander and the most senior man in the entire Regiment, the day promised to be one that would live long in the Joe's memory and would go some way towards determining his subsequent career path. As Joe began to ascertain just what was going on and why he was here, his team and the Signal specialists started to assemble their equipment, Tommy and Brian stood off to one side where they were soon joined by Andy Jenkins, "hello lads" he said smiling grimly, as he came across to shake hands, "seems that you just can't let sleeping dogs lie can you?" "I tell you what" said Brian with an unmistakable menace in his voice, "if I get my hands on whoever is behind this, so help me God I will kill them myself". "We were here when they were planting the bloody thing" said Tommy "and we never noticed a thing, it was only JJ who clocked them but by then they were gone". Andy looked about him, "what do you reckon to a firing point?" he asked, both Tommy and Brian looked across to the high ground they had identified earlier, "somewhere over there" said Brian, "offers all the usual amenities these guys would be looking for", "seems to be the likely choice" agreed Andy, "Can the Police get access to a helicopter do you know", "we asked but it's not likely" said Tommy. Joe had by now marshalled his team and a small remote controlled robot was being made ready, from the safety of the vehicles this could be manoeuvred into the tightest of positions and could render safe most types of bomb including ones that were remote controlled, this and similar machines had had helped to save countless lives since their inception in the early 1970's. Andy turned to Brian, "how is Jo doing?" he said gently, "have we been able to keep this away from her?" "She is staying with her Mum so is at present unaware this is going on, and if possible I think we should keep it that way. She is hurting" went Brian "but she has good people around her, today will be hard as hell and the next few days and weeks won't get any easier". Both Andy and Tommy fell silent as Brian spoke of how he had been their Andy and Jo's best man and the times he had shared with the pair of them. As he fell silent he turned away as if to watch the Bomb team at work, Tommy quietly placed a hand on his mates shoulder a silent but reassuring touch that told Brian he was not alone.

The trio were joined by both the Commanding Officer and the Major who was the Catterick Teams Squadron Commander, they had been busy talking to the senior Police Officer on scene about the need to dominate likely firing positions and had just seen their efforts rewarded, it had been agreed that given the importance and potential severity of the situation not only would an armed response team be sent to the scene but a force helicopter was being scrambled to take up an over watch position above the hills and woods to the south. JJ had been talking to a couple of Police Officers who had been assigned cordon positions he had been able to organise coffee and bacon sandwiches to be sent from a nearby cafe. He returned to find Brian and Tommy talking with the Officers, introductions were made and handshakes exchanged, when JJ heard of the plan to cover the hills he argued that if the police were to venture up there he should be included, given the fact that he was the only one who could identify the man they were looking for. The men stopped talking as the unmistakable sound of the remote controlled "wheelbarrow" trundled out of the incident control point and made its way down to the suspect mound of earth. They could see Joe Riley and his number two control box in hand deftly steering his way around the cemetery gates, both men peering intently at the small TV monitor in the back of the bomb van watching the barrows progress. The remotely operated vehicle or to use the ever loved military use of an acronym ROV stopped at the foot of the pile of earth, using a combination of skill and dexterity the number two deployed a number of sensors around the mound, this done Joe walked the short distance to the Bleep wagon, inside sheltering inside the air conditioned shell which was necessary to keep the radio detection and jamming equipment cool the signal specialists was endeavouring to find the one signal from the millions that were in the ether that would identify itself as hostile. Tommy and the rest of the operators stood watching, had been through this routine hundreds of times, they all knew it required a wealth of specialised knowledge, perseverance and sometimes luck, but by finding the correct signal Joe would be better protected when he came to put on the bomb suit and make that long walk.

Whilst the hunt was on for the elusive radio wave, Joe's number two carefully removed the tarpaulin cover that had been placed over the mound, this was always a dangerous moment as the team had no way of knowing just yet precisely what type of device was hidden below, what its condition was and what reaction any sudden movement might have on it. The wheel barrow claws gripped one corner of the cover and once grabbed the ROV operator slowly rotated the wrist of the claws thus ensuring a firm grip that would not easily be broken. The cover was lifted high above the mound in order to prevent any slippage of the soil which may dislodge whatever was hidden inside, and once clear deposited off to one side. The ROV now returned to the exposed soil looking for any signs of a bomb lurking beneath the surface. The Bleep opened the door to his vehicle and beckoned Joe across, after a few minutes Joe and the bleep looked anxiously in the direction of the assembled operators, as they did the Major excused himself and made his way towards them, Tommy could see but not hear the ensuing conversation, the Major asked a few questions of the signal specialist and the three of them then returned to his van where they all climbed into the rear compartment once again shutting the door behind them. "Looks they got something" said Brian out loud. "We will know soon enough" replied the Colonel. The Major jumped out of the van and quickly walked across to the waiting onlookers, "we got a positive from the mound" he said, a positive was the word for a suspect signal, "what frequency?" asked the Colonel, "looks like a mobile phone" replied the Major, "I have given permission to use all necessary cover, and made sure that Sergeant Riley makes no manual approach until he spoken to me or the SAT here direct". "Well I guess this now means the helicopter and armed units are an urgent requirement" said the Colonel walking off to once more talk with the Police Commander. The ROV operator now being guided by Joe began to carefully scrape away the top layer of soil, the earth that was dislodged spilled messily onto the gravel path and green grass that had been so carefully swept and cut only the day before.

The armed response unit turned up in two fast looking cars, after a brief introduction and learning that JJ was not just an ordinary soldier and could positively identify one of the men, they agreed to allow him to accompany them on their search of the hills. They would be supported by a helicopter who would guide them on to anyone seen loitering in the area, it promised to a possible rude interruption for any would be lovers who were hoping to find some quiet time alone that morning. JJ bade goodbye to the operators, promising to be back in good time for the service and to keep them informed as to what or who they found. As they headed out of town JJ opened the ordnance survey map the Police had brought with them, using his military tacticians head he had estimated there were three or four likely spots that afforded not only good line of sight but also a means of easy escape and protection from casual observers, the first of these was a small parking spot which doubled as a picnic area, it was unlikely that anyone would be there at this time of the morning but it was on the way and it was never wise to totally disregard a possible target area. The two cars sped southwards on the B6528 as the ROV continued scraping away the soil; the service was due to start in less than five hours.

Zayeed had been silent since they had left the graveyard, he was troubled by what they had done, and he had killed men before, many men so it wasn't the killing that concerned him it was more the way of the killing. Hassan had no such concerns and had been telling Zayeed how he was looking forward to setting the device off just when the grieving widow and the army were about to say goodbye to their comrade. Hassan had called the Father an hour earlier to tell him that all was in place, they planned to be in the firing point at about mid day, the two men were sat in a car that had been stolen earlier from Newcastle and had parked outside a 24 hour supermarket, the sort of place where nobody noticed cars coming and going at all hours of the day and where they could easily drive the short distance to an area called Ashbank Woods where they would be able to sit undetected with a mobile phone in hand, a number pre set into its memory bank to send a coded signal to an identical phone currently laying inside a plastic box buried deep inside a pile of dirt, next to the plastic box and linked via an electrical cable lay a second box, larger than the first containing over ten kilograms of explosive around which had been packed hundreds of steel ball bearings, the explosive charge was not overly large, but the damage wrought by the steel balls racing outwards at the speed of sound into the packed unprotected bodies crowded around the grave would be catastrophic. The impact would be felt around the world, nowhere was safe, as the Father had said even in death there is a time to die.

The two police cars stopped at a secluded picnic spot on the north side of Claytons woods, at any other time JJ would have relished the peacefulness he found there, but today was not any other time, radioing back to the police control room, the senior armed Officer asked if any Officers could be spared to safeguard the picnic area, true to form he was told that all Officers on duty were assigned to other tasks, they had no choice but to drive on, still the chopper once airborne would be able to circle around and be able identify people hanging around the area, then it would be up to the cars to get there as quick as they could. The second spot identified by JJ was an overhang reached only on foot, however the closest road was only a short sprint away if you had to reach it in a hurry and from there a waiting car could have you away and heading towards airport port or the motorway links in no time at all. As the two marked police cars turned yet another sharp bend that seemed to be a feature of these roads, they saw a car parked carefully in one of the few passing places dotted along the verge, at any other time a car parked here would be unusual today it was definitely suspicious. The Police car stopped and JJ accompanied by two armed Officers approached the car, the engine block was still warm to the touch, it hadn't been parked here long remarked one of the Officers, on the back seat was a suitcase and in the passenger foot well lay an AA road atlas open at a page that showed amongst other places Newcastle airport. The three then headed into the woods towards the rocky outcrop, using a narrow path that clearly showed signs of being recently used, they stopped short on hearing voices up ahead, the tactics used by the police were almost identical to those used by JJ and his men in the task Force and he quickly fell in behind the two Officers as they formed an open Vee formation to approach the overhang, JJ wished fervently he had a weapon with him felt dangerously unarmed and vulnerable, grabbed a short stocky branch as he picked his way across the open ground. They had gotten themselves within a few metres of the now clearly heard voices but the origins of which remained hidden by a bank of bushes, "I told you we should wait" one said to which the other voice replied "we can't wait it has to be now, we can't hide this forever, someone will see it eventually" the police found their way to a small opening and through it could see two people one male, a mobile phone clutched in one hand, the second a woman, one Officer stepped through the gap in the bushes holding his pistol in front of him as the second barked a command ordering the two to stand still, the woman shrieked loudly as the man looked him clearly as shocked as she was by the sudden appearance of an armed policeman. A few minutes later the two Officers left promising to not tell either the woman's husband or the man's fiancée of their impending midwife aided delivery no doubt realising that very soon there would be no need for telling.

Joe had by now had his ROV deep inside the mound of freshly dug earth, as he probed deeper, the TV monitor showed a length of electrical cable the white plastic sheathing standing out clear as day against the brown of the soil, "gotcha" he whispered, let's get the barrow back we need to fit a cutting charge, having issued his directive he moved away to find his commander and the police to tell them of the latest developments. The cutting charge a small length of plastic cord filled with high explosives would be used to break the link between the two major components of the bomb, making it, in theory anyway, safer to approach and eventually deal with; The team worked efficiently to bring the wheelbarrow back and turn it around complete with a fresh set of batteries and the required cutting charge, it wasn't quite formula one pit stop standard but it never failed to amaze Tommy how four guys working in unison towards a common goal managed to get a fully loaded ROV out and heading towards a suspect device in less time than it took most people to reverse into a tight supermarket parking space. Joe had already warned the Police incident commander of his intent to explosively cut the link and he had arranged for his Officers to shelter behind what was referred to as hard cover, the possibility of something going wrong and causing a device to function was a real one and precautionary measures were always better than reactionary ones when dealing with high explosives. Breaking the link would not completely render safe the device and it would go no way to removing the explosive risk but it was a start, Tommy once again remembered the old refrain drummed into him and other operators by the always hard to please but wise and experienced instructors at the Felix centre," if its Time—React, Victim Operated-take your time and Command—Take control" and this was one way in which some semblance of taking control could be achieved. Joe watched closely as his number two positioned the charge as close to the centre of the electrical cable as possible, satisfied that everything was in place and the police had taken whatever shelter they could find, he gave the order for his assistant to initiate the charge; JJ heard the sound of the charge from the hills where he was standing looking down on the cemetery, he looked towards the sky as the familiar sound of whirring rotor blades signalled the arrival of the police helicopter, the Officers established contact and once again boarded the vehicles to continue the search. The service was due to start in less than four hours.

As the dust settled Joe could see clearly that where there had been a wire twenty seconds ago, now there was nothing but dirt and soil, it was not uncommon for the cutting charge to throw the now separated ends of the wire both left and right of the cut, what Joe had to do now was find and trace both ends to their respective origins on one end he was hoping to find an explosive charge on the other the firing switch that would have initiated it. He had the ROV poke around the earth until he could see one frayed end of cable, taking care not to dislodge too much earth he had his number two trace the wire, digging down and using a combination of claws and manipulator he managed to clear enough soil to uncover a blue plastic drum into which the wire ran, the drum was too firmly wedged to be able to remove it with the ROV, but at least he now knew where it was, the other end of the cable ran towards a second plastic box this, much smaller than the first undoubtedly contained the firing switch, he now had two options he could use one of his disruptive weapons and shoot the box thus ensuring complete separation or he could assess the box to contain no explosive threat and leave it to be X Rayed and preserve maximum forensics, the first option was always the safest and after taking the advice of his Commanding Officer who argued that there was no telling what these guys are capable of, told the operator "let's hit it and we will pick up the pieces afterwards". Police SOCO's, Scenes of Crimes Officers, nowadays were more than capable of putting disrupted devices back together and seldom very little was lost in the way of forensic evidence. Joe had already pre empted this advice and had ordered his team to position on of the weapons on the small plastic container, the contest was never an even one and the box quickly disappeared as the disruptor tore through it separating box from phone form power source and throwing the remnants over an area covering two square metres. There was little more that the ROV could do now for Joe apart from confirming what he had just achieved with this shot, he had the team park the robot off to one side and began to prepare for the next phase of the task which would see him don the heavy suit and approach the device. As Joe wiggled his head into the helmet his bleep and number two whispered last minute instructions and made sure that everything he had asked for was in place, he set off slowed down not only by the weight of the suit but by the equipment he was carrying, weapon, a radio control jamming system, and a bag containing assorted ropes, hooks, pulleys and karabiners that he would use to remove the explosive charge from its current resting place. His first act was to see for himself the results of his remote actions, he confirmed the cut on the wire and more importantly ensured it was the only wire there, he then moved around the mound to have a look at the disrupted firing switch, it quickly became apparent that there on the floor now in dozens of pieces lay a mobile phone with a small electronic circuit board attached to its face, a couple of electrical wires had originally ran from the circuit board into the interior workings of the mobile phone seemingly through a small hole that had been drilled through one side, however these had now been well separated by the powerful disruptor. He heaved himself from the crouching position he had adopted whilst inspecting the phone and associated circuitry and moved back to the mound. He had already identified a likely pulley point nearby, the grave had been dug conveniently close to a sturdy looking tree and a prussic loop around the trunk would serve very well as both a high point to lift the container and as a change of direction to move it away from the earth. He rigged his line and pulleys before moving across to the blue drum, taking care not to move the drum whilst attaching his line he connected the free end of the rope to the handle, leaving enough slack in the line to not risk getting tangled as he stood up, he then placed a large plastic sheet at the base of the tree and made his way back to the safety of his vehicle.

CHAPTER NINETEEN

Zayeed and Hassan left the car park at eleven o clock and driving carefully set off for Ashbank Woods, finding a secluded spot they reversed the car off the road and made their way towards the top of the hill from where they would have a clear view of the churchyard. The helicopter pilot saw a car driving slowly along the minor road that led to the woods and subsequently let the armed Officers know of his sighting, having nothing else to look at he continued to monitor the vehicles journey, the two patrol cars were travelling from the east and were currently crawling along behind a small tractor, the tractor driver headphones firmly clamped to his ears had no idea that behind him were two cars full of by now increasingly frustrated policemen, he eventually heard the impatient tooting of horns and sirens and veered suddenly off to one side to allow the two cars to speed by. The pilot had by now reported that the car had stopped and two occupants had gotten out and were on foot heading towards the top of the hill, Zayeed heard the helicopter and grabbing Hassan by the arm forced him to stop, "wait" he hissed "let him fly past, we have plenty of time", the pilot using his thermal imagery equipment could see clearly that the two men had now stopped deep inside the trees, the cars tore along the B6528 and turned onto the small track that would lead them to the woods, they reached the spot where the men had left the car, leaving one man to watch the car, which following a plate check showed it to have been reported stolen from an address in Newcastle the day before, the remaining Officers with JJ in close attendance made their way through the woods upwards being guided by the ever watchful eye in the sky, Hassan was impatient to get to the hill top and broke free from Zayeed's grasp, "don't worry about them he said they don't know who we are, we could be anyone lets go" as he reached the summit he could see what should have been an almost empty churchyard full of white vans, police cars and men in uniform, swearing angrily he pulled the mobile phone from his pocket determined to at least get someone with the bomb they had so recently planted, Zayeed ran up alongside him seeing immediately that the plan was spoiled made to grab the phone telling Hassan they should leave before the police start blocking the roads, Hassan broke away from Zayeed and searched quickly for the number that would cause the bomb to detonate if he couldn't kill the mourners he would kill the man in the bomb suit who was kneeling next to the pile of earth. Hassan had found the number he wanted and had stepped towards the edge of the steep hill, as he did so the trees and bushes behind him burst open as a group of police Officers brandishing guns suddenly appeared, the shouted commands of Armed Police Stop, stand still caused Zayeed immediately to fall to the ground hands held high in surrender, he is the one from the village said JJ pointing towards the now spread-eagled figure on the floor, Hassan phone in one hand and intent on ignoring the urgent orders from the police went to press the call button he never got that far, seeing an immediate and real threat to life three Officers opened fire, the impact of the bullets threw Hassan off the hill and sent him sprawling to the valley floor below, the mobile phone having been dropped on to the floor where he had been standing.

The sound of gunfire reached the graveyard causing all those there to look sharply towards the South from where the sound had come from, immediately the police commanders radio sprang into life with messages from all units reporting gunfire, switching to the channel used by the armed response unit he quickly called the team to find out just what was going on. The Commander listened intently to what he was being told then walked across to the Colonel "The team have just shot one man who was attempting to detonate the bomb with a mobile phone one man has been arrested and seems to want to talk, it was him who told the Officers of the bomb, the area will be secured until we know just what is really happening" he said "Thanks" said the Colonel "were any of your men injured?" "No" replied the policeman and moved away to brief his men, "Carry on Sergeant Riley" said the Colonel, "let's get this bomb out shall we? How good is your rope work?" "pretty good Sir" answered Joe confidently with two men pulling on the line and Joe watching the action through the cameras off the ROV the drum slowly but surely rose from the earth, and was deposited squarely on the plastic sheet next to the tree that Joe had positioned for this very reason, "mmm not bad" murmured the Colonel clearly impressed with the young operators actions. The rest of the task passed quickly although not hazardous the immediate threats had been diminished by the disruptive actions of the operator's weapon systems and the police marksmen. JJ reappeared after a short while and was able to brief Tommy and Brian as to just what had happened, Zayeed had hardly stopped talking telling tales of safe houses in

Newcastle, someone called the Father and with every second breath asking for political asylum saying that if he ever went back he would be killed. "I would put him on the plane myself" said Brian with feeling.

The service passed smoothly, the honour guard formed by the British Legion was expertly marshalled by an old but still very smart and efficient Warrant Officer proudly wearing his old badge of rank and a collection of medals that spoke of his long and distinguished life of service to King, Queen and Country, as the flags dipped Tommy felt a sense of pride that there were men such as these who still held core values and beliefs he could understand and strive to live by. Jo had asked Brian to say a few words, words which he never hoped he would have to say, he spoke of sacrifice, of courage but above all else of a man who loved life, his wife, his friends and what he did. The Regimental Colonel read a sermon that spoke of sacrifice and duty and the vicar, reacting fully to the family wishes never veered away from a sermon full of sentiment and warm humour. As the family and former comrades filed out of the church they made their way towards a mound of earth that stood next to an open grave, as colleagues formed a silent vigil Andy was laid to rest. Jo leant on Brian's arm as they walked back to the gate where the old guard still stood, flags raised to form an arch of colour through which the grieving party silently walked. Jo turned to Brian and whispered her thanks, her eyes full of tears, Brian just looked at her unable to trust his voice to speak without breaking; instead he simply gave her arm a squeeze. Tommy and JJ were walking alongside the Colonel, who had managed to get dirt all over his best dress shoes, dirt spread by the tracks of the remotely controlled vehicle only a few short hours before, "you would think they would have swept the path first wouldn't you?" he said with a smile, "not to worry sir I will have a word with the police I am sure the gravedigger will be dealt with accordingly" said JJ with a grin.

Over the coming days a man inside a secure London police station spoke freely of his life in Afghanistan hoping that with every revelation he was step closer to never having to return there. From the information he so willingly gave, operators in a far off country were able to watch an unmanned surveillance drone beaming back images of a house where Zayeed had once heard a man killed for failing to prevent a man being captured. The Commander of task force twelve had seen the images and read the reports coming out of London and in a few hours time in two helicopters would be waiting just across the border in Afghanistan, on board sat JJ and his men waiting for the go go go message that would finally close a chapter.